Queen of My Hart

Headstrong Harts, Book 2

by Emily Royal

Dragonblade Publishing, Inc. is an imprint of Kathryn Le Veque Novels, Inc.
P.O. Box 7968
La Verne CA 91750
ceo@dragonbladepublishing.com

Produced in the United States of America

First Edition November 2020
Mass Market Paperback Edition

ARE YOU SIGNED UP FOR DRAGONBLADE'S BLOG?

You'll get the latest news and information on exclusive giveaways, exclusive excerpts, coming releases, sales, free books, cover reveals and more.

Check out our complete list of authors, too!

No spam, no junk. That's a promise!

Sign Up Here

www.dragonbladepublishing.com

Dearest Reader;

Thank you for your support of a small press. At Dragonblade Publishing, we strive to bring you the highest quality Historical Romance from the some of the best authors in the business. Without your support, there is no 'us', so we sincerely hope you adore these stories and find some new favorite authors along the way.

Happy Reading!

CEO, Dragonblade Publishing

Additional Dragonblade books
by Author Emily Royal

Headstrong Harts
What the Hart Wants, Book 1
Queen of my Hart, Book 2
Hidden Hart, Book 3

London Libertines
Henry's Bride, Book 1
Hawthorne's Wife, Book 2
Roderick's Widow, Book 3

Dedication

for Mum, in the hope that you
won't blush too much in heaven

Acknowledgements

To Neil, Jasmine and Frankie, thank you so much, as always, for your support, plus all the cups of tea and nachos which fuelled my writing sprints. Thanks, once again to my tribes, the Beta Buddies and UKRomChatters for moral support, and feedback on pitches and blurbs.

To Sarah: our virtual writing & wine sessions have kept me motivated when I was in danger of suffering from writers' block, and lastly, to Grandpas Benjamin and Harold, who encouraged me to play chess and gave me several tough games—I dedicate my heroine's chess prowess to you.

Chapter One

"**O**H, I SAY, bad luck, Alderley! The bounder must have cheated to best you like that—but considering his origins, we shouldn't expect anything less."

Dexter glared at the speaker. Viscount de Blanchard had a reputation for snobbery—among other, less palatable, traits, and, like most of the room, loathed Dexter for nothing more than his humble birthright. After all, what right had the grandson of a blacksmith to attend a society party?

The man across the card table wore a gray pallor. And well, he might. For tonight, Dexter had relieved his enemy of his fortune.

His plan was working. One final move and victory would be his. He cared little for the money. His eye was on the real prize—the woman standing demurely beside her father—the honorable Elizabeth Alderley.

Honorable in title, if not in behavior.

And when Dexter finally took possession of her, he'd use her title to further his business where titles drew investors as surely as carcasses attracted flies.

He lifted his gaze, and Elizabeth's eyes met his. Her eyes had been described as *captivating*, but they held a calculating expression as if continually searching for the outcome which best suited her, and to hell with anyone standing in her way.

She curled her lips into a smile—red lips, which she scraped her teeth over to give them a swollen look she clearly imagined to be attractive to the opposite sex.

Foolish woman. Once she became Dexter's, she'd discover who the true master was in their relationship. She had used her sexuality to increase his need for her, and he'd willingly played along, taking pleasure from her admin-istrations.

Elizabeth would make the ideal wife, for he'd never be at risk of falling in love with *her*. And he'd enjoy teaching her humility. All those nights she'd given him the cold shoulder to increase his desire, every instance of her flirtations with others to incite his jealousy…

He would teach her what it was like to be on

the receiving end of her games—then she'd find out how a true master of seduction operated. Her need would be his plaything. To toy with, to pay her back for how she'd tried to play him.

And to pay her father back for the humiliation Dexter had suffered at that man's hands—to see Alderley willingly give his precious daughter to the boy he'd once spat on in the dirt.

"Mr. Hart?"

Their host's voice returned him to the present.

Dexter pulled out his pocket watch, making a great show of staring at it, then he yawned and snapped it shut. "I'm afraid I must be going. I had no idea how late it was."

He rose to leave. Elizabeth's smile slipped, and she narrowed her eyes. He'd seen that look on her before—aimed at a servant she admonished, and, lately, directed at Dexter himself as her way of showing disapproval.

She nudged Alderley, and the older man glanced up, a flash of irritation in his eyes. Dexter smiled to himself. If it were any man but Dexter Hart, Alderley would be glad to rid himself of his daughter. At twenty-six, and on her fifth season, with a reputation for being a shrew, she was heading for spinsterhood.

"Papa," she prompted.

"I have nothing else to wager," Alderley said. "Everything else is entailed. The bastard's cleared me out."

Dexter drew back his chair and stepped away.

"Wait!" Alderley cried. "Give me a chance to win it back."

"What with?" Dexter asked.

Alderley's shoulders slumped. "You cannot leave when I have nothing," he said, a plea in his tone. "Have mercy, for pity's sake!"

Why was it that the worst bullies turned into sniveling wrecks when bested?

A ripple of unease threaded through the room. Dexter glanced across to where Earl Stiles stood next to their host, a look of disapproval on his face.

But neither man knew the root of the hatred between Dexter and Alderley. Neither knew the scars he bore as a result of the beating he'd sustained as a boy at that bastard's hands. His back still itched at the memory of the lashes.

Fifteen years was a long time to wait for vengeance on the man who had almost killed him.

He closed his eyes, reliving the memory of the lash slicing into his flesh.

Have mercy, sir!

Mercy! To a filthy brat? You deserve all this and more!

Dexter resumed his seat. "You beg for mercy, Alderley?" He sneered.

"I'll do anything to win it back!" Alderley

cried.

Dexter leaned forward and drummed the table with his fingers.

"There is, perhaps, one thing you might care to wager…" He hesitated, then shook his head. "No—it's foolish of me to mention it."

Alderley's eyes grew bright with desperation. The fish had caught sight of the bait. All Dexter need do was reel him in.

"Tell me," he said.

Dexter picked up his brandy glass, took a slow sip, then set it down. The room fell quiet as every pair of eyes focused on him. "Very well, Alderley," he said. "One turn of the card. If you draw high, I'll return your stake."

"And if I lose?"

"You'll give me your daughter's hand in marriage."

An expression of horror crossed Alderley's face.

"M-my *daughter?*"

"Yes." Dexter savored his enemy's horror. "Her hand, with your blessing, delivered to me in front of as many witnesses as I choose, to acknowledge your eagerness to welcome me into your family."

Elizabeth feigned surprise and gasped, but hunger glittered in her eyes. Their host barked an order, and a footman rushed forward and refilled Alderley's glass. The old man took it and drained it in a single gulp, then spluttered, his face growing red with rage.

"How dare you!"

Dexter shrugged. "You're under no obligation, Alderley. I care not either way."

Alderley glanced at his daughter and narrowed his eyes.

"I'm prepared to be generous," Dexter continued. "If you lose, I'll return a portion of your funds in recognition of your daughter's worth. Shall we say five hundred guineas?"

He leaned back in his chair and crossed his arms, letting the idea sink in—that he'd just offered to buy Alderley's daughter as if she were a commodity.

The trait which served him best in business was patience. The winner in any business deal was the party with less need for it. With countless creditors snapping at his heels, Alderley was at a disadvantage. Dexter merely needed to wait for him to acknowledge it—to himself and the whole company.

Alderley stared at the table for a full minute. Then he lifted his head and met Dexter's gaze.

The expression in his pale blue eyes was that of sly triumph.

"Very well, Hart," he said. "We have a deal. One turn of the cards. Highest wins. I'll wager my firstborn child's hand in marriage."

Something about his expression gave Dexter

a feeling of unease, as if Alderley had the advantage.

"Not yet, Alderley," he said. "Your pledge must be legally binding."

"I hardly think we can draw up a marriage contract tonight," Alderley scoffed.

"We can draw up a promissory note that both parties can sign," Dexter said. "If we can find two men willing to act as witnesses."

Alderley nodded. "I'll agree, provided the note places an obligation on us both. If I lose, you must promise to honor the marriage. In turn, I shall march the bride down the aisle myself and hand her over with my full blessing."

"Of course." Dexter turned to their host. "Lord Strathdean, would you be so kind as to act as witness?"

Their host nodded. "Alderley should choose the other witness," he said.

"Very well," Alderley said. "I choose Stiles."

By the time the note had been drawn up and handed to Stiles for safekeeping, the music from the room next door had stopped, and the other guests had entered the drawing room. Alderley was playing into Dexter's hands. As a professed man of honor, he couldn't rescind his offer if he lost. Not with the eyes of half the ton on him.

Alderley reached for the cards.

"A new deck, if you please," Dexter said. "I want this to be a fair game. Honor demands it."

"What do you know of honor!" Alderley hissed.

"A damned sight more than you."

"Steady on, Hart," Strathdean said. "There's no call for that kind of talk with ladies present."

A footman passed him a new pack of cards, and he shuffled it, then cut the deck.

"Alderley, you first."

The older man picked a card and looked at it. A slow smile crept across his face, and then he placed it face-up on the table.

"The queen of diamonds," Strathdean said. "Now you, Hart."

Focusing his gaze on Elizabeth, Dexter picked a card and dropped it on the table.

He had no need to look at it. The look of glee on Elizabeth's face, and the whispers threatening through the room, told him all he needed to know.

"The ace of hearts."

"Let me be the first to congratulate you," Alderley said.

Why was the bastard smiling?

Dexter rose and extended his hand toward Elizabeth. "Miss Alderley, would you do me the honor…"

"Wait!" Alderley said. "What are you doing?"

"I believe I'm now engaged to your daughter."

"That's right," Alderley said, a smile on his

face. "My *first* daughter."

Elizabeth turned to her father. "Papa, surely you cannot mean…"

"I have another daughter," Alderley said.

"Have you taken leave of your senses, old chap?" Strathdean asked. "I've known you for over twenty years. You have two children—a son and a daughter."

"I have three children," Alderley said. My *natural* daughter is my firstborn. Her harlot of a mother blackmailed me into recognizing her as my own."

"Surely, you're jesting!" Stiles said.

"I'm perfectly serious," Alderley replied. "And now I can reap my reward in lieu of the expense of her keep. Thank the devil I'll no longer have to waste any more funds on her."

Elizabeth had gone pale with rage. "Papa!" she cried. "Tell them you're jesting! I'll marry Hart to preserve your reputation. I am happy to sacrifice myself—for you. And nobody need mention that *bastard* again!"

A volley of tutting resonated around the room at her coarse expression.

Hypocritical creature! It was she who'd suggested the scheme to extort her father's funds in order to secure his overt blessing on their marriage. Yet now, she was playing the martyr!

"Elizabeth, I won't throw you away on that uncouth brute when I have someone far more expendable," Alderley said. He turned his gaze to Dexter. "You wouldn't dream of going back on your word, would you, Hart? Imagine the damage it would do to your reputation! What other contracts might you be willing to break?"

The man was right. In a roomful of men—existing and potential investors—Dexter had signed a pledge. There was no going back without losing his reputation. And for a banker, reputation was everything.

Alderley struggled to his feet and held out his hand. Though Dexter longed to slice it off with a steak knife, he had no choice but to take it.

"It was a *pleasure* doing business with you, Hart," he said. "I trust you'll find satisfaction with your purchase. I'd call it the perfect match, but would argue that even the bastard daughter of a viscount ranks above the grandson of a black-smith."

"CELEBRATING ALREADY, HART?"

Dexter looked up from his brandy. His friend Harold Pelham stood before him, a broad smile on his face.

No, Dexter was most certainly *not* celebrating.

His plans to marry himself and his siblings to

titles had been destroyed. Dorothea was too old to consider a respectable union that didn't stink of desperation. Delilah had fallen pregnant out of wedlock. As for Daisy—that horse had already bolted.

"May I join you?" Pelham asked.

"It's a free country," Dexter growled. "A man can come and go as he pleases."

"Not in Whites." Pelham settled into a chair. "Fortunately, some havens exist to give a man sanctuary from the rest of the world."

"Are you here to escape the world, Pelham?" Dexter asked. "Or do you seek sanctuary from your wife?"

Pelham let out a laugh. "The secret to a successful marriage is each party having a haven in which to be themselves for a few hours, rather than one half of a couple. Of course, you'll soon learn this yourself, won't you, Hart? We should toast your good fortune."

Dexter sighed. "News travels fast."

"Most men win cash in a wager," Pelham said, "though Stiles won a horse last Season at the cast of a die. But I know of no man who managed to win himself a *wife*."

"I'd have preferred the horse."

Pelham laughed. "I'm sure you'll ride the woman just as well. Though, if I'm permitted to be honest, I'd say you'd be hard-pressed to find happiness shackled to the honorable Elizabeth

Alderley."

"I'm not marrying Elizabeth."

"Aren't you betrothed to Alderley's daughter?"

"Elizabeth has an older sister."

"There's a brother in the army," Pelham said, "but I know of no sister. Surely she'd have had her come-out by now?"

"It seems Alderley has a *natural* daughter," Dexter said.

"You jest."

"Unfortunately, not."

The humiliation at being bested still stung. Alderley had played a longer game than Dexter thought him capable of, revealing his piece on the chessboard when least expected.

"It seems he tucked her away in some obscure little village," Dexter said, "to be brought into play when he had use of her."

"Have you met her?"

"No," Dexter said. "With luck, I'll never have to."

"You'd be excused if you refused," Pelham said. "Alderley's on shaky ground if he takes out a lawsuit."

"It's a matter of honor," Dexter said. "I signed an agreement in front of some of the most prominent men of London society to wed Alderley's eldest child. With a business founded on reputation, I cannot risk breaking the promise

I gave my signature to." He drained his glass. "My only hope is that she'll do me the honor of jilting me at the altar."

Pelham let out a laugh. "That would increase your eligibility tenfold, my friend. Next to a title and a substantial income, there's nothing more attractive to a lady than a man with a broken heart."

"Then I'm safe," Dexter replied, "for I have no heart—at least not for a woman."

"I almost feel sorry for her," Pelham said.

"Don't," replied Dexter. "If she agrees to this marriage, then she'll prove she's as avaricious as her sister."

And he would take pleasure in teaching her what happened to women driven by avarice.

Chapter Two

"I DON'T UNDERSTAND!"

The child pouted and folded his arms. Meggie knelt beside him and placed a hand on his arm.

"It's quite simple, Thomas," she said. "The bishop moves along the diagonal—see? So if you place your knight within his eye line, then my bishop can take your knight."

She picked up the knight and moved it across the board.

"But, place him *here*," she said, "then not only does he threaten the queen, but he's safe from being taken by other pieces. That's the beauty of the knight, you see. Because he moves differently to the other pieces, he can capture them by deception and wit, rather than an outright attack."

"Like the knights in the story of King Arthur, which you taught me last week?"

"Yes!" she said. "Clever child!"

The door opened, and a simply-dressed woman with iron-gray hair walked in.

"Good afternoon, Mrs. Preston," Meggie prompted.

Nine little voices struck up in unison. "Good afternoon, Mrs. Preston!"

"Thank you, children," Mrs. Preston said. "That's enough lessons for today. But before you go, what do you say to Miss Alder?"

"Thank you, Miss Alder," the children chorused, and they filed out of the schoolroom.

Meggie tipped the chess set into a box.

"I'll never understand why you insist on teaching the children that game," Mrs. Preston said. "It's too difficult for them."

"As with anything," Meggie said, "it's easier to learn the basics while you're young. Thomas is a bright lad."

"But what opportunities will a child of his class have to play chess?"

"Perhaps none," Meggie replied. "But chess is a game of strategy, and as such, it can equip us for life. Learning the moves is simple. The complexity arrives when one begins to understand how all the pieces interact with an end goal. You must plan several moves, anticipating your opponent's moves, and adopt counter-strategies if necessary."

She hesitated, the flash of a memory stinging at her heart. "It also teaches us the necessity of sacrifice."

A look of sympathy crossed Mrs. Preston's eyes. She took Meggie's hand and gave it an affectionate squeeze. "Dear child." Mrs. Preston began tidying the books and papers.

"Oh, no," Meggie protested. "Let me."

The old woman let out a sigh. Since yesterday, she seemed to have aged.

"Is something the matter, Mrs. Preston?" Meggie asked.

"I'm just a little concerned about Mr. Adams."

"Our landlord?"

"His solicitor wrote to demand an increase in our rent," Mrs. Preston said, "and I have accounts in the village to settle. Mr. Jones is a kind man, but he's insisted that he'll supply us with no more meat until I've paid him. And Mr. Timmings asked me only yesterday where the payment was for the last bag of coal. It seems as if every tradesman in Blackwood Heath is demanding we settle our accounts, and I don't have sufficient funds."

I could ask Mr. Clayton for extra work," Meggie said. "A few more hours at the Rose and Crown will soon add up.

"Best get going," Mrs. Preston said. "You were due at the Rose and Crown five minutes ago."

Meggie glanced at the clock on the desk and gave a low cry.

"On no—what will Mr. Clayton think of me?"

"Doubtless the same as I," her companion said. "That you devote too much of your time to others. Now, run along and tell him he's not to utter a single harsh word unless he wishes to answer to me."

Meggie grabbed her shawl and dashed out of the tiny building. By the time she reached the inn, her sides ached. But she welcomed the exercise, which helped to stave off the bitter cold. With winter well on its way, the country was gripped by frost.

A side door opened, and a voice called out. "Afternoon, Meggie!"

"Mr. Clayton, forgive me, I…"

"No matter, lass," he said, "you're here now. Come in quickly. We're in sore need of your stew tonight with this cold weather, and we have a full house—plenty of empty bellies. Mary's got a nice bit of scrag end."

"I'd best get started," Meggie said. "That'll take some time to cook."

The innkeeper took her arm.

"Before ye go to the kitchen, lass, best make yourself presentable. There's a gentleman to see you."

"A gentleman?"

"I recognized him right away, though it's been eight years. I took him to the parlor where you can attend him in private."

Meggie's stomach clenched. Mr. Clayton could only mean one man—the man she feared above all others. A man who'd only ever looked at her with dislike, as if she were an insect he'd rather stamp out.

The last time she'd seen him had been eight years ago when she'd lain in a hovel, ruined, broken, and bleeding. Impervious to her grief, he'd lectured her on the shame she had brought upon his name while she grieved for an innocent life.

Billy...

In the years since, Alderley had given her a small stipend that contributed toward her board and keep. But she would have exchanged it in a heartbeat for a single word of affection from the man who was her father.

"How long has he been waiting?" she asked.

"About half an hour."

"I'd best go directly, for he'll be angry."

"Tidy yourself up first, lass. Ye look like an urchin!"

"I doubt he'll care."

"A little effort on your part won't hurt," he said. "Gentlefolk set too much store on manners and looks, but it's not our place to disagree. And you must understand why he could never publicly acknowledge you, don't you?"

"Of course," she said, blushing at his reference to her birth.

After splashing her face with cold water, she approached the parlor and knocked on the door.

"Enter!"

A shiver of fear rippled through her. Eight years had passed, but she still recognized the voice—a cold, nasal tone with a sharp edge as if every word were barking out an order.

He sat in a chair, the light from the fireplace casting sharp shadows across his face. With a huff of irritation, he struggled to his feet, his knuckles whitening as he gripped his cane.

She dipped into a curtsey. "Lord Alderley."

"Come here, child!" he snarled, tapping his cane on the floor. "Let me see you."

She approached him until he raised his hand.

"That's far enough." He looked her up and down, then circled her, muttering to himself about her appearance, as if he were a farmer inspecting a cow at auction. Thin, bony fingers grasped her chin and tipped her head up. His eyes narrowed in concentration, then he released her.

"I'd hoped for better," he said, "but you'll do."

"For what?"

"It's not your place to ask questions."

"It is if the answer affects my life," she said.

His face darkened, and he curled his hand into a fist. For a moment, he looked as if he was going to hit her. Then he sighed and sat down again, gesturing to a chair.

She folded her arms and tipped her chin up. Maybe a show of defiance would persuade him that she'd not be suited to his purposes, whatever they may be, and he'd leave her alone.

"Are you not going to sit?" he asked.

"Why should I?"

"Out of common courtesy, if nothing else. After all, I've been supporting you all your life. I can withdraw that support in an instant."

"Then why don't you?" she cried. "Why don't you leave here?"

"Because I have use for you. The time has come for you to show your gratitude."

"Gratitude?"

"Who fed and clothed you from the day you were born?" he asked. "Who took care of you after your sordid little disgrace when you showed yourself to be a slut, just like your mother?"

She flinched and stepped back.

"Stop right there, girl!" he said. "It'll be worse for you if you continue to defy me."

He gestured toward the chair. "Don't try my patience," he warned, his grip tightening on the cane.

She took a seat.

"That's better," he said. "Perhaps, after eight

years, you've learned your lesson."

The memory of loss overcame her will to defy him, and a tear splashed onto her cheek.

If Billy had not died—if she'd not killed him—would he be here now?

"Now's not the time for self-pity," Alderley said. "Your life is about to change for the better."

"I have a good life here," she said.

"What, tucked away in an obscure little village?"

Wasn't that what he'd wanted? Obscurity for his bastard?

"I have occupation and fulfillment here," she said. "It takes my mind off..."

He raised his hand. "Do *not* speak of it! You do me great injury by referring to it now. I'll forgive you this once, but shan't be lenient a second time. As for your husband, he'd have you horsewhipped if he discovered your sordid little secret."

"My *what?*"

"Your husband," he said, triumph in his voice. "You should thank me for finding someone willing to take you on."

"You expect me to marry?"

"I do," he said. "He's a respectable man—given his origins. And he's wealthy. You'll want for nothing, as long as you behave as a wife should."

Dread rippled through her. Despite his

words, it was clear that Alderley didn't like the man he'd promised her to.

"I don't want to marry," she said.

"It's not your place to question my judgment."

She rose to her feet. "I *won't* marry him!" she cried. "I can see you don't like him."

He jumped out of his chair and gripped her arm.

"You'll do as you're told," he snarled, "and Hart will take you, even if I have to drag you down the aisle in chains! I've wasted enough money on you, and it's time I reaped the reward!"

"What do you mean?" she asked.

"Did you never question the identity of the landlord for that pathetic little school you value so highly?" He gestured around the room. "Or who owns the freehold of this tavern?"

He pushed her back, and she stumbled against the door. "I'm sure Mrs. Preston will be most aggrieved if Mr. Adams raises the rent to a prohibitive level—or turns her out altogether—and Mr. Clayton will have much to say if his landlord, Mr. Attlee, evicts him on grounds of running a house of ill repute."

"You mean…"

A slow smile crossed his lips, and he nodded. "Yes, my dear child," he said. "I've owned you—and those on whom you depend—from the day your mother dumped you."

She drew in a sharp breath as the enormity of his words settled upon her. She thought she'd been enjoying a free and independent life. But in reality, it had never been her own. And now, she had two choices—to submit to the demands of the man who'd resented her all her life or to defy him and watch as he destroyed the lives of the few people she cared for.

He strode toward the door, and she moved aside, unwilling to feel his hands on her once more. A smile of victory glittered in his eyes.

He knew he'd cowed her.

"We leave immediately," he said.

"What about my things?" she asked. "My friends?"

"I've wasted enough time on you, girl, and wish to return home before nightfall. The marriage takes place next week."

Next week! Good lord!

"At least permit me to say goodbye," she pleaded.

"Don't be a fool," he snapped.

He opened the door to reveal two liveried footmen. They stood a head taller than Meggie and had brutish thick-set frames. As Alderley pushed her through the door, they flanked her on either side and, like gaolers, they escorted her down the stairs and through the main parlor. Her cheeks warmed with shame as the patrons ceased their chatter and stared.

"Meggie?"

She heard Mr. Clayton's voice and turned to catch a glimpse of his shocked white face. He moved toward her, but the footman blocked his path.

"Best make no fuss, sir," she said, "if you want to avoid trouble with your landlord, Mr. Attlee."

The footman grasped Meggie's arm and hauled her toward the waiting carriage, then he pushed her inside and squashed himself beside her.

Alderley climbed in after them and sat opposite.

Meggie leaned out of the window. "Mr. Clayton!" she cried.

"That's enough, miss," the footman said. "We don't want to upset his lordship, do we? Not when he's been kind enough to take care of you."

"Lord Alderley," she pleaded. He ignored her.

"Father!"

"Control your charge, Wilkes," he said to the footman. "Teach her the consequences of disobedience."

"With pleasure, your Lordship."

Wilkes tightened his hold on her. Scars and bruises adorned his hands—the trophies of a man who used his fists. His thickset body pressed against hers. Brute strength radiated from him.

He could control her body with one hand, and Alderley held the fate of those she held dear in his hands.

What could she do but yield? Even if she escaped, the few friends she had in the world would suffer.

The carriage set off, and she lurched forward with the motion. Thick fleshy fingers grasped her arm and yanked her back to the seat.

She tried to free herself, but his grip was too firm. "Do you intend to have me incarcerated?" she asked.

Alderley snorted. "Wilkes will tend to you until you're no longer my responsibility. Once you belong to Hart, there will be no necessity for correction on *my* part."

The footman licked his lips as if he relished the prospect of *correcting* her.

A week under Wilkes's command was almost too much to bear.

But what would come after?

And what man could be such a fearsome prospect for a husband that even Alderley felt the need to assign a gaoler to prevent her from escaping him?

Chapter Three

EXTER AND HIS business partner climbed out of the carriage, and both stared at the building.

The Alderley family chapel.

"Hell's teeth, Peyton, did you ever see such a godforsaken place?"

His companion laughed. "You'll find it a fitting environment for your black heart."

It was a testament to Peyton's usefulness that Dexter didn't call him out for such disrespect.

Oliver Peyton employed his business brain during the day with the accuracy of a master swordsman, and he was the only worthy opponent in chess in London. But by night, he was a dandy, who set reason aside and pursued women with gentle charm instead of a hunter's ruthlessness.

Unlike Dexter, to whom the game of seduction was just another chess match, where he could read a woman's intentions and desires several steps in advance.

Nobody could beat him at chess.

Or at seduction.

Oliver gave him a nudge.

"Cheer up, old boy. Alderley might swap the brides back!"

"Let's hope not," Dexter replied.

Oliver laughed. "You prefer to shackle yourself to a dried-up old maid from a country village than the honorable Elizabeth?"

Perhaps. Dexter had reconciled himself to his fate. However unpalatable she was—and a natural daughter raised in the gutter could not be considered anything but unpalatable—his bride would, most likely, be so grateful for being elevated from the mud pile that she'd submit to his every command.

"I daresay you'll relish the gratitude of a peasant," Oliver continued, "and I'm sure she'll be obliging enough to remain indoors while you explore London's bawdy houses to dine on sweeter meat!"

"That's enough!" Dexter growled. "In less than an hour, the woman will be my wife."

Oliver's smile disappeared. "I'm sorry, my friend, I was only trying..."

"I know," Dexter sighed. "To make light of

this godawful situation, I find myself in."

"You could always call it off," Oliver said. "None would think the worse of you."

"It's a question of honor," Dexter said. "And this way, I can keep Alderley in my sights. If he wishes to sacrifice one of his pawns, let it be to *my* advantage. He must have a purpose for giving her to me. Once I discover that purpose, I can use her for my own ends."

Oliver shook his head. "I almost feel sorry for her."

His words, unwittingly repeating Harold Pelham's observations of a fortnight ago, pricked at Dexter's conscience.

Dexter gestured toward the chapel. "Best get this over with."

The chapel was empty save for the parson and a black-clad man Dexter didn't recognize. He stood and issued a stiff bow as Dexter approached him.

"Mr. Hart," he said. "Permit me to introduce myself. Mr. Turner, at your service. I'm his lordship's steward."

"What happened to your predecessor?" Dexter asked.

The man colored and averted his eyes.

"Never mind," Dexter said. "No doubt the challenge of restoring Alderley's finances proved too much for him. I wish you greater success, though unless you're practiced in alchemy or witchcraft, you'll have a struggle on your hands."

"Which is why I'd be most obliged if you saw fit to discuss his lordship's debt with…"

Dexter raised his hand. "First, I deem it unseemly to discuss finances on what is supposed to be the happiest day of my life. And second, any plea on behalf of the Alderley estate must come from his lordship's mouth, for me to consider it."

A creak echoed around the church as the doors opened. A solitary figure stood, silhouetted in the light. Dexter sighed in irritation. He'd recognize that shape anywhere, given the numerous occasions on which it had been shown to him.

The newcomer walked down the aisle, slowly, as if in a procession, and the parson let out a nervous cough.

"I was right," Oliver whispered. "Alderley has swapped daughters."

The woman tipped her head up, greed and desperation in her eyes.

"What are you doing, Elizabeth?" Dexter hissed.

"I'm come to demand you see reason." She reached out her hand, and he brushed it aside. Her lips thinned into a frown, and it struck Dexter how unattractive she really was. Her sharp handsomeness displayed a meanness of spirit, which only served to emphasize what a lucky escape he'd had.

"What's done is done," he said. "You do yourself no favors being here, and your father would object to his prize possession, tainting herself with my presence."

"I can still persuade him," she said, her tone taking on a nasal whine. She grasped his wrist, her hand moving too quickly for him to avoid her. But where he'd once hardened at her touch, his skin only tightened in revulsion.

"You cannot want to marry that little harlot," she pleaded. "Think of your reputation! You'll be a laughing stock, tied to a woman of no parentage."

"She's your sister," he said, shaking off the offending hand. "You have at least one parent in common."

"She's a whore."

Elizabeth's voice bore all the cultivated brittleness of a lady, but the coarse expression gave her voice a shrewish tone.

He pushed her aside and strode to the front of the aisle where the vicar stood, waiting. Oliver joined him, and he stood, motionless, staring straight ahead.

The chapel clock struck two, and the doors creaked open, then shut with a bang. The vicar straightened his stance and gave a sigh of relief. Sharp, confident footsteps approached, accompanied by a lighter, softer footfall, moving at an irregular pace, as if their owner were being dragged along.

It seemed the bride was as reluctant as the groom.

"I'll be damned!" Oliver cried. "Guttersnipe she may be, but she scrubs up well."

"Spare me the humor," Dexter growled.

"I'm not jesting," Oliver replied. "Of all the indignities this union has piled upon your head, I can think of several women who'd be a worse prospect for warming your bed."

"Perhaps you'd care to take my place."

"I wouldn't dream of it." Oliver laughed. "But it looks as if your reputation has preceded you."

"What do you mean?"

"I've never seen a woman so miserable."

Dexter could no longer resist the temptation. He turned and caught sight of his bride.

Chapter Four

"DO NOTHING TO disgrace my name," Alderley said. "Do you hear?"

He leaned forward. "I'll hear you say it, girl."

Wilkes gripped Meggie's wrist until tears of pain stung in her eyes.

"Yes, *Papa.*"

Alderley's eyes darkened at her flash of defiance. But if she were to be sold as chattel by virtue of being his daughter, then the devil take him if he expected her to address him by his title.

Wilkes released her, and she slumped back in her seat as the carriage swayed to and fro en route to the chapel.

For the past week, she'd been living in a cottage on the Alderley estate, hidden from the main house. Wilkes attended her daily. Her 'personal footman,' Alderley had described him.

In reality, he was her gaoler, threatening her with punishment if she tried to flee—a punishment he'd carried out with relish.

Instinctively she pulled her sleeve down. The delicate lace cuffs on her bridal gown almost obscured the bruise on her wrist.

Alderley had made it plain that he'd have Mrs. Preston's school burned to the ground if she defied him.

The carriage halted outside the chapel. Wilkes climbed out, pulling her with him, and led her to the chapel door.

"Give her to me, Wilkes," Alderley said. "Remain by the door in case of trouble."

He glanced at Meggie, and she lowered her gaze. What was the point in causing more trouble? It would only earn her another bruise.

Alderley took her wrist and squeezed the bones together.

"Remember what I said," he hissed.

She nodded, and they set off down the aisle.

A lone woman sat in the front pew, dressed in a crimson gown, and matching wide-brimmed hat. It must be Meggie's half-sister, the honorable Elizabeth. She glanced over her shoulder, a sneer on her face, then resumed her attention on the front of the chapel.

Four men stood at the end of the aisle, including the vicar, holding an open bible in his hand. Meggie recognized the man to his left as

Alderley's steward. The other two had their backs to her. As Alderley pulled her along, her feet tripping as she tried to keep up, one of them turned and looked at her.

He had an open, expressive face, framed with light blonde hair. Soft, brown eyes crinkled into a warm smile, and she could have wept with relief. Her fears had been unfounded. Friendly, welcoming, and kind—before her stood a man with whom she had a chance at happiness.

He nudged his companion, who turned and stared at her.

The second man stood half a head taller. Thick, dark hair framed angular features. Dark brows formed a slash across his face. His mouth, full and sensual, creased into a scowl. Cold blue eyes fixed on her, anger in their expression. She shivered as if all warmth had been sucked out of the air.

He looked as if he lived in perpetual shadow as if a thundercloud hung continually above him.

In short, he looked the very embodiment of the devil.

A cold slab of ice solidified in her stomach, and she caught her breath and stopped.

Alderley tightened his grip.

"Do not disgrace me, girl."

The devil's eyes narrowed, and his brow furrowed into a frown. His jaw gave a tic as if he clenched his teeth. Meggie bit her lip to control her fear and resumed walking. He continued to stare at her, and her skin tingled as if his gaze burned. But she swallowed her concern and focused her attention on his companion. Surely, *he* was the groom. The devil did not seem the type of man who'd be bested in a game of cards.

Or in anything.

The angel made no move.

The vicar coughed, and the angel nodded and stepped aside, leaving her alone, standing beside the devil.

Dear god!

She had to crane her neck to see him. He had resumed his original position, body stiff, staring over the vicar's head, as if the whole ceremony bored him.

But he was not bored. His body vibrated with anger—shoulders stiff, arms by his sides, hands fisted.

She didn't know what was more frightening—the fury he harbored or his ability to suppress it almost to invisibility.

And in a matter of moments, she would belong to him.

Chapter Five

A S THE VICAR droned on, Dexter glanced at his wife.

Such a miserable-looking creature! What the devil had she to complain about? She was being lifted from poverty and illegitimacy.

He was the one with cause to be miserable.

But it wasn't her fault. She was just a pawn in Alderley's game, to best his enemy and win back his fortune.

Curse it! Dexter had been so diligent at feigning boredom that he'd missed most of what had been said, including his bride's name.

She was speaking now. Her voice was softer than he'd expected—unlike the throaty rasps of the women in the village he'd grown up in.

The vicar resumed his speech, and Dexter glanced at her. She seemed to have withdrawn into herself as if she were trying to disappear. Were she capable of that, Dexter's problems would be solved, and he could return to London with Oliver and enjoy a night's hard drinking.

She clutched the posy in front of her, knuckles white as her fingers curled round the stems. Not the expensive hothouse orchids Elizabeth had always demanded, but a simple array of wildflowers and grasses procured from a hedgerow. She lifted her hand and caressed one of the blooms, her fingertips tracing an outline of one of the petals.

An almost unnoticeable gesture, but one which conveyed tenderness. Had Dexter possessed a heart, the simple act might have touched it.

But he didn't. Hearts were for weaklings.

She lowered her hand again, and he glimpsed a darkening bruise on her wrist, not entirely concealed by the lace of her cuff. He cleared his throat, and her body stiffened. She moved the posy to hide the mark.

The chapel fell silent, and then the vicar closed his bible with a snap.

"Are we done?" Dexter asked.

The vicar nodded.

"Thank God. Then we can leave."

He reached for his bride's hand, then drew back, remembering the bruise.

"Follow me," he growled.

He retraced his steps along the aisle, not bothering to look back. Soft footsteps followed him. At least she understood her vow of obedience. And the greater the distance he put between himself and the Alderleys, the better. With luck, he need never see Elizabeth or her father again.

Alderley stepped out of his pew and blocked Dexter's path.

"Where are you going, Hart?" he asked.

"I'm anxious to return to London."

"You must grace us with your presence at the hall," Alderley replied, "for the wedding breakfast. My home is at your disposal—at least, for the next hour."

"For what purpose?"

"Honor," Alderley said. He lowered his voice. "Did you not demand it of me as part of our arrangement? I would not have you claim that I broke my word."

"You sound reluctant, *Father-in-law*," Dexter said.

Alderley flinched at the address, and Dexter smiled inwardly at the man's discomfort. Alderley may have foisted his by-blow on him, but he'd forever suffer the indignation of their being related by marriage.

"Say what you like of me, Hart," Alderley said, "but let it not be said that I was ungracious in victory."

"Victory?"

Alderley's lips thinned into a spiteful smile. "We both know you've secured the poor end of the bargain."

Dexter's bride said nothing. How could she display such stoicism? Or, perhaps, she'd weathered enough insults at Alderley's hands to be rendered immune. Her fingers curled round her posy, and she moved closer to Dexter until their bodies almost touched.

He caught his breath at the onset of an instinctive need to protect her. What had she suffered at Alderley's hands, that she sought comfort from a stranger—the man she had looked at with such fear in her eyes?

But the last thing he wanted was a weak, needy woman clinging to his coattails.

He glanced toward Oliver, who frowned, his eyes conveying disapproval. His bride—*what the devil was her name?*—would have been better off with Oliver, for he had something Dexter did not possess.

A heart.

But it was too late, now.

"Very well, Alderley," he said. "I would be delighted to accept your invitation."

THE WALLS OF the drawing room were smothered with portraits. Everywhere Meggie looked, a grim face stared back at her with haughty disapproval. Alderley's ancestors.

And hers. The blood of these reptiles ran through her veins.

Reptiles…

She giggled to herself, drained her glass, and set it aside. Almost immediately, a footman was upon her, sweeping aside the glass with a disapproving glare.

She pulled a face, then took a full glass from his tray and crossed the floor to inspect the ugliest of the portraits. A wrinkled face filled the frame, his skin a gray pallor, reminiscent of the lizards in Mrs. Preston's zoological textbooks. Pale eyes with yellowing whites stared down at her. The wrinkles around the nose gave the impression as if a bad smell lingered in the room. She read the inscription, carved into a metal plate at the base of the portrait.

Phineas Ignatius, fifteenth Viscount Alderley.

Meggie's great grandfather. Perhaps he turned in his grave at the notion of his grandson's bastard staining the shades of Alderley Hall.

His lips had a bluish tinge, and to Meggie, it looked as if at any moment, a long reptilian tongue would leap out and snatch a fly.

And Meggie was that fly—viewed by the rest of the party as nothing more than a minor irritation. Not even her new husband wanted anything to do with her. After he'd steered her into Alderley Hall, a possessive hand on the small of her back, he'd removed his hand as if she might burn him, then abandoned her to talk to the vicar.

She took a mouthful of champagne. The bubbles burst on her tongue, warming her throat and softening her senses. Though she struggled to focus, the ache in her wrist and heart lessened with each glass until she felt the uncontrollable urge to laugh and cry at the same time.

"Enjoying the champagne?" a female voice spoke in clear-cut tones.

Up close, the honorable Elizabeth was even more elegant. Her hair shone with a rich luster and had been fashioned into a mass of elegant curls that must have taken her maid hours to perfect.

In comparison, Meggie was a grubby urchin.

Elizabeth wrinkled her nose and lowered her gaze to the half-empty glass in Meggie's hand.

"Well? Do you have nothing to say?"

Meggie dipped into a curtsey, and Elizabeth gave her a cold smile. "At least you recognize our difference in rank," she said. "Let me give you a little friendly advice. When a young woman has supped on gin and ditchwater all her life, it's most unseemly to demonstrate the kind of enthusiasm for quality champagne that can only be equaled by a toper."

Meggie shook her head. What was wrong with these people that they spoke in riddles all the time? Was unintelligible speech a trait of the upper classes?

From the cold smile twisting on Elizabeth's lips, it was plain that she had issued an insult.

"Finest quality?" Meggie said. "I'm sure piss tastes better."

Elizabeth's lips thinned, and her eyes hardened, their pale blue the color of ice.

"Let me give you some more advice, my dear," she said, lowering her voice. "As a friend, I feel it only kind to warn you. Prepare yourself for a painful introduction to the marriage bed."

Meggie's hand shook. "A-a what?"

Elizabeth smiled. "He's like a bull," she said. "A bride will bleed like a pig on her wedding night, and you'll be no exception—assuming, of course, that he can stomach the notion of touching you."

At that moment, Alderley's steward approached them to issue his congratulations. Elizabeth gave him a haughty smile, waiting until he was out of earshot before resuming.

"My Dexter has a voracious appetite," she continued. "But marriage is not as lucrative an enterprise as whoring, my dear. Dexter is a miser when it comes to parting with his cash. And a wife is expected to spread her legs for free."

Meggie drew in a sharp breath and lifted her glass, but Elizabeth snatched it away.

"I think you've had enough of that."

"Who are you to say whether I've had too much?" Meggie asked. "You're…"

"I'm someone far above you in station," Elizabeth interrupted, her words coming out in a snarl. "And I'll be there to service Dexter when he tires of you."

"Elizabeth!" a voice spoke sharply.

Meggie turned and came face to face with Alderley.

"Papa," Elizabeth said, her cultured tone of voice returning. "I was just wishing my sister all the happiness she deserves."

"Quite so," he said. "But you mustn't neglect the other guests." He frowned at Meggie as if he believed her mere presence would taint Elizabeth.

Meggie drained her glass and curtseyed. "Let me take my leave instead."

Before they could respond, she moved away, pausing only to place her empty glass on a tray brandished by the footman who'd glared at her before. She set it down with a clang and gave him a sweet smile when he flinched.

Let him flinch! Let them all cringe at her presence! She had never felt so bold. But her boldness came hand in hand with dizziness. The room had grown overly hot, and she moved toward the window where, at least, the air was cooler.

Nausea rippling through her, she focused her attention on the view from the window. But the manicured lawn surrounded by hedges clipped into ugly, angular shapes only served to emphasize her inferiority.

"Mrs. Hart," a male voice said.

Ignoring it, she watched a pheasant stride across the lawn, trailing a long tail of brown feathers, the iridescence on its glossy blue-green head resembling an exotic jewel. A large dog bounded onto the lawn, and the bird launched itself off the ground with a series of squawks and flapping of wings.

If only Meggie could do the same and launch her ungainly, inelegant person through this very window and away from these people.

A hand touched her elbow, and she jumped and gave a low cry.

It was the angel from the chapel.

"Forgive me, Mrs. Hart," he said. "I didn't mean to startle you."

Mrs. Hart.

No longer was she Meggie, or even Margaret Alder. She had lost her name as well as her freedom. She was now defined by the man who owned her, Dexter Hart.

"I'm sorry," she said. "I find it strange to find myself…" she gestured to herself, "…to find…"

"...that you must be addressed by a name which, until a sennight ago, you'd never heard of?"

Her cheeks warmed with embarrassment. "N-no, of course not."

"There's no need for apologies," he said. A gentle hand touched her arm, and he smiled. "Those of us able to direct our lives often fail to appreciate that others are not so fortunate. I understand the fear you must feel."

"I'm not afraid, sir."

He smiled, and she blushed. His direct gaze seemed to penetrate her thoughts and recognize the lie. "Then you're braver than most, in having conquered it."

He gave a deep bow and clicked his heels together. "Permit me to introduce myself," he said. "Oliver Peyton, at your service."

She held out her hand. "Mr. Peyton."

He took it and lifted it to his lips. "A pleasure, madam," he said. "May I take the liberty of giving you some advice regarding the state of fear?"

"Please do."

"Knowledge," he said, "is the most effective cure for fear."

"I have knowledge enough," she said. "Just because I'm beneath everyone here, including the footmen, doesn't mean I lack education."

He smiled. "Intelligence and knowledge don't always walk hand in hand," he said. "An excellent

Latin scholar may know nothing of modern languages. He—or she—may quake with fear when faced with the French tongue, lest his ignorance of it is exposed to the world."

"And on what topic do you consider me lacking in knowledge?"

"On my friend." He nodded toward the groom, who was deep in conversation with Alderley, while Elizabeth watched from a distance, a dark scowl on her face.

"Let me increase your level of knowledge as far as I can," Mr. Peyton continued. "My friend listens more than he speaks. He lives in a difficult world and has to be hard to thrive within it."

"Why are you telling me this?" she asked. "Do you wish to make me afraid?"

"Quite the opposite," he replied. "Don't take much notice of his demeanor. He may be uncompromising, but he's not a cruel man. He's straight and true, and I know of none fairer, nor as honorable."

"And do fairness and honor lead to happiness?" she asked, her husband's words about victory and bargains ringing in her head. "A quest for fairness is little more than a thirst for retribution. Honor is no better, for it's a concept used to justify vengeance."

He smiled. "You're not what I imagined you to be, Mrs. Hart."

"What did you imagine?" Meggie asked, her

temples throbbing with the onset of a headache. "A guttersnipe? Or a harlot?"

The conversation stopped, and she looked round to see her new husband staring directly at her, his expression dark. Behind him, Elizabeth watched her, a cold smile on her thin lips.

Mr. Peyton was wrong. No amount of knowledge would conquer her fear. Her husband loathed her and desired another.

Mr. Peyton touched her arm in a gentle gesture. "Are you well, Mrs. Hart?"

"I have a headache."

"Perhaps you indulged in a little too much champagne," he said. "I loathe the stuff. Overpriced, harsh on the palate, and guaranteed to elicit the most shocking pains behind the eyes. But society raves over it. By convincing each other of its prestige, viscounts and earls perpetuate the myth that only the best people drink the best champagne. The wine merchants must be laughing at their stupidity—laughing as they drive to their banks with their profits."

"Banks such as my husband's?"

He smiled. "The very same."

She continued to watch as Elizabeth approached the groom and curled her fingers round his arm.

"Pay no attention to her," Mr. Peyton said.

"He wanted *her*, didn't he?" Meggie asked.

"Perhaps at first, when formulating his plans, but he feels very different now. He said so this morning."

"His plans?"

Mr. Peyton colored and looked away.

"Forgive me, I've said too much," he said. "Please permit me to offer my congratulations, and wish you every happiness. I have no reason to doubt you'll be happy. You strike me as a very honest young woman. And my friend values honesty and sincerity above all." He lowered his voice and winked. "Which is why the *honorable* Elizabeth would have proved a disastrous match. The adjective which applies to her title bears no reflection on her character."

"Honesty, Mr. Peyton?"

"Of course," he said. "You'll find such a characteristic is sorely lacking among society. It seems that the higher born a man is, the less honesty he possesses. My friend may be an imposing sort of man, but his anger only comes to the fore when he finds himself deceived. I assure you, good lady, that *you* have nothing to fear from him, as long as you remain truthful and honest."

He bowed and took his leave.

Well-meaning he might be, but he'd confirmed one thing—that her husband had wanted another woman.

As to fairness and honesty—Mr. Peyton's words sent a shiver of dread through her. What would her husband think if he discovered her secret?

Chapter Six

RATHER THAN SOOTHE Meggie's already strained nerves, the carriage only increased her nausea.

Elizabeth had been right. Not only was it unseemly to drink so much champagne, but unwise. The dulling of the senses, which she'd welcomed, had turned into an ache in her temples.

Her husband—the man to whom she now belonged—sat opposite, body stiff, jaw set into a firm line. Ever since ushering her inside the carriage and barking an order to the driver, he'd remained silent, his gaze fixed out of the window.

Mr. Peyton had opted to travel separately. After shaking the bridegroom's hand and giving him a pat on the back, he'd bowed over her hand and offered her a smile of reassurance before taking his leave.

But looking at the stern, dark scowl before her, Meggie felt anything but reassured.

While his attention was fixed on the landscape outside, she could watch him unobserved. Taller than most, his broad frame filled out his jacket which, though cut in a clean, elegant style, was such a dark shade of blue one might mistake it for black. Even his waistcoat was a deep gray, devoid of color as the rest of his attire. Her husband clearly preferred stark, sharp colors. His boots, which had been polished until they gleamed, were black.

The only splash of color was his eyes—clear blue made all the more intense due to the lack of color elsewhere.

And his lips.

His mouth creased in a frown. Below, a small scar curled over his chin. But rather than render him unpalatable, it gave him a dangerous, piratical air.

What might that mouth look like if he smiled? Could those eyes, which carried such intensity, sparkle with joy?

Was he capable of happiness?

She lifted her gaze to find those eyes staring directly at her. He held her look as if she were an animal caught in a net.

She was no match for him, and he knew it. Her cheeks flaming, she looked away. When she glanced back, he had resumed his attention on the view from the window.

After a while, the tension in the atmosphere thickened until she could no longer bear it.

"I-I wonder," she said. "Might I ask…"

Her voice trailed away as his head snapped round. She closed her mouth and swallowed.

He raised an eyebrow. "Yes?"

"Might I ask how far we are from our destination?"

"We're going to my house in London."

"I don't know where that is."

He rolled his eyes and sighed. For a moment, his expression softened. "I take it you've *heard* of London," he said, not bothering to wait for a response. "It's twenty miles from Alderley Hall."

He turned his head away again.

"How long will it take to…"

"It'll take as long as it takes," he interrupted gruffly. Then he hesitated and narrowed his eyes as if in concentration. "Forgive me," he said. "Would you remind me of your name?"

If she required further proof of her irrelevance, he had just given it.

"Meggie," she said.

"What the devil's sort of name is that?"

"Margaret Frances Alder," she said. "Shall I write it down for you? I can write, you know."

His eyes flashed, and he leaned forward. She shrank back, and he shook his head and sighed.

"With your permission, I shall call you Margaret," he said. "I cannot abide by an excess of formality."

She could hardly refuse, for he'd spoken it like an order, rather than a request.

"And," he said, "my name is…"

"Dexter William Hart," she finished. "With your leave, I shall call you husband."

He arched an eyebrow.

"Unless you'd prefer sir," she said. "Or my lord. Or master."

His eyes darkened. "You're my wife, not my servant. And I dislike formality. You may call me Dexter."

"Husband, it is."

His mouth twitched, and for a moment, she thought he might smile. A twinkle flashed in his eye, a glimpse of the sun hidden behind a thundercloud, which strived to break free.

Then his expression returned to that of indifference, but she now saw it for what it was, the outer shell of a man who concealed his thoughts from the world. Once again, she struggled to understand how Alderley could have bested such a man at cards.

But was indifference worse than anger? Anger implied that she was, at least, worthy of notice.

Back at Blackwood Heath, she'd served a purpose. She'd made a difference to the lives of the children at Mrs. Preston's school, and Mr. Clayton had appreciated her help.

But the man before her needed no one, least of all Meggie. At best, she was an inconvenience—at worst, a constant reminder of how Alderley had duped him.

The poor end of the bargain.

A tear splashed onto her cheek. She turned her head to conceal her expression and wiped away the tear.

"Margaret."

She jumped at the harsh tone in his voice but fixed her gaze on the wall of the carriage.

He sighed, and his voice softened. "It seems as if our marriage—and whatever the circumstances, we must call it such—has not begun well."

He paused as if waiting for a response, but she remained silent. If she spoke, her voice would betray her despair.

"We must make the best of it," he said.

She closed her eyes as another tear spilled onto her cheek.

He sighed.

"I'm no fool," he continued. "You're as reluctant about this arrangement as I. But I consider myself a fair man. I'll ask nothing of you, other than you abide by the vows you uttered today. I know little of your capabilities, but provided you treat me with respect, I see no reason why we cannot find a suitable degree of contentment in the situation in which we find ourselves."

His words, spoken in the manner of a business proposal, might have deepened her despair eight years ago. But she'd learned the hard way that the passionless words of a man who disliked her were preferable to the pretty speeches of a man bent on seducing her.

She summoned the courage to look at him. Clear blue eyes stared uncompromisingly at her. Her skin tightened under his frank appraisal, unburdened by social niceties. Raw power vibrated beneath the calm, controlled exterior.

He had no need to seduce. The air around him vibrated with vitality and virility, a mesmerizing power as addictive as any drug. Most likely, businessmen fell over themselves to gain his approval, and women competed to secure his attention.

Her cheeks warmed under his gaze, and her body flushed, sending heat to other parts. He lowered his gaze, and a little pulse of need throbbed deep inside her as if invisible fingers caressed her skin. The breath caught in her throat, and she turned away.

His eyes elicited a secret thrill, the prospect of awakening new sensations…

"Do we have an agreement?" he asked.

"Y-yes," she said. "I will abide by my vows. And…" steeling courage, she looked at him again to prove she was not afraid, "…and you shall abide by yours."

The corner of his mouth twitched.

"Then we have an agreement," he said. "Above all things, I value the truth. In business and," he gestured toward her, "in a marriage. Abide by that, and I'll give you no cause to regret our union."

She leaned back and relaxed, only then realizing she'd been tensing her body. Perhaps there was hope after all.

"Tell me what happened to your wrist, Margaret." A flicker of compassion gleamed in his eyes.

Instinctively, she reached for her sleeve and pulled it down to conceal the bruise—evidence, as Alderley had said, of her willfulness and disobedience.

The last thing she wanted was her husband's pity.

And what had Alderley said?

He'll have you horsewhipped…

"I-I sprained it," she said. "I slipped and fell."

Almost at once, his expression hardened, and he sat back, curling a hand into a fist.

He hadn't inquired out of compassion. He'd been testing her honesty.

And she had failed.

Chapter Seven

DEXTER OPENED HIS pocket watch and checked the time.

Again.

Where the devil was she? Hadn't she understood the need for punctuality? Not to mention the fact that he was starving.

He looked up as he heard a noise. Still in her wedding gown, she stood at the top of the staircase with the posture of the unrefined.

It was worse than he thought.

He held out his hand. "Come here, then."

She hesitated, then descended the stairs and took his hand. Her little fingers were ice cold, and for a moment, he was struck by an overwhelming need to warm them. Then, propriety recalled, he grasped her wrist with his free hand and placed her hand on his arm.

The color rose in her cheeks, but she said nothing, and he led her into the dining room and escorted her to a chair at one end of the table, then took his seat at the opposite end.

A footman entered, brandishing a tureen of soup.

"Do we have guests?" she asked.

"Whatever for? I hardly want to be accompanied on my wedding night."

"W-what about your family?"

"My sisters are currently residing in Bath," he said, "and my brother chooses to live elsewhere. We are alone."

She looked down. "The table is so big," she said. "Will we dine here every night?"

"We can hardly dine in the kitchen."

The footman approached her and presented the tureen. She eyed it with suspicion.

"You help yourself," Dexter said. "Do I need to show you?"

"No."

The footman's lip curled in a sneer as she grasped the ladle, hands trembling, and lifted it. She deposited a ladleful of soup into the bowl in front of her. A drip of bright green liquid splashed onto the tablecloth. The footman tutted and stared at it markedly. Dexter glared at him. However lacking in grace his wife was, the servants had no right to point it out.

"John, see that wife is tended to properly," he

ordered. "Send someone to clean her place."

"Very good, sir." The footman gave a sly grin and slid out of the room.

Yet another servant needing to be dismissed. If they insulted his wife, then they also insulted him.

He'd seen their stares as she'd stumbled out of the carriage on their arrival, uttering a curse when she tripped on the steps. Word would spread around London that Dexter Hart, the man who aspired to rub shoulders with the aristocracy, had married a peasant, born on the wrong side of the blanket, who used the language of the gutter.

It wouldn't do to dismiss a servant every day, or there'd be none left by the weekend.

He lifted his wine glass and drained the contents. How could a man such as he even begin to make this timid little thing happy?

Unpleasant as Elizabeth might be, he could, at least, have been able to satisfy her needs. All he'd need to do was furnish her with enough pin money to adorn herself with jewels, bed her four times a week, and turn a blind eye to the string of lovers she'd inevitably take once she realized how much he despised her.

In many respects, Margaret reminded him of his sister Daisy. But his wife was not his sister. Daisy had chosen to live a life of obscurity in the country and, try as he might, he'd never been able to persuade her to enjoy the comforts his successes could now afford them.

And as for Delilah—pregnant out of wedlock and now languishing in Bath, awaiting her confinement with Dorothea—his hopes to align his family with the ton were all but destroyed.

He glanced up and noticed his wife watching him. She looked away and remained motionless in her seat. Perhaps she wasn't hungry, though he'd heard her stomach growl in the carriage.

He reached for the soup spoon and lifted it. Almost immediately, she did the same, her eyes focused on his hands. He dipped the spoon into the soup and lifted it to his lips. She mirrored the gesture. Her spoon caught the edge of her bowl, and she flinched.

How could he begin to transform her into the type of wife he'd wanted? He needed a hostess to charm dinner guests and prospective clients' wives with her accomplishments in the drawing room while he wooed the men over port and cigars. He had no use for a country milkmaid who couldn't even cope with consuming a simple bowl of soup.

But she did not entirely lack in charm. The sight of her in that wedding gown had sent a bolt of lust through his body until his breeches became too tight. And now, as she leaned over the soup bowl, he caught a glimpse of the valley between them. His mouth watered at the notion of exploring the flesh concealed beneath her lace tuck, seeking out her little buds. Would they bead for him in anticipation of his touch?

And when he took her to bed—would she blossom like a ripe, pink flower, opening up at his touch? Could he mold her into the shape he desired—fashion her into the perfect bed partner—a willing, eager mate, to spread her legs at his command?

The meal concluded, he rose from his seat.

"It's time for you to retire while I take my port," he said. "I'll send for Mrs. Draper to attend you.

He could almost taste her relief. He issued a stiff bow, then exited the dining room and headed for his study. He needed time away from her to clear the fog of lust, which, if unchecked, would result in him tossing her skirts up and thrusting himself into her from behind over the dining room table.

His manhood twitched in need.

Curse his body! He reached for the decanter and poured a brandy. At all costs, he needed to soothe the raging ardor. He was a large man, and the sight of him fully erect would likely send her into a fit of apoplexy. Though the aristocracy might deem him uncouth, he at least understood that etiquette demanded that his bride *not* be unconscious with terror when he deflowered her.

MEGGIE STARED AT the dressing table mirror, but she didn't recognize the woman staring back. Her hair hung in unruly strands about her face, and her gown sported a green stain down the front.

Her wedding gown. The only fine gown she'd ever had, and now she'd ruined it.

But there was nothing to be gained from self-pity. The sooner she was asleep, the sooner she could face tomorrow and the rest of her life. Her husband might be an unpleasant sort of man and a darkly handsome one at that, but he lacked the air of cruelty which had lingered around Alderley.

She reached behind her back to undo the buttons of her gown. The action lifted the cuff of her sleeve to reveal the bruise on her wrist, the bruise her husband had noticed.

Would he correct her, as Alderley had done? Is that what society husbands did?

She jumped at a knock on the door and paused, her stomach fluttering. A female voice called out.

"Ma'am? May I come in? It's Mrs. Draper."

The door opened to reveal a plump woman in an iron-gray dress, a clean white apron, and a bunch of keys hanging from her waist. She was one of the few servants who'd looked at her with kindness—unlike that footman.

"I hope you don't mind my forwardness, ma'am," the woman said, "but seeing as you didn't bring a maid with you, I wondered if you needed assistance."

"Assistance?" Meggie asked. "What with?"

"With getting undressed, of course."

"I don't understand."

Mrs. Draper shook her head, tutting. "The master could at least have warned us…"

She sighed. "Never mind. Tomorrow I'll set about finding a maid for you. Do you have any preferences?"

Meggie shook her head. "I-I don't know. I've never…"

A gentle hand touched her shoulder. "Of course, my dear, I understand. We can discuss it tomorrow. Shall *I* help you tonight?"

Meggie shook her head. Her nightgown was frayed, and she'd endured enough contempt and pity in the past few hours to last a lifetime.

"Very well," Mrs. Draper said. "I'll leave you to ready yourself for the master."

"Ready myself?"

"Yes. Best be quick. He'll be here soon."

"B-but he has his own chamber!" Meggie said.

"That he does, but you must know he'll be visiting you tonight." The housekeeper gestured toward the door at the far end of the chamber. "He'll use the adjoining door. Did your mama never speak of your wedding night?"

Heat warmed Meggie's cheeks. "I never knew my mother."

"Then let me advise you as a mother would," Mrs. Draper said. "Undress quickly, blow out the candles, and await him in the bed. Once your chamber's in near darkness, he'll know to enter. But be quick, my dear. He's not a man who likes to be kept waiting."

As if on cue, a murmur of voices rose behind the adjoining door.

"That'll be him, with his valet," Mrs. Draper said. "Hurry now!" Before Meggie could protest, she opened the trunk and pulled out Meggie's nightgown. If she noticed the frayed hem, she said nothing, but her eyes conveyed sympathy as she handed the garment over.

"If I may be so bold, ma'am, let me reassure you that it will be over quickly. I'll send Tilly to tend to you in the morning in case of any— discomfort. There's nothing a good dish of sweet tea won't fix. You needn't worry about rising early. A new bride is expected to rest after her wedding night."

Discomfort...

Mrs. Draper excused herself and left Meggie alone. Mindful of the voices next door, she removed her wedding gown, slipped off her underclothes, and pulled her nightgown on. Then she extinguished the candles, and the room was in darkness, save for a sliver of light at the bottom of the adjoining door and the orange glow from the fireplace.

The voices stopped.

Meggie slipped under the bedsheets and waited. Her heart pounded in her ears at the eight-year-old memory of pain and heartache.

Her husband was such a large man. How much more would he hurt her, compared to…

She closed her eyes, praying sleep would claim her. A clock chimed in the distance, and she counted eleven notes. On the final stroke, the adjoining door creaked open, and a tall shape entered the chamber. The bed shifted with his weight, and he slipped in beside her. His body heat seeped through the bedsheet, and she turned her head to face him.

He lay on his back, the outline of his profile silhouetted against the diffused light from the fireplace. He blinked, and his eyes glittered as he stared at the ceiling. The tick-tick of the clock on the mantelshelf seemed to grow louder, but he made no move.

At length, he sighed and rolled toward her, and she felt his breath quickening against her cheek.

But still, he made no move to touch her. Eventually, she could bear the silence no longer.

"Are you g-going to touch me?" she blurted. "You don't have to…" she waited, but he remained silent, "…if you don't want to."

"Take off your nightgown. I'll be as gentle as I can."

His voice was a low growl, but his tone was kinder than it had been all day. He moved closer, and she drew in a sharp breath.

She hadn't realized he was naked.

She grasped the hem of her nightgown and pulled it over her head. Perhaps if he'd promised her gentleness, she might be able to trust him. What reason would he have to lie, given the power he had over her?

He moved on top of her and nudged her thighs apart with his knee. She turned her head aside, unwilling to see the expression in his eyes—to have it confirmed that he saw her merely as a tool by which to best Alderley.

He placed his elbows on either side of her, and she felt something hot and hard nudging against her thigh. She parted her legs wider and waited for the onslaught.

He thrust forward, and she cried out in anticipation of the pain. But there was no pain—not like before. Only a tight pinch. He thrust into her again and again, his breathing growing hoarser with each movement. The discomfort as he'd entered her intensified, but before it grew unbearable, he let out a groan and collapsed on top of her.

When he withdrew, she opened her eyes to

find him staring down at her, his eyes glowing in the dark.

"You deceived me," he said. His voice, though quiet, held a note of danger.

"I don't know what you mean."

"I think you do. Another man was there before me."

Fear spiked through her. "Who told you?"

"It seems *you* just did. A man knows, and you've confirmed it with your response."

He climbed off the bed and strode toward the fireplace, seemingly oblivious of his nakedness. The firelight caught the planes of his muscles, showing his finely sculpted form. He placed a hand on the mantelshelf and studied the fire, his back to her.

"Does Alderley know you weren't a maid?"

"Yes."

He sighed. "I'll wager he's laughing at my expense."

"Your expense?"

"Yes," he said. "Not only has he deceived me into wedding his by-blow, I find that she's sullied."

Almost as soon as he'd spoken the words, he flinched.

"Forgive me," he said. "I shouldn't have said that."

"Why not?" she cried. "My father tricked you into wedding his bastard when you wanted his legitimate daughter—the one who told me that you'd soon tire of me and ask her to service you instead."

"She said *what*?" He sat on the bed, and she drew her knees up and pulled the bedsheet to her chin as if to protect herself.

"Who was he?" he asked.

"It's not important."

"It is to me if I'm to wake in the morning to find some low-life sniffing at my door."

"There's no chance of that, I assure you."

"Then I must be content with that," he said, "if somewhat disappointed that I was not your first."

His words cut through her heart. Why was it that a man could deceive a naïve young girl with pretty speeches to seduce her, only to abandon her afterward—yet she was the one who must live with the consequences?

"It happened once," she whispered. "A long time ago."

The bed shifted under his weight. "Why should I believe you?"

"I have no reason to lie."

"Yet, you lied to me today."

"No, I didn't!" she cried. "I made a vow to honor and obey a stranger—a man of few words and sour disposition, who had no wish to take me for a wife. A man who loathes me almost as much as the father who sold me to him. I will stand by my vows. And I am not afraid of you."

"Aren't you?"

She slipped her hand beneath the bedsheet to conceal the bruise on her wrist. "I've known enough of cruelty to learn the futility of fear. The inevitable will happen, whether I fear it or not."

"You're wrong," he said.

"In what way?"

"I don't loathe you. Far from it."

He crawled across the bed, his muscles rippling with each movement as if he were a lion, poised to devour his prey. Then he grasped the bedsheet.

"Will *you* show me cruelty?" she asked.

"No." He tugged at the bedsheet, and it fell away, exposing her body. His eyes darkened with hunger as he dropped his gaze.

He reached toward her and cupped her breast. Her skin tightened with an unfathomable need, and her nipple beaded against his palm. He flicked the peak with his thumb and curled his mouth into a smile. A wicked sensation pulsed between her thighs at his touch.

"Will you show me mercy?" she whispered.

"No, my dear," he said. "I will show you pleasure."

Chapter Eight

DEXTER'S MANHOOD HARDENED at the sight before him. Her skin was smooth as cream, glowing in the firelight. She had the body of a courtesan, built to tempt and ensnare a man.

And another had claimed that body first.

Yet the fear in her eyes had all but obliterated the anger and betrayal he'd felt on hearing her confession. The expression in her eyes spoke of innocence, and she was the exact opposite of Elizabeth.

No, his little wife was innocent in spirit, even if her body had been used. But Alderley had tricked him thoroughly and was, most likely, expecting Dexter to confront him. That old bastard would do anything to destroy Dexter's reputation and would relish spreading tales around the clubs of London of how he'd conned him.

The woman sitting before him now was not to blame for her father's machinations. Doubtless she lacked the wit to understand what was happening. Tucked away in obscurity lest her status as a bastard threaten her father's good name, she was, most likely, uneducated and naïve—an unwitting pawn, a minor piece which Dexter's opponent chose to sacrifice at a minimal cost.

Every chess player knew that a pawn had little value compared to his other pieces. Pawns were disposable. Alderley would never have consented to give him Elizabeth, for she was a more powerful piece. A queen—the one piece a chess master was reluctant to sacrifice.

A mere pawn his wife might be, and she must be removed from London with all haste.

Removed for her own well-being. Tucked away in the country, in the confines of Molineux Manor, she'd want for nothing, and she'd be safe. She may be the last woman he wanted for a wife, but he had no wish to make her life a living misery. He'd seen the bruises on her wrist. And he'd seen the fear in her eyes each time she looked at him. She was like an injured animal— and he was the last person in the world capable of giving her comfort.

But, for now, as promised, he would give her pleasure.

He grasped the bedsheet and pulled it back. At first, she resisted, then she met his gaze and yielded. Though she was thin, her body had lovely curves. Her breasts were full and shapely, and the prospect of tasting them pleased him. His gaze wandered across her body—the softly rounded belly, the delicate flare of her hips, and the nest of curls at her core.

"Lie back," he commanded.

Her lips parted in surprise. At first, she remained still, then she complied. He lay beside her and reached toward her face. She flinched, and he stopped.

"Are you afraid?"

Her eyes glistened, but she shook her head. He placed his palm on her face and caressed her skin in the manner of a stablemaster taming a filly. Her body tensed as he continued, following the lines of her body, stroking her neck, her throat, until he reached her breasts. Her nipples were already peaked for him. She gave a little whimper of surprise.

"W-what's happening?"

Whoever claimed her first had known nothing of pleasure. The true mark of prowess was the ability to give a woman pleasure rather than merely rutting her. And he could think of nothing more pleasurable than having his wife writhing underneath him, begging him to take her.

He placed a light kiss on her breast. She gave

a little gasp, and he circled her nipple with his tongue. When he covered her breast with his mouth and sucked hard, she bucked and gave a sharp cry. The air filled with a sweet, musky smell, the unmistakable aroma of female need, and he found himself caught in a wave of powerful lust.

Jealousy overcame his lust, and he suckled harder, relishing the cries which erupted from her throat. He thrust his hand between her thighs, and she parted them for him. He almost came undone as he touched the damp curls at her center, and his fingers met her needy heat. She may not know it, but she was ready for him. He ran a fingertip along her flesh until he found the secret bud, and her body jerked, and she cried out.

How could he resist? He lowered his head, drinking in the sweet, exotic smell of female desire. Why the perfumers of Paris saw fit to distill flowers and spices was beyond him. All they need do was bottle the essence of female need, and they'd make a fortune.

He placed a light kiss inside her thigh, and she drew in a sharp breath and tried to clamp her thighs together.

He held her firm, and she let out a whimper. "Please…"

"Please what?" he asked, relishing his conquest. He knew he'd have her begging for him but had not imagined victory would come so quickly.

"Please, don't let it hurt again."

Her desperate plea doused his need for conquest.

He lifted his head. "Did I hurt you before?"

She nodded. "Does it always hurt?"

"Usually only the first time."

"But the second time hurt also."

"Did your mother not tell you about the marriage bed?" he asked.

"I never knew my mother."

"Then I must show you myself. Hold still, and trust me."

Hardly silver-tongued words of seduction, but she complied, and he slipped a finger inside her.

"What are you…oh!" she cried out as he teased her little nub.

Once more, she parted her legs. She may not beg with words, but her body knew what it wanted. He lowered his head and dipped his tongue into her folds, breathing in her sweet scent. She shuddered, the tremors of her body vibrating through him. Her legs shifted in a slow dance as she reached her peak.

Little mewing cries escaped her lips, and she thrust her hips toward his face. Her body rippled and contracted around him as she peaked again while he kissed and licked her.

Eventually, her cries subsided, and her body relaxed. By the time he lifted his head, she had fallen asleep, a woman well pleasured.

Her mouth had curled into a small smile of contentment. It was the first time he'd seen her smile, and the peaceful expression tore at his heart. His manhood strained with the need to be buried inside her, but he clenched his hands and sat back. Though she was his to do whatever he liked with, he had no wish to see that beautiful smile disappear. What might she look like if she smiled when awake?

Would she ever smile at him?

He shook his head. He was turning into a sentimental fool, ruled by a pretty smile and a willing body. Better for her if she learned her place sooner rather than later—and it was better if she did that in the country.

WHEN MEGGIE WOKE, the fire had gone out, and the chamber was in darkness. She smiled to herself. Her predicament was not as bad as she'd feared. When her husband had realized she wasn't a virgin, he'd been angry at first—those cold, blue eyes had flashed like a steel blade. But then he seemed resigned to it.

The memory of her pleasure pulsed through

her, and she shifted her legs to recall the delicious sensation of his intimate caresses, his mouth on her flesh…

And he'd joined her in bed. Rather than be abandoned and unloved, hope sprang forth that she would be cherished and cared for.

She reached across the bed to find it empty.

Her husband had abandoned her during the night.

He was no different from the others. Her mother had abandoned her when she was a baby. Her father had tucked her away out of sight. As for *him*…

She cursed herself. Resurrecting that memory only led to pain.

Like the rest of them, her husband had taken what he wanted, then had no further use for her.

He hadn't even kissed her.

What might he do now? Find another to satisfy his appetite, just as Elizabeth said he would? Was that why he had a separate chamber, so he could enjoy women he desired, while the woman he'd never wanted slept next door?

She rolled onto her side and succumbed to the tears.

Chapter Nine

DEXTER LOOKED UP as his wife entered the breakfast room.

"Good morning, husband."

She sat at the end of the table. Though her voice was flat, she looked as if she'd been crying.

"Are you well—Margaret?" he asked.

She glanced at the footman, then nodded. Dexter gestured to the servant.

"Please serve breakfast to your mistress," he said. "Forgive me, what's your name?"

"Charles, sir."

"Charles," Dexter said. "Perhaps some eggs and a little bacon, unless my wife objects."

She looked up, her nut-brown eyes watching him with uncertainty. "Thank you," she said, "that would be most kind."

She waited until the footman had left before

she started eating.

"You look tired," he said. "Forgive me. I assumed you'd remain in your chamber this morning."

She colored but said nothing.

"Would you like some tea?" he asked. "I can ask..." he hesitated and gestured toward the door. What was the damned man's name?

"Charles," she said.

"Charles, yes, that's it. I can ask Charles to pour you a cup."

"Are you in the habit of forgetting the names of those you deem unimportant?"

Ah! There it was. She possessed spirit, though it had, no doubt, been suppressed most of her life.

He lifted his teacup and drained the contents. "I make it my business to know every one of my employees personally," he said. "It ensures their loyalty. The root of a successful business is a contented and fulfilled workforce."

"And what is the root of a successful marriage?"

"That depends on the marriage," he said. "But, at the very least, a marriage cannot survive without honesty."

Her hand trembled as she lifted a forkful of eggs to her mouth. She might have spirit, but it seemed as if he could crush it with a single sentence if he wanted.

But he did not.

He set down his teacup. "In answer to your question, today is the first day I've set eyes on Charles. He's new to my employ."

"Don't you have enough servants already?"

"I do," he replied. "Charles arrived this morning to replace John."

"John?" she asked. "The one who served us at dinner? Has he had an accident?"

"I had him dismissed," he said. "Another essential quality an employee must possess is respect for his employer. And his employer's wife."

She nodded and resumed eating. But this time, he noticed a little relaxation in her shoulders.

"I trust you'll be ready for your journey," he said.

She stiffened. "My journey?"

"To Molineux Manor," he said. "We leave in two days. I'd have preferred sooner, but I have business to attend to, today and tomorrow."

"Molineux Manor?"

"My country seat," he said. "You'll want for nothing there."

"You're sending me away?" she asked. "Is it because…" she hesitated. "Because of last night?"

"Partly."

She flinched, and he cursed himself. The brutal honesty which elicited the desired result when conducting business was, perhaps, not the best quality in a marriage.

Which only confirmed the need to send her away. She was poorly equipped for the harsh realities of the world in which he lived, and he had neither the time nor the ability to deal with her. She needed a tender hand, and he was not a tender man.

"You'll be better off in the country," he continued. "You're not suited to life in London."

"I understand."

She continued to eat, but her stricken expression threatened to melt his heart.

"You'll enjoy the trappings of a wealthy wife if you have concerns in that quarter," he said.

She stopped eating and pushed her plate away.

"You can learn the arts of being a lady in relative peace," he said. "With no fear of ridicule."

She set her mouth in a firm line.

"In fact, you're at liberty to do everything you want," he said. "On one condition."

"Which is?" She spoke so softly, he almost believed he'd imagined it.

"You must keep yourself tidy," he said.

"As in clean and presentable?"

"No…" he hesitated.

Damn it—naïve little creature! Why hadn't some other woman explained it to her? Why did he have to speak of such matters?

"After what I discovered last night…in your chamber. About you…"

Understanding flooded her expression, and she sat back and folded her arms, her cheeks flaming.

"I would hear your promise," he said.

"I've already said I'll stand by my vows," she replied. "Why demand I repeat what I've already said?"

"You cannot deny that you came to the marriage bed impure."

"Can *you* deny any previous liaisons?" she asked. "With Elizabeth, perhaps? We should be judged on equal terms."

"Men and women are judged differently," he said. "And as for Elizabeth, whatever you think of her, she understands enough of the rules of society to know that she must remain—intact—before she marries. She is a maiden, still."

"How do you know?"

He pushed his plate aside. "That's not a subject on which a respectable married woman should speak."

He picked up his napkin and dabbed the corners of his mouth, then rose from his seat.

"I have some business to tend to in my study," he said, "and I wish not to be disturbed. But you are at liberty to explore the rest of the house if you so wish."

Before she could respond, he gave her a stiff

bow and left the room.

MEGGIE TURNED THE page, her gaze following the lines of verse. She'd never read Byron before. Some of the phrases made her heart race. Such passion!

There had been so few books at Mrs. Preston's school that any new book was a treasure.

And her husband had a library full of them. She closed the book and picked up another, tracing the gold lettering on the spine.

Mo Chridhe
A collection of verse
by
Delilah Hart.

Delilah Hart. It must be one of her husband's sisters. Meggie smiled at the glimmer of hope. If he permitted his sister to employ her intellect, then he must believe a woman capable of more than simply submitting to the man who ruled her.

She heard a knock on the main doors.

Not another visitor! That was the fifth today. Why were so many people curious to see her? Was she a prize exhibit to be paraded along the street so that they could look down their nose at her?

Clutching the book, Meggie crossed the floor and peered out of the window.

A woman stood on the doorstep. Elegantly dressed in a purple coat with matching bonnet, she spoke to the footman, cradling a bundle of fur in her arms. She was small, perhaps an inch or two shorter than Meggie, but bore an air of elegance that gave her stature.

The woman lifted her gaze to the window. Meggie shrank behind the curtain, her heart racing with shame and embarrassment. Had she seen her? The voices stopped, and the door slammed. Meggie moved into the window and looked out again. The woman was walking away, but before she reached the end of the street, she stopped and turned.

She'd known Meggie was there.

Shortly after, the footman entered the parlor, brandishing a card on a silver tray.

"You had a visitor, ma'am," he said, bowing. "I said you were not at home."

"Thank you, Charles."

She picked up the card and read the inscription.

Mrs. Harold Pelham.

The name was familiar. Meggie's husband

had mentioned a Mr. Pelham as one of his business associates. No doubt, the man's wife wished to glimpse the unsuitable woman her husband's banker had married.

Charles gave another bow and left. Meggie set the book aside. Heartfelt poetry may stir the emotions, but it threatened to exacerbate her melancholy. A historical volume full of dry, soulless facts was to be preferred. Or maybe a copy of Dr. Johnson's dictionary to increase her vocabulary. She slipped out of the parlor and made her way to the library.

Voices came from within. Her husband and Mr. Peyton, the kind man from the wedding breakfast.

"Hart, you work too hard," Peyton said. "Why don't you take a vacation with your bride? The bank would be in safe hands with me."

"I know that," came the response, "but it's best if my wife is settled in Hampshire as soon as possible."

"Much as I loathe to admit it, I agree with you," Peyton said. "It's your move."

"I know." Meggie detected irritation in her husband's voice. "Are you so eager to conclude the game?"

"Not particularly," Mr. Peyton replied. "Damn it! It seems as if you've beaten me again."

"You concede too easily, Peyton. That's why so few businessmen are successful. They're too willing to accept defeat."

"Whereas you fight until the end?"

"Perhaps."

"Will you apply the same principle to your marriage?" Mr. Peyton asked. "Or have you conceded defeat already?"

"I'll not concede defeat until it's an insurmountable certainty."

The two men paused, then Peyton spoke once more. "Do you intend to resume your liaison with the honorable Elizabeth once your wife's tucked away in Hampshire?"

"I hardly think that's any of your business."

"Oh, but it is. Any man with your voracious appetite would starve if deprived of bedsport for too long. And you'll not want for partners. Lady Cavenham was asking after your health last night."

"Perhaps she's concerned I'll catch cold."

Mr. Peyton laughed. "Hardly! An inquiry about one's health is her calling card, saying she's available. What I cannot understand is how, after one meeting, she believes you can service her better than I."

"You're welcome to her."

"How are you so skilled in the bedroom?" Mr. Peyton asked.

"Women are easy to read."

"I find them an enigma, myself. For example, how can you tell whether a woman will welcome your attention?"

"By her reaction, Peyton." Meggie's skin tightened as her husband deepened his voice. Her blood warmed at the memory of his whispered words when he'd caressed her so intimately last night.

"A woman will speak with her body if she's ready," he said. "Her skin will flush, a soft pink to advertise the soft pinkness elsewhere. Her lips will part, just a little as if to welcome you in. When her thighs part just as eagerly, then she's ready."

"And then?" Peyton's voice came out in a strain.

"Then, you listen. Each sigh, each little mewl, will speak of her need. When her body cries for you—then, and only then—you take her."

Meggie's pulse throbbed deep inside with a wicked heat. She lifted her hands to her throat, where her skin was hot and flushed, just as her husband had described.

"What then?" Peyton asked.

"Then, if you have any sense, you leave. You return to your bed and leave her wanting."

"You're serious?"

"Perfectly. For a woman, nothing will surpass the first time you bed her. The memory of it will remain with her and become the bit and bridle with which you can control her."

Her husband's cold words doused Meggie's desire, and she stepped back, ashamed at her body's reaction, both last night and now.

"Perhaps you should teach me," Peyton said.

"So you can conquer Lady Cavenham?" Meggie's husband let out a laugh. "Nothing will dampen a woman's desire more than the knowledge that her lover is a greenhorn."

"And you're more experienced than most."

"Only through experience can one gain sufficient prowess. Both in business—and the art of seduction—it's a matter of knowing what your prospective partner desires the most and giving them enough of a taste to leave them craving more. With business, the needs vary a little, but with seduction—women all want the same thing."

"And what about the seducer?" Mr. Peyton asked. "Is he in danger of being ensnared himself?"

"A successful businessman is not hampered by emotions. To succeed at seduction, one must adopt the same principle."

"What about love?"

"A man who falls in love is a fool."

"On that note, I think I'll be going," Peyton said. Meggie heard a chair scrape, and she darted back into the parlor.

Footsteps passed by as her husband saw Mr. Peyton out. She heard mumbled voices, then the footsteps faded into the distance.

She crept out and ventured toward the library. It was empty. A decanter stood on the edge of the desk, next to two empty glasses.

A chessboard had been set up on the desk, the pieces scattered about as if a game was in progress. She studied the pieces. White had the advantage, with two castles and a bishop surrounding the black king. With a single move, white would checkmate black by bringing the queen into play.

She picked up the white queen and studied it. Carved from wood, the piece was more functional than decorative, but beauty was always to be found in simplicity. The most powerful piece on the board, players guarded the queen jealously, often at the expense of the lesser pieces.

Sighing, she replaced the queen and picked up a pawn—an overlooked piece that players often sacrificed on a whim for no real gain, to be cast aside on the edge of the board and forgotten.

Like a bastard daughter.

Or an unwanted wife.

A splintering crash came from outside, followed by a curse.

"Damn!"

She opened the door to see her husband holding pieces of a vase, the remainder of which lay at his feet. His eyes narrowed as he caught sight of her.

"What are you doing?" he asked.

"Fetching a book," she replied. "What have you done?"

"What do you think?" he asked, irritation in his voice. He dropped the shards. "Hated the bloody thing anyway. It contained the remains of the seventh Count Von Hirschtein."

"And you didn't like him?"

"Rumor has it he murdered both his wives."

"Then, a fitting end for him might be to get swept up and discarded with the rest of the rubbish," she said.

His mouth twitched into a smile.

"It seems as if the count has effected one last injury," Meggie said, nodding toward his hand where a patch of red had appeared. He lifted his hand and blanched.

A long gash covered his palm.

Charles appeared from a side door. "Is everything all right, sir?"

"What the devil does it look like!" he roared, an edge of panic in his voice. "Do you think I've been playing…"

"Charles," Meggie interrupted her husband. "Would you be so good at to fetch a bandage or some strips of linen and some honey, if there's any in the house?

"I don't know, ma'am."

"Ask Mrs. Draper if you're unsure," she said. "We'll be in the library. And I'll need some alcohol." She glanced at her husband. "Preferably something the master places little value on."

Charles gave a bow and disappeared.

Meggie gestured toward her husband. "Will you come into the library?"

He remained still.

"Please?"

He sighed. "I can deal with it myself, Margaret."

"I don't doubt it, but I'm sure you'd not want any more of your blood mingling with the ashes of a murderer."

A smile played on his lips again, and he followed her into the library.

Chapter Ten

DEXTER SAT AT his wife's direction while she inspected his hand with silent, detached professionalism. Unlike most ladies, she came to the fore at the sight of blood, rather than fainting in a fit of hysterics. Elizabeth would have swooned, throwing herself into his arms in an attempt to elicit chivalry—even though he was the most unchivalrous man in London.

When Charles appeared, brandishing a tray laden with a small pile of linen, a jar of honey, and a decanter, she took it and bobbed a curtsey. The footman raised his eyebrow, but more out of surprise than contempt. She flushed and lowered her gaze.

Dexter dismissed the footman, but he hadn't the heart to admonish his wife for her faux pas. He made a mental note to instruct Mrs. Draper to warn Charles not to gossip about his wife's unladylike demeanor.

"May I?" she asked.

At his nod, she knelt at his feet and set the tray on the floor. Then she reached for his hand. Gentle fingers uncurled his, and he grimaced at the sight of the red liquid pooling in his palm. He closed his eyes, but the memory was too strong—the stream of red at his feet and the pain across his back, which burned like a flame.

"Husband?"

He opened his eyes to see her staring up at him, concern in her expression. Her eyes, which he'd thought an unremarkable brown, bore the warm, comforting hue of chocolate, punctuated by golden flecks that reminded him of the sun.

For a brief moment, another memory flashed past him—a different woman at his feet, taking him in her mouth to exert her sexual power over him. But rather than lust, he felt only shame at the memory when faced with the purity of his wife's expression.

Would he never be free from Elizabeth?

"Get on with it," he growled.

The light in his wife's eyes died. She reached for the decanter and tipped it up, soaking a piece of linen. He wrinkled his nose at the smell.

Whisky—disgusting stuff. Fit for cleaning the silverware, and little else.

"Hold still," she said. "This might hurt."

"I know that."

She pressed the soaked linen against his palm. A sharp sting caught him unawares as if a knife were being drawn across his hand.

"God's teeth, woman!" he roared. "Did you have to do that?"

"It's necessary to prevent putrefaction."

"Don't tell me you're a doctor."

She didn't answer. Instead, she continued to clean the wound, then dropped the blood-soaked bandage on the tray. He turned his head away and swallowed. When he looked back, he saw she watched him, understanding in her eyes. Yet she said nothing of his weakness. She dipped her fingers into the honey and smeared it over his palm.

"To aid healing," she said, anticipating his question. "It forms a barrier over the wound."

"It'll make my hand taste sweet if nothing else."

She smiled and picked up another strip of linen, then bound his hand, finishing with a neat knot.

"Where did you learn to do that?" he asked.

"At Mrs. Preston's."

"Who the devil is Mrs. Preston?" Shame at his weakness at the sight of his own blood fueled the harsh tone to his voice. She frowned, and for a moment, he glimpsed, once again, the fire in her eyes.

"She runs the school."

"What school?"

"The school at Blackwood Heath," she said. "The one my father threatened with ruination if I didn't marry you."

She stood, rolling up the rest of the bandages, and moved toward the desk where she set the tray next to the chessboard.

He lifted his bandaged hand. "Thank you," he said.

She gave a tight smile, then gestured to the chessboard. "This is beautiful."

"Don't touch the pieces," he said.

"I wouldn't move them without your leave," she replied, an edge of irritation in her voice. "I presume you're playing a game with someone."

"Have you heard of chess?"

She nodded.

"Do you know how the pieces move?"

A smile curled at the corner of her mouth. "A little."

"Shall I show you?" he asked. "I can teach you the basics, but the game of chess itself is somewhat complex."

"Oh?"

He could swear he heard amusement in her voice.

"It's a game of tactics and strategy," he said. "Not something most women would be able to understand."

Her smile disappeared. "You think women lack understanding?"

"Most women of my acquaintance believe themselves to be masters of manipulation," he said. "But they lack the foresight or understanding to form a strategy for success."

"Perhaps that's a function of your choice of female acquaintances rather than a general rule applicable to the whole of my sex."

For such an ignorant creature, her level of perception unnerved him.

"Perhaps it is," he said, "but it needn't concern you. You're leaving for Hampshire tomorrow."

"I thought we were leaving the day after?"

"I'm staying here," he said. "I have business to attend."

"You're not coming?"

"You needn't worry," he said. "You'll be safe on the road. I have a private coach and will instruct my men to watch over you at all times."

"And you want me gone?"

He averted his gaze before she could assault his heart with those pleading eyes of hers.

She sighed. "May I ask you a question?"

"That depends on the question."

"Had you married Elizabeth, would you have sent *her* away?"

"No," he sighed. "But Elizabeth is not…"

"A bastard?"

"I'd prefer you didn't use such language."

"But it's true, is it not?"

"By taking names to yourself, you give them credibility," he said. "You are my wife, and as such, should command respect. Who you were before that is of no consequence. Nevertheless, it would be better for both of us if you retired to the country, and I remained here."

"Very well."

She bobbed a curtsey, then left the room.

Yes—it would be better if she left for the country. Why, then, did he regret his decision to send her away?

Chapter Eleven

MEGGIE JERKED AWAKE. The carriage door opened to reveal a footman.

"Ma'am?"

She rubbed her eyes and sat up, stretching to ease the ache in her back.

"Where are we?" she asked.

"We've arrived," he replied. "At Molineux Manor."

Thank the Lord.

The journey had taken the better part of three days, and she'd had nothing but her own company to amuse herself with. In addition to the boredom, she'd battled the fear of being accosted on the open road. Tales of highwaymen had been rife in Blackwood Heath, and without her husband's protection, she'd been convinced she wouldn't survive the journey.

He must have given strict instructions to his servants, who almost continually checked on her and didn't let her out of their sight. She even suspected they'd stood guard outside her room at each inn while she slept. The younger of the two had, that morning, looked like he was going to fall asleep.

She climbed out of the carriage. At least this time, she didn't stumble. The memory of her arrival in London still stung. Only by virtue of her husband's swift reaction, she'd avoided falling flat on her face on the pavement. As it was, she'd let slip a curse, incurring a hard stare from the butler and a disappointed sigh from her husband.

At least here, she wouldn't be subject to his disappointment.

She drew in a breath of air and looked up at the building before her. A monstrosity of dark gray stone, it stretched almost as far as she could see. She'd never seen a structure so large.

And it was her new home.

Even to her untrained eye, she could tell the place had not been maintained. Ivy grew on the walls, thick tendrils surrounding the windows to choke the soul out of the building. The garden was overgrown—shaggy, unkempt bushes lining the perimeter—and weeds sprouted from the gravel drive.

It was as if the home had never known love.

The footman led her toward the main doors

where a small group of servants stood in line. A young man stood at the end. With soft brown hair and a clear gaze, he gave her a bright smile. Beside him stood a young woman in a maid's uniform. She cast him a look of devotion, then gave Meggie a nervous smile.

A plump woman stood at the far end, next to a tall, stiff-looking man dressed in black, who must be the butler. At a sharp word from the woman, the rest of the servants bowed and curtsied in unison.

"Welcome, ma'am," she said. "I trust you had a good journey."

Meggie dipped into a curtsey, and the woman's eyes widened.

"Forgive me," Meggie said. "I'm Mrs. Hart. I-I don't know how to..."

"I understand, my dear," the woman said. "I'm Mrs. Wells. Is the master with you?"

Meggie shook her head. "He's still in London." She gestured toward the building. "I didn't expect it to be so large!"

Mrs. Wells smiled. "Of course not, my dear," she said. "Neither did I."

"You've not been here before?"

"The house was unoccupied until a fortnight ago," Mrs. Wells said, "when the master took up the tenancy."

"Oh!" Meggie exclaimed. "So that explains why..." she trailed off, embarrassed.

"Why the place is in a state of disrepair?" Mrs. Wells smiled. "The interior is in need of attention, and we don't have a full complement of staff. Now that you're here to direct me, we can make progress in time for when the master joins you."

This woman, kind though she may be, clearly expected Meggie to act as lady of the manor, but Meggie knew nothing about such things. Would the servants soon show the same disappointment at her inadequacies as her husband did?

Mrs. Wells took Meggie's hand. The butler cleared his throat, and she shot him a warning look.

"We'll work it out together, shall we, my dear? I'm at your disposal. To take your instruction, but also to give guidance should you need it." She lowered her voice to a whisper. "There's nothing to fear from managing a large house. It's the same as any home, only with a few extra rooms."

Meggie looked into the woman's eyes and saw nothing but kindness.

"Thank you."

"There's no need to thank me," Mrs. Wells said. "Now, my dear, I suspect you're exhausted after your journey, particularly if you're unused to traveling. Perhaps some sweet tea? Mrs. Brown has a fruitcake freshly baked this morning. A slice would restore you, I'm sure. I'll have it brought to your chamber."

She led Meggie inside.

If the exterior emitted an air of gloom, the interior was no better. The hallway was all marble and polished metal—the epitome of elegance, and something Alderley and Elizabeth would relish. But to Meggie, there was no soul in the harsh, stern lines.

"Mama, mama!" Excited voices echoed, and two children appeared at the end of the hallway.

"Jack! Betsy!" Mrs. Wells cried. "Didn't I tell you not to disturb me today? The mistress doesn't want to see you abovestairs!"

"No, please," Meggie said. "Let them."

"It's not done," Mrs. Wells said.

"Did you not say *I* was to direct *you?*" Meggie asked.

The housekeeper's mouth twitched into a smile.

"That I did, ma'am. I know you're unused to the life of a lady, so I'll help you all I can."

"You know about me?"

Mrs. Wells had the grace to blush. "Begging your pardon, but circumstances such as yours attract the interest of people hereabouts."

"You mean I'm the subject of gossip?"

"Not here, I assure you," Mrs. Wells said. "I've instructed the household to give you the respect your position commands. But I'd advise you to maintain the distinction of rank between yourself and the tenants and servants. They'll respect you all the more for it."

The children approached Meggie. The boy looked up with expressive blue eyes, and the girl stood beside him, her thumb in her mouth.

Mrs. Wells gave a sharp sigh. "Jack, did you not hear me? The mistress doesn't want you under her feet!"

"No, please, let them," Meggie said. "I love children." She addressed the boy. "Do you like it here?"

The boy grinned. "Oh, yes!" he said. "Since we arrived, I've eaten fruitcake every day."

"Then I must have some with my tea if you recommend it so highly."

"Run along now, Jack," Mrs. Wells said. "The mistress is tired."

"Perhaps you'll take tea with me tomorrow," Meggie said. "You can tell me all about this house. Are you taking lessons?"

"Mama has taught us how to read," the boy said.

"And what about your numbers?"

He pulled a face. "I don't like numbers."

"Oh, that's a shame!" Meggie exclaimed. "Numbers are so useful in everything we do. Perhaps, with your mama's permission, I might teach you. I used to help out at a school where…where I lived before."

"I don't know…" Mrs. Wells said.

"Please," Meggie said. "I want to be useful, to do something familiar, which…"

She broke off, unwilling to finish the sentence.

Something which I will not fail at.

A reassuring hand touched her arm. "Of course, my dear," Mrs. Wells said. "Don't worry. You'll soon adapt to your life here. And now, you must rest. There's nothing a pot of tea and a good night's sleep cannot fix."

She nodded to the children. "Run along, dears," she said. "You can see the mistress in the morning. We must make her feel welcome. Sarah, see to it, would you?"

"Yes, Mrs. Wells." One of the maids took the children's hands and led them away.

Mrs. Wells took Meggie's arm and escorted her upstairs. They stopped at a large paneled door, and she pushed it open.

"This is your chamber."

The room was enormous. Dark wooden paneling lined the walls, absorbing the light. A stone fireplace occupied almost all of one wall. Red curtains lined the windows overlooking the estate. A pile of logs filled the fireplace. How much did it cost to heat a room of this size?

"I cannot stay here," Meggie said. "Is there a smaller room I could have?"

"A smaller room?"

"This room doesn't feel right."

"But it's yours," the housekeeper said.

"Can't I choose my own room?" Meggie asked. "This one's so dark and gloomy."

"I can put you in one of the guest rooms," the housekeeper said. "But most of them overlook the woods. Don't you want a view of the lake? It's what Molineux Manor used to be admired for among society."

"I don't belong in society," Meggie said.

"You do, Mrs. Hart," the housekeeper said. "Nobody can dispute your right to be here."

"Then nobody can dispute my right to choose my own room."

The housekeeper sighed. "Very well, I'll have Milly make up another room for you. Do you wish to rest here while you wait?"

At that moment, Meggie's stomach groaned.

"Or, perhaps, you'd like to take supper? I can set a place for you in the dining room."

"There's no need to do that," Meggie said. "I can eat in the kitchen."

"It's not done…"

"But it's my decision."

"Very well," Mrs. Wells said. "Just this once. I'll take you to the kitchen. By the time you've had your supper, the room will be ready."

She closed the door, shutting out the chamber of darkness, and led Meggie back down the stairs.

The kitchen was generously sized. In fact,

Mrs. Preston's whole school building could have fit into it. The fireplace dominated the far wall, and copper pots and pans lined the walls, gleaming in the firelight.

A black cauldron hung over the fire at which a woman in a plain gown and smart apron stirred continuously. Two servants sat at the table in the center—the young man and woman who'd attracted Meggie's interest when she arrived. The woman blushed when she saw Meggie, but the man stood and gave a warm smile, which she couldn't help return.

"What's the soup tonight, Mrs. Brown?" the housekeeper asked.

The woman at the cauldron turned and gave an exclamation when she saw Meggie.

"Oh, it's the mistress!"

"Mrs. Hart will be taking her supper in the kitchen," the housekeeper said.

The cook gave Meggie a curious expression, then waved her spoon at the couple at the table.

"Milly, Ralph, be off with you. You can eat later."

"But..." the young woman protested.

"That's enough, Milly!" the housekeeper said. "Come and help me with the mistress's room."

"But I've been preparing it all day," Milly protested. "Is it not ready?"

"It's not your place to question my orders," Mrs. Wells said. "Come on!" The young woman's mouth turned down in a sulk, but she rose to her feet.

"And you too, Ralph," she added. "There's plenty you can be doing in the stables while the mistress takes her supper.

"Don't leave on my account," Meggie said.

He smiled. "That's very obliging of you."

"Ralph!" Mrs. Wells said. "It's not your place to address the mistress in such a familiar fashion." She turned to Meggie. "It's best this way, ma'am," she said. "And the master would agree if he were here."

"But he's *not* here," Meggie said.

The housekeeper nudged the young woman. "Come on, Milly. The sooner we've prepared the room, the sooner you can have your supper. It smells good. What is it, Mrs. Brown?"

"Beef and vegetable broth."

The cook ladled out two bowls of soup and placed them on the table, together with two spoons and a bread plate.

Meggie picked up the bread and dipped it in the soup. The housekeeper gave a pointed cough. Meggie's cheeks warmed with embarrassment as she recalled her first night in London and the footman's contempt. She picked up the spoon.

The housekeeper nodded and smiled, then exited the kitchen, followed by Milly.

"Mrs. Brown makes the best soup out of London," Ralph said. "Probably the best in the country."

"Oh, stop it, Ralph!" Mrs. Brown laughed. "You're a one. No wonder Milly's so sweet on you."

Ralph winked at Meggie, his blue eyes shining. He reminded her of the angel at her wedding. Mr. Peyton, though Ralph was perhaps a few years younger.

He leaned forward and lowered his voice. "Now that Mrs. Wells is no longer here to admonish us, you can eat the soup how you'd like."

"I'll stick to the spoon," Meggie said. "I am, after all, supposed to be mistress of the house."

"Yes, ma'am." Another wink.

"What do you do here, Ralph?" Meggie asked.

"I'm head groom," he replied, dipping bread into his soup.

"Is that like an ostler?" she asked, remembering the young lad who'd tended to the horses at the Rose and Crown.

"Better," he said. "I'm in charge of the stables."

A snort came from the fireplace. "In charge of yourself!" Mrs. Brown said. "Unless you count the horses, who don't answer back."

"When the estate's fully staffed, I'll have at least two stableboys under me," Ralph said.

"So, you tend to the horses?" Meggie asked.

"I didn't know there were any."

"We have nine."

"So many?"

"Six for the coach, plus the master's stallion, the steward's gelding, and a mare," Ralph said. "Do you ride?"

"No," Meggie said.

"I could teach you. The mare has a good temperament. She'll do for you."

Meggie shook her head. "I don't think it would be proper."

"A lady should know how to ride. Isn't that right, Mrs. Brown?"

"Aye, lad," the cook said. "But perhaps the master has someone in mind to teach the mistress."

"I doubt he's thought of it at all," Meggie said.

Ralph and Mrs. Brown exchanged glances, and heat rose in Meggie's cheeks. She'd spoken out of turn again. Would she ever learn what was the right or wrong thing to say?

"The soup's delicious, Mrs. Brown," she said.

"I do my best, ma'am."

"You must make this when..." Meggie hesitated. How should she refer to the man who'd exiled her here? "...when the master comes."

Another exchange of looks.

She nodded toward the window that overlooked an enclosed garden full of plants arranged in neat rows.

"Are the grounds extensive?" she asked.

"Sixty acres," Ralph said. "Are you fond of the outdoors?"

"Oh, yes!" she replied. "I used to enjoy picnicking in the woods, back when…"

She broke off, the housekeeper's warning ringing in her ears.

"I'm sure Mrs. Brown could arrange a picnic," Ralph said.

"It's not your place to make such suggestions, young man," the cook said. "Be off with you now. You've finished your supper, and there's no reason for you to be lingering around the mistress. You can take some of my bread back to your cottage."

"Very well," he said. The cook handed him a loaf wrapped in a cloth. "Mind you bring back that cloth," she said. "I won't have you using it to polish your boots like the last time."

He put his arm round the cook's shoulders and drew her close.

"Where would I be without you, Mrs. Brown?" he laughed. He placed a deep kiss on her cheek, and though she squealed in protest, her eyes shone with merriment. She pushed him away with a laugh.

"With your leave, ma'am, I'll retire," he said. "But my offer still stands. I'd be honored to teach you how to ride, then we can explore the grounds properly. The estate is beautiful."

"I'd like that," Meggie said.

"And, if I may be so bold," he continued, "the master is not only fortunate to have such a fine estate, but also in his choice of wife."

"Ralph!" the cook admonished.

"Begging your pardon," he said. "Mrs. Brown, I'll see you tomorrow. I trust there will be a bit of bacon awaiting me as usual."

"And a clip round the ear, if you're not careful."

He bowed once more, then exited the kitchen, whistling a merry tune.

"He's a charmer, that one," the cook said.

"And he's offered for Milly?" Meggie asked.

"We all expect him to," came the reply. "It's not fair to keep the lass waiting. Perhaps when the estate's fully staffed and young Ralph isn't so busy with the horses, he'll find time for courting."

"I could help," Meggie said.

"Begging your pardon, ma'am, but it wouldn't do to get too friendly with the staff," Mrs. Brown said. "Ralph will offer for Milly when he's good and ready. Let him teach you to ride, by all means, but as mistress and servant. You can never be friends."

Mrs. Brown was right, of course. But the thought of a lifetime of loneliness in this gloomy house was more than Meggie could bear. A little companionship from the souls living on the estate was not too much to ask, surely? And if her husband had wanted her to learn how to be a good wife and mistress of the house, then he should have accompanied her himself rather than abandon her here, alone.

Meggie rose to her feet and pushed her soup bowl aside. "It's time I retired."

She left the kitchen and found Milly, who led her to a small guest chamber at the back of the house. She dismissed the maidservant, then undressed and slipped into the bed. She had much to look forward to—the countryside to explore, picnics, and the prospect of learning to ride. She'd been fond of the horses at the Rose and Crown and had often helped Mr. Clayton with them when he needed extra hands. But she'd never believed she might get to ride one.

Perhaps life at Molineux Manor wouldn't be so bleak after all.

Chapter Twelve

DEXTER WAVED AT the carriage as it disappeared round the corner. His sister Delilah—now Duchess Molineux—was on her way to a new life in Scotland. Away from him.

Though Dexter had wanted a large wedding for her, Lilah's husband had insisted on a quiet affair. It was probably for the best, given how close Lilah was to her confinement. And it meant that he was spared the good wishes of guests he neither liked nor cared about. Why should he be congenial when he felt far from it? Weddings presented an opportunity to display marital bliss—not only that of the happy couple but of the guests who stood proudly together in perfectly formed pairs.

And the last thing Dexter needed was a reminder of the marital bliss he was never going to have.

Not that he'd envisaged such a state—at least not with Elizabeth.

But with Margaret...

Beneath the rather shabby exterior of the woman he'd been tricked into marrying lay a sweet girl with kind eyes.

And a delectable little body which had responded to his caresses as if she'd been made for him. Though he was skilled enough to elicit moans of pleasure in all manner of women, the cries of passion in his quiet little wife had taken him unawares. Like the finest wines, they had ruined his taste for any other woman.

It wasn't only honor that prevented him from seeking relief in the arms of others. It was her.

He missed her.

His breeches tightened at the memory of her, splayed before him on the bed, thighs parted.

A hand touched his arm, and he jumped.

"You seem out of sorts, brother."

Dorothea looked at him, her brow creased into a frown.

"Aren't you happy for Delilah?"

"Of course," he replied.

"And you should be." She set her mouth into a thin line. "After all, her child won't be born a bastard."

A spike of anger rippled through him at Thea's crude expression and the memory of the shame in his wife's eyes as she'd taken that name upon herself.

"Am I right in thinking we should also be wishing *you* joy?" Thea asked.

News traveled fast.

"How did you find out?"

"Does it matter?" she asked. "What I want to know is why you kept it a secret."

"My life is nobody's business but my own," he growled.

"Yet, you think you've the right to dictate my life," she replied. "According to you, I'm too old to find a husband, yet you, who are older than I am, are content to marry the bastard daughter of the man who tormented our family when we were children!"

"It's not as simple as that," he said.

"I'm told you won a wife in a game of cards," Thea said. "Perhaps I should enter a gaming hell and present myself as a prize."

"I see Anne Pelham has been gossiping again."

She snorted. "All of London's gossiping about it. I don't understand why you didn't invite any of us, and why you banished your bride within two days of the wedding. You've always said that as a family, we should stick together."

"I married while you were in Bath with Lilah," Dexter said. "And our brother wouldn't have agreed to come."

"But you didn't even see fit to *tell* us!" she said. "Are you ashamed of her? Or of us? Is that why you bought me a house of my own? Not out of love, but of shame?"

"I'm not ashamed of anyone," he said. "But it's better if she remains in the country."

"For her, or for you?"

"Both."

"I suppose I should have expected it," Thea said, "given that you didn't invite Daisy today."

He looked at her, and she flinched as if she knew she'd stepped too far.

"I sent Daisy an invitation," he said. "She didn't respond."

"Why should she?" Thea asked. "Imagine how she'd feel—the sister who disgraced the family name, being forced to congratulate the sister who married a title."

"Lilah's happy."

"Not because she's a duchess," Thea said. "You're the only one of us who believes that a title would make you happy. How must it feel to be so disappointed?"

"I'll manage."

"I'm sure you will," she said. "I don't know who I pity the most. You, or your wife." She gave a bitter laugh. "Perhaps spinsterhood isn't the worst state a woman can find herself in."

Ah, there it was. Beneath the skin of the obedient sister lay the resentment of a woman too old for marriage.

He sighed. "I can set about finding a husband for you, Thea."

"What, advertise me for sale to any man who'd take a woman nearing thirty?" she asked. "No, thank you, I'd rather look for myself. At least now I have a home of my own, so I'll be spared your oppression."

She flinched as if she expected an outburst of anger, but what was the point in arguing with Dorothea if she spoke the truth? He led her back inside, to the morning room, where Charles was already clearing the crockery.

Dorothea was right. Dexter had failed. Not only in securing suitable matches for them all, but in keeping his family together. Daisy lived in obscurity, refusing to see him, and Delilah had barely spoken to him today. And Dorothea exuded unhappiness.

As for Devon…

A solitary man sat beside the fireplace, his face almost entirely concealed by a black silk mask, a half-full glass of brandy in his right hand. He acknowledged Dexter's presence with a grunt, then resumed his attention on the fireplace, the light from the flames reflecting in his eyes.

At least Devon had made an appearance today.

"I'm glad you came, brother," Dexter said.

Devon curled his lip into a sneer, the action

revealing part of his scar.

"I came for Lilah. Not for you."

"Perhaps you've heard," Dexter said. "I'm lately married, also."

Dexter sipped his brandy. "What do I care? Yet another woman to scream at the sight of me."

"You're unlikely to meet her."

"Stuffed her away in the country, have you?" Devon asked. "So you can fuck that Alderley woman with a clear conscience?"

A splintering crash made him jump. Charles dropped to the floor, mumbling an apology while he cleared up shards of crockery from the floor. Dorothea shot Dexter an angry look, then rushed to help the footman.

"If you must know, I have no intention of seeing Elizabeth again," Dexter said.

"You think me a fool?" Devon asked. "You've been obsessed with that harlot almost as soon as you were old enough to realize what your cock was for."

Brandy always brought Devon's temper to the fore. Any other man and Dexter would have called him out—or at least planted a shiner on his face. But Devon had experienced enough in his twenty-five years to be unfazed by physical threats.

"I hardly think you're in a position to lecture me on obsession, Dev," Dexter said. "Tell me, what has the Lady Atalanta been up to today?

Does she know you creep after her in the shadows?"

Devon jumped to his feet and flung the brandy glass at the door.

"For heaven's sake!" Dorothea cried. "If you two are going to fight like dogs, do it outside—or better still, down at the docks where I believe such activities take place."

"Forgive me, Thea," Devon said. He shot an angry look at Dexter. "I find the company here oppressive. Shall I escort you home?"

"With pleasure," Thea said.

"Aren't you accompanying me tonight?" Dexter asked. "Dinner with the Pelhams."

"I've had enough for one day," Thea said.

"How so?"

"Like it or not, Dexter, none of us have been able to live up to your expectations," she said. "You value Delilah only because she's married a title. In your eyes, the rest of us have let you down, and I've had my fill of being reminded of it today."

She swept out of the room on Devon's arm.

Dexter stood at the window, watching them walk down the street, while Charles continued to clear away the shards of glass and crockery. The poor man had only been in Dexter's employ for a fortnight. What must he think of them—the notorious Harts who didn't belong in society?

Dorothea was wise enough to understand the

root of Dexter's ill-temper, but in one aspect, she was wrong. It was Dexter who'd let his siblings down—not the other way round.

And he'd also let his wife down.

Chapter Thirteen

"So, Mr. Hart, what transgressions did your wife commit to warrant her banishment, so soon after your marriage?"

Mrs. Pelham sliced through her beef as if thrusting a sword into the belly of an opponent while focusing her steady gaze on Dexter.

Not only was he subject to criticism from his family—but also his friends.

"Anne, my love!" her husband warned.

"Forgive me, Harold," she said sweetly. She picked up her wineglass. "To my friend, Delilah," she said. "May she be one of the few women in the world fortunate enough to be valued and cherished by her husband."

Pelham rolled his eyes but said nothing. Doubtless, he hoped his wife would leave it at that. But Anne Pelham was an insistent little thing.

"I paid a call on your wife a fortnight ago," she continued. Her tone was light, but the determined set of her mouth told Dexter another assault was forthcoming.

"Oh, did you?" he asked, his voice just as carefree. He reached for his wine and took a sip. "An excellent claret, Pelham," he said. "But I suppose, when you deal in the stuff, you develop a more discerning palate."

"Thank you," his host said.

"And do you keep the best of your imports for yourself, Pelham? I can imagine many of your clients are unable to discern a fine French wine from something more mediocre."

Anne gave a little huff, betraying her exasperation at Dexter's attempt to change the subject.

"I was told your wife was not at home," she continued. Her husband shot her a warning look, which she ignored. "But she was. I saw her watching me from the parlor window. Had you told her not to admit me?"

"No," Dexter replied.

"Or had you refused her permission to receive visitors?"

"Of course not!"

"Perhaps she felt ashamed," she continued. "After all, she's guilty of the crime of being the wrong Alderley sister."

"Anne, please!" Pelham admonished. "This is

hardly the subject for the dinner table. Hart's here to mark the occasion of Delilah's marriage, not be criticized for *his*."

"Forgive me." She resumed her attention to her meal.

But she'd struck a nerve. The day after Margaret had left for the country, Dexter had found Mrs. Pelham's card in the parlor. Charles had been forthcoming enough to explain that when Mrs. Pelham had come calling, he'd 'happened upon the mistress hiding behind the curtain.'

The meal concluded, the gentlemen rose to take their port in Pelham's study, while Mrs. Pelham retired with a glass of Madeira to the drawing room.

Pelham picked up a decanter containing a straw-colored liquid.

"I thought it was fitting to have a glass of whisky in honor of your new brother-in-law," he said.

Dexter could hardly refuse, though he loathed the stuff.

Pelham handed him a glass, and he wrinkled his nose at the smell, which evoked a memory—a sting on his palm, and his wife's eyes, full of compassion as she knelt before him and tended to his injury.

The wound still itched, but it had faded to a pale scar.

He took a mouthful of whisky and almost

choked as it rasped against his throat.

"Not to your taste, Hart?" Pelham laughed. "Your new brother-in-law will be most offended."

"I doubt it," Dexter replied, "given that my bank's his biggest creditor."

"And Alderley's biggest," Pelham said. He drained his glass and picked up the decanter. "Another?"

"Not unless you want me to expel the ragout on this rug."

Pelham chuckled and poured himself a glass. "I don't envy Alderley his next meeting with his banker, given that you're now his son-in-law."

"I doubt that old bastard will sully his hands by dealing with me," Dexter replied. "He'll send his steward, who, at least, seems a sensible fellow. He might avoid bankruptcy, provided Alderley keeps his spending in check."

"Which will be a challenge given that the Honorable Elizabeth is still his responsibility," Pelham laughed. "At least she's not *your* responsibility. I wonder if Alderley realizes the mistake he made?"

"His mistake?"

"A by-blow's cheaper to maintain than a legitimate daughter," Pelham said. "Alderley sold you the wrong one."

Dexter bristled at his friend's casual reference to his wife's circumstances. The poor girl couldn't help her origins. He set his glass on the table with a smart thud. "Elizabeth would have been a disastrous wife, but she would have stepped into the role of hostess with ease."

"She wouldn't have gained you many friends," Pelham said. "My Anne can't stand her. And a man doesn't just need a wife for society parties. He needs a companion. In that respect, at least, I must agree with Anne's opinion that sending your wife away was a mistake."

"It's easy for you to judge," Dexter said. "You married a viscount's daughter."

"So did you," Pelham replied. "I don't love Anne for her lineage. I love her because she's generous and caring. She'll do anything I ask of her. Not because she vowed obedience—but because she *wants* to. You may think you're in need of no one, my friend, but have you never wondered what it might be like to place your trust—your heart—into the hands of another? The time may also come when you understand the fulfillment of being able to provide comfort to another, such that they might trust *you* completely."

"Trust only leads to betrayal," Dexter said.

"Only if you place your faith in the wrong person. My Anne didn't trust me when we first married, but I have seen her grow to trust me completely over the years. You will never understand what a gift that is, my friend, until you've experienced it."

Pelham made a dismissive gesture. "The qualities Elizabeth possesses—manners, fine speech, and ladylike deportment—can be taught. But do you know what can never be taught, no matter how hard you try?"

"What?" Dexter asked.

"Kindness," Pelham replied. "Goodness. It's either there or it's not. If a woman's soul is rotten to the core, there's nothing to be done."

"You don't believe in redemption?"

Pelham shook his head. "Redemption is merely the process by which a man gains a greater understanding and appreciation of the world around him. He can only change if he wishes it."

"What the devil are you trying to say, Pelham?" Dexter asked.

"That you shouldn't judge your wife by whether she knows the exact position of a fork on a dining table. You should judge her by whether she has a good heart—by her innocence if you like."

"My wife came to the marriage bed impure," Dexter said.

"And? Anne was married before."

"Married, yes," Dexter said. "My wife was not."

"And is she in love with the fellow?"

Dexter remembered the look of fear in his wife's eyes.

"No," he said. "I got the impression she'd rather forget."

"Then forget it," Pelham said. "You're affronted because another man got there before you. You've hardly lived a chaste life."

"Ye gods, Pelham, you sound like my wife."

"What did she say when you confronted her about it?" Pelham asked.

Her response had been a tearful confession, followed by a plea that he not hurt her.

Pelham had spoken of trust. Dexter's little wife, though frightened and anticipating pain, had given him her trust.

And a woman such as her—with no title, no fortune, no name—her trust was all she had to give.

Dexter lifted his gaze to see his friend looking directly at him, understanding in his eyes.

"Come on, my friend," Pelham said. "I think we ought to join Anne before I do something unforgivable, such as unearth your conscience."

As soon as they entered the drawing room, Anne Pelham rose from her seat.

"Coffee, Mr. Hart?"

"I can help myself, Mrs. Pelham," he said. "Please don't trouble yourself."

She glanced at her husband. "Mr. Hart," she said, "I didn't mean to criticize you this evening. Though I hope you see me as a friend, I've no right to tell you how to behave in your marriage."

"No," he replied. "I value frankness above decorum, Mrs. Pelham. Too often, others seek to manipulate me by telling me what they believe I want to hear. I would prefer you to speak frankly, even if I don't like what you have to say."

She smiled. "Then, with your leave, may I suggest you refrain from neglecting your wife?"

"My wife is in the best place she can be," Dexter replied. "The world believes I sent her away because I don't care to have her with me, but the country is the kindest environment for her. London is populated by sharks, whereas Molineux Manor harbors much safer waters."

She lifted the coffee pot and poured him a cup, dropping three sugar lumps in.

Just how he liked it. Some women were capable of silent observation, using their keen eye for others' benefit and comfort.

Like his wife. She had noticed his aversion to the sight of blood and had managed to soothe his fears without even mentioning them, thereby not only helping his hand to heal but also preserving his pride.

It took a rare woman to achieve that.

"Mr. Hart," Mrs. Pelham continued, "despite your efforts at concealing it, a kind heart beats beneath the fine cut of your jacket. Why not bestow a little of that kindness where it might be needed the most?"

"My love, you've lectured our friend for long enough," Pelham said. "How about some music?"

"Very well." She crossed the floor to the pianoforte, and shortly after, the soft melodies of a Mozart sonata filled the room. Dexter leaned back in his seat, closing his eyes to savor the melody.

Anne Pelham was a handful. But her husband could be forgiven for being smitten with her.

WHEN DEXTER RETURNED to his townhouse, he stopped in the main hall and looked around him. Though servants bustled about belowstairs, he'd never felt so alone. His sisters had moved out, and now he'd exiled his wife.

He handed his greatcoat to Charles and climbed the stairs, his footsteps echoing as if to emphasize his solitude. When he reached his wife's chamber, on impulse, he pushed the door open.

The room had been cleaned, and the bed made—not a crease or a thing out of place. The shabby little trunk that had resided in the far corner was no longer there, exiled in the country with its owner.

A small object caught his eye on the floor underneath the bed, and he moved closer to get a better look.

A single stocking.

He plucked it off the floor and held it up. A thread had pulled apart, running along the stocking, toward a hole, halfway up.

He rubbed the soft silk between his finger and thumb, then lifted the stocking to his face, breathing in the faint aroma of earth and fresh air. The material was soft to the touch, as soft as the smooth, pale skin of the thigh it had once covered. Closing his eyes, he caressed it, relishing the memory of her skin, which had flushed a delectable shade of rose at his touch.

"Mr. Hart? Sir?"

He jumped to his feet, shifting position to conceal the erection tenting his breeches. It wouldn't do for his valet to discover him fisting himself in his wife's chamber.

"You may retire for the night, James," he said. "I can see to myself."

"Very good, sir," came the reply.

When the valet's footsteps faded, Dexter returned to his chamber, clutching his prize. After he'd undressed and settled into bed, he rolled the stocking up and stuffed it under his pillow.

Chapter Fourteen

MEGGIE BOUNCED THE little girl on her knee. "So, Betsy, if you gave Jack nine apples and he cut each one into seven pieces, how many pieces would there be in total?"

"She'd have none if I ate them all!" Jack cried, sticking out his tongue at his sister.

"Jack!" Meggie admonished. "That's not very civil. Very well, *you* must answer this. If you then ate nine of those pieces, how many would there be left?"

"I know!" Betsy cried. Jack pulled a face.

"I'm sure you do, my dear," Meggie said, "but your brother must give us the answer. You can whisper it in my ear if you like."

She bent her head, and the little girl cupped her hand over her mouth and whispered softly.

Fifty-four.

Meggie nodded. Betsy possessed an extraordinary intellect. As a girl, and one of her class, what opportunities would she have to make use of her talents?

Jack frowned. "Seven."

Betsy giggled.

The door opened, and Ralph entered the kitchen, and Meggie detected the now-familiar smell of saddle-soap and leather.

Jack squealed in delight. "Ralph! Is it time for me to help feed the horses?"

"Not yet," the groom replied. "Mrs. Hart has prior claim. And your lesson isn't over."

"Thank you, Ralph," Meggie said. "Now, Jack, can you remember what I said about the nine times table? About how easy it is to remember it?"

"Is that the bit when you add the numbers up?"

"Yes, that's it!" Meggie said brightly. "What did I teach you?"

Jack screwed his eyes up in concentration. "You said that if you wanted to know whether a number was in the nine times table, you add its digits together to see if it comes to nine."

"That's it," Meggie said. "Shall we try one now? How about fifty-four?"

The boy counted on his fingers. "Yes!" he cried. "If you add five and four together, you get nine."

"So, what do we know about fifty-four?" Meggie asked.

"It's in the nine times table?"

"Clever child!" Meggie said.

"Why do we need to know our times tables?" Jack asked.

"There are many reasons," Meggie said. Jack didn't look convinced, and Ralph knelt beside him.

"I have nine horses to look after," he said. "So, if each horse eats four bales of hay a week, you can use your nine times table to work out how many bales I need."

"Thirty-six!" Betsy cried. Jack frowned at his sister, then he looked up and gave a cry of delight.

"Mama!"

Mrs. Wells stood in the doorway, arms crossed, a broad smile on her face.

"Come along, children," she said. "You've taken up enough of the mistress's time today. Tidy your books and take them to your room."

The children obeyed, then rushed to the door.

"What do we say?" Mrs. Wells prompted.

"Thank you, Mrs. Hart!" they chorused.

Meggie's heart gave a little lurch as the words brought forth memories of the school at Blackwood Heath.

How was Mrs. Preston faring? Had Alderley

left it alone—or had he burned it to the ground?

"You're a born teacher, Mrs. Hart," the housekeeper said. "Jack and Betsy adore you. But I wonder at your spending so much time downstairs. You have to get used to the main house."

"Why?" Meggie asked. "It's cold and dreary. Think about how much it costs to heat the whole place! There's just me—and the house is big enough for a hundred. I'm sure my husband would not appreciate funds being wasted."

The housekeeper frowned, but Ralph nodded in encouragement. "I agree," he said. "Money shouldn't be spent needlessly."

"And what do you know of such things?" Mrs. Wells snapped. "It's not your place to tell the mistress how to manage the household."

"Neither is it yours," Ralph replied.

Mrs. Wells's lips thinned.

"I think it's time you got on with your work," she said. "The mistress doesn't want to hear any of your nonsense."

"But…"

"Ralph," Mrs. Brown interrupted, wiping her hands on her apron. "Why don't you help me with the logs? This fire's almost out, and I need someone strong to carry them."

He hesitated, and Mrs. Wells folded her arms. "Do as you're told," she said.

"Of course." He cast a quick smile at Meggie,

then followed the cook out of the kitchen.

Mrs. Wells sat beside Meggie.

"My dear," she said. "Permit me to be so bold, but I must caution you."

"In what manner?"

"It simply won't do for the mistress of the house to spend so much time downstairs."

"I thought you were happy for me to teach your children," Meggie said.

"Of course I am, but the lady of the manor should spend her time in the main house. I didn't want to press the matter before because I felt you needed time to settle in. But you must assume your responsibilities eventually. Your husband would expect it."

"My husband is not here."

The housekeeper raised her eyebrows.

Meggie had been at Molineux Manor for almost a month, and he'd not even written to her. Had he cast her from his mind to make room for others?

"Forgive me," Meggie said, "I spoke out of turn. But my husband might not take kindly to my incurring expenses by employing staff we don't need. I don't want to give him cause to…" she hesitated and felt the heat rise in her cheeks.

…to be angry.

"The master wouldn't oppose an increase in the staff," Mrs. Wells said. "He'll understand the need for it."

Meggie shook her head. "But *I* don't understand."

"When it comes to the running of an estate such as this, one must consider every possibility, rather than the direct impact of a single decision," the housekeeper said.

"And employing more staff in the house will help?" Meggie asked.

"Yes, it will." Mrs. Wells gestured toward the kitchen door. "Do you think it's Mrs. Brown's job to bring in the firewood? Or Ralph's, for that matter? By undertaking tasks to which she's not suited, she might be rendered incapable of performing her duties. If we can employ a young lad to fetch and carry, then not only have we benefited Mrs. Brown, but we give him gainful employment."

"So, we can benefit a young man?"

The housekeeper smiled indulgently. "Not just one man, Mrs. Hart, but the whole estate. By employing a full staff, we are giving work to many men—and women—enabling them to feed themselves and their families. More tenants will come to the estate, and it will prosper. A farmer can afford to live here and tend to the land if his sisters are employed in the house. And if his land prospers, it yields rent for the estate, and produces to benefit everyone."

"And I must manage all that myself?"

"Lord, no!" the housekeeper laughed good-naturedly. "Your place is to direct. I can manage the household, and we'll leave the rest of the estate to Mr. Billings, the steward. The purpose of the lady of the manor—and the lord, for that matter—is to tend to the people."

"I didn't realize," Meggie said. "I always thought…" she broke off, embarrassed.

"You thought ladies merely sat in their parlor and looked down on the rest of the world? Doubtless, there are some who neglect their duty, which is why so many estates hereabouts are failing. But, if you look at the prosperous estates—such as Radley Hall, Earl Stiles's seat—you'll notice that the principal inhabitants rule with benevolence, rather than tyranny."

She gave Meggie's hand an affectionate squeeze. "You have the character and temperament to take care of every living soul on this estate, Mrs. Hart. All you need do is learn how all the pieces in an estate can work together."

Understanding flickered in Meggie's mind. "Such as in a game of chess?" she asked.

"If you say so, ma'am," the housekeeper said. "I know nothing about the game."

"In chess, a player has many pieces. She shouldn't consider each piece in isolation. She must look at the board in its entirety and plan several steps to form a strategy to deal with every eventuality."

"Then you understand," Mrs. Wells said.

"And I'll be here to help you. I'd suggest, as a first step, you spend your time in the main house. You could start small—perhaps open up a suite of rooms. This is your home, and it belongs to you—not the other way round. You mustn't be afraid of it."

The housekeeper was no fool. She understood Meggie's fears.

"I'd also caution you not to take too much direction from the servants," Mrs. Wells continued. "Your role is to take care of them, not be instructed by them."

Mrs. Wells was right. If Meggie could consider herself as a caretaker of the souls who depended on her, rather than a superior being, then she could find fulfillment in her role as the mistress. Perhaps that would provide consolation for the lack of satisfaction in her role as a wife.

The cook appeared, followed by Ralph, brandishing a basket full of logs. The young maid, Milly, trotted behind him like a lovesick puppy.

"Milly, love, help me with these plates," Mrs. Brown said. "They've been soaking all day and should come up nice and clean, now."

"Yes, Mrs. Brown," came the reply. "Ralph, would you help me?" She turned wide expressive eyes at the groom, but he ignored her, set the basket on the floor beside the fireplace, then turned to Meggie.

"Mrs. Hart," he said, "it's time for your riding

lesson. It looks like it'll rain soon, so it's best if you come now.

Mrs. Wells raised an eyebrow and gave Meggie a pointed look.

"No, thank you, Ralph," Meggie replied. "I've neglected my duties upstairs for too long."

His smile slipped, but Mrs. Wells nodded encouragement, then exited the kitchen.

"Perhaps tomorrow, if I have time," Meggie continued.

"It would be my pleasure," Ralph replied.

Now it was Milly's turn to scowl, though Meggie recognized it for what it was. Simple jealousy.

"You're becoming quite the proficient," he continued. "I think tomorrow we can try mounting unaided, now that you're used to the saddle."

Meggie laughed. Her first riding lesson had revealed her ignorance when Ralph had presented her with a peculiarly shaped saddle designed for ladies. Having only seen gentleman riders at Blackwood Heath, she'd assumed ladies rode in the same fashion.

"I still think riding astride would be more comfortable," she said.

"I prefer it myself when a woman straddles her mount properly." His eyes gleamed, and for a moment, she thought she saw hunger in them.

A crash echoed round the kitchen.

"Milly!" Mrs. Brown cried. "You clumsy girl! What the devil do you think you're doing?"

The young maid stood in the center of the kitchen, a pile of crockery at her feet.

"That'll have to come out of your wages," Mrs. Brown said.

Meggie opened her mouth to protest, then closed it again, remembering the housekeeper's words.

"Sorry, Mrs. Brown." Milly stooped to pick up the broken pieces. Her mouth was down-turned, and Meggie glimpsed moisture in her eyes.

"I'm not going to help you." Mrs. Brown continued. "I'm due my break. And Ralph, you should get back to the stables—those horses won't feed themselves." She turned to Meggie. "Ma'am, perhaps if you retired to the parlor, Milly can bring you some tea when she's finished here."

Before Meggie could answer, Mrs. Brown left, taking Ralph with her. Meggie approached the door leading to the main house and grasped the handle. She heard a sniff from behind and turned.

"Milly, are you all right?" she asked.

"Yes, ma'am," came the reply. "Sorry, ma'am, for the mess."

"Plates can be replaced," Meggie said. "You'll be careful not to cut yourself, won't you?"

"Yes. Thank you, ma'am."

"Milly, are you fond of Ralph?"

The maid's cheeks flushed red. "It wouldn't be proper," she whispered.

"What does propriety matter when you're in love?"

Milly let out another sniff.

"Does he return your feelings?" Meggie asked.

"I-I don't know," Milly said. "Sometimes, I think he wants me. He's said he'll offer for me—once he's got a bit put by."

"That's good, isn't it?" Meggie asked.

"I suppose. He always says he's too busy for courting, but I've seen him looking at other girls. At the Radley dance last month, he danced twice with Susan."

"Susan?"

"The under-gardener's niece at Radley Hall," Milly said. "I hate her! She knows I'm sweet on him."

"And how many times did he dance with you?"

"Six."

"Well then!" Meggie said, smiling. "That just goes to show he's kind enough to ask a girl to dance so that she might not be shamed for want of a partner—but he'll spend the majority of the evening with the one he loves."

Milly's eyes widened with hope. "Do you

think so?"

"Of course!" Meggie laughed. "And there's much I can do to help you both, starting with engaging an under-groom. With an extra pair of hands in the stables, he'll have no excuse not to court you. And I have the perfect idea to bring the two of you together."

"And what's that?"

"A picnic," Meggie said. "Ralph has mentioned a lake hidden in the forest, which is the perfect spot for courting. I'll insist he accompany us, then I can leave the two of you together."

"I'd love that!" Milly exclaimed. "The secret lake's perfect for bathing. The water is so clear, and you can see the bottom. But I've asked him to come with me before, and he's refused."

"He can hardly refuse the request of his mistress," Meggie said.

"Oh, thank you, ma'am!" Milly said. "I never knew you could be so kind! If it pleases you, I'll bring you a pot of tea as soon as I've cleared this mess up."

The maidservant stood and bobbed a curtsey, and Meggie exited the kitchen and climbed up the stairs into the main house.

A shaft of sunlight beamed across the hallway, illuminating a painting on the wall, highlighting the background's warm colors.

For the first time, the house didn't feel cold and unwelcoming. Perhaps, if she heeded Mrs.

Wells' advice, and brought about the happy union of the two young servants, Meggie might begin to feel she belonged here.

AS MEGGIE SIPPED her tea, she heard hoofbeats outside, and she peered out of the window. Her heart gave a little jolt of anticipation, but the rider was too slight to match her husband's powerful frame. After engaging in a few words with the footman, he mounted and set off as quickly as he came.

Shortly after, the footman knocked and entered the parlor, brandishing a silver salver.

"You have a letter, ma'am."

Hope rose within her as she grasped the envelope.

He'd written! Her husband hadn't forgotten her, after all.

What might he say? Would he ask after her health? Whether she was happy? Perhaps he'd written to say he was on his way to see her.

She tore open the envelope, and her joy faded.

The cold, soulless words, written in a spidery hand, were those of Lord Alderley.

In three short sentences—as if he wished to waste as little paper and ink on her as possible—

he informed Meggie that he and Elizabeth intended to visit Molineux Manor, 'in order to discuss a business matter and further family relations.'

Did he think her a simpleton? He'd made it plain on her wedding day that he despised her and loathed her husband.

Mrs. Wells entered the room.

"Was that a letter from the master?" she asked. "Is he coming?"

"It was from my father," Meggie said. "He'll be staying for a few days."

"When?"

Meggie picked up the letter and reread the words as if she could will them to say something else.

"He arrives in a fortnight."

"Then we'd best get the place ready, Mrs. Hart," the housekeeper said, "and you must write to the master as soon as you can. He'll want to be with you when they arrive, won't he?"

Meggie set the letter aside.

Three sentences on a piece of paper. That was all it took to shatter the illusion that Meggie could feel as if she could be happy here.

She would have to endure the company of the man she thought she'd never have to see again—the man who had sold her to his enemy. And she'd have to play hostess to the woman who looked down on her—the woman who'd boasted, with such relish, of her conquests, past, and future, of Meggie's husband.

In one aspect, Mrs. Wells was right. Meggie's husband would want to be here.

But not for her.

Chapter Fifteen

DEXTER TURNED THE letter over in his hand and read the bland, soulless words on the page.

But did he expect any different from Daisy? She might be happier than she would have been had that wastrel not abandoned her, but by refusing to pay the man, Dexter had brought about that abandonment.

And she still blamed him.

He fingered the scar on his chin. A mere echo of the marks on his back, but administered by the same hand, albeit some ten years later. It served to remind him how he'd let Daisy down.

He picked up his pen and held it over a blank sheaf of paper. What could he say to her? He wasn't a man of feeling. Any expression of regret penned by his hand, she'd view as insincere. And the last time they'd spoken, Daisy had made it clear she never wished to set eyes on him again. The shame of her situation had been too much, and she'd imposed herself in exile until she had been saved—by a better man than her brother.

If he delved into the deepest recesses of his heart, he might discover that he was capable of love. But love—even for a sister—was a weakness that could be exploited.

Something compelled him, this time, to write a few words of affection. Perhaps an inquiry after her health. He wrote a sentence, then almost immediately scrunched the paper into a ball and tossed it on the floor. He picked up a clean sheaf and scribbled a few words.

Dear Sister,

Herewith I enclose two pounds.

Yours,
Dexter

Soulless and practical, but money was all he had to give her. He opened a drawer in his desk, pulled out two notes, and folded them together with the letter. After scribbling the directions on an envelope, he set it aside and rang the bell.

Soon after, Charles appeared.

"Post this for me, please," he said.

"Very good, sir."

"Are there any letters?"

"Just the one." The footman handed Dexter an envelope, then bowed and left.

The hand which had penned the directions was unfamiliar—a neat, cursive style, devoid of unnecessary flourishes. He traced the shape of the words, then tore open the envelope.

The letter was from his wife. Her penmanship was remarkable, considering her background.

He gave a little sigh. His origins weren't that different to hers, save for the fact that he'd been born on the right side of the blanket. Surely, he wasn't turning into a snob?

He read the first paragraph.

"Damn!"

The curse slipped out before he could prevent it.

She had invited Alderley to stay and was demanding Dexter join her in the country as soon as possible. He slammed the paper on the desk.

She was her father's pawn after all, and this must be his first move.

But what game was he playing?

"YOU SEEM OUT of sorts, Hart," Oliver Peyton said as a footman arrived, brandishing a tray and two glasses.

Dexter plucked a glass off the tray. Before he'd taken a sip, Peyton drained half his glass and nodded to the footman to fetch another.

"I hope I won't have to carry you home," Dexter said.

"Am I not permitted a celebration?" Peyton asked. "I've secured us the Westbury account. That family's banked with Coutts for over fifty years."

The Westbury account was a boon, and it increased the chances of other notable families moving their accounts to the Hart Bank. Oliver Peyton excelled at the personal side of banking—maintaining relationships with the account holders and wooing clients. And Dexter would be the first person to admit that he lacked Peyton's congeniality.

"You don't seem too thrilled," Peyton said. "Anything the matter?"

"I have been summoned to the country," Dexter said.

"Who by?"

"My wife wrote the letter," Dexter replied, "but I suspect it was dictated by another."

"What do you mean?"

"She writes to tell me that Lord Alderley will be visiting 'in order to further family relations'—whatever the hell that means."

"It means your father-in-law is in need of cash," Peyton said.

Dexter snorted. "There's hope for you yet, Peyton, if you're capable of such healthy cynicism."

"Is he bringing Elizabeth with him?" Peyton asked.

"It would appear so," Dexter said. "Having moved his pawn to my end of the board, he's bringing his queen into play."

The footman reappeared with another glass, and Peyton took it.

"Are you having another, Hart?"

Dexter shook his head. "I need a clear head. I leave at dawn."

"You're *going?*"

"I must engage with Alderley at some point," Dexter said. "Where better than on my territory? Alderley may believe he has the upper hand, but a player can overestimate the effectiveness of his pieces."

"And you think he intends to use both daughters against you?"

"He'll fail," Dexter replied. "Alderley may think he has control of the board, but I can just as easily use his pieces against him."

"How long will you be away?" Peyton asked.

"A fortnight."

"And you trust me not to run the bank into the ground while you're battling your father-in-law?"

"You can view this as a test of your prowess,

Peyton," Dexter said, "and I want you to join me in a week to report on activities."

"Naturally," Peyton said, grinning. "You could never relinquish control for too long. Is there anything, in particular, you wish me to report on?"

"Keep an eye on the MacGregor account," Dexter said.

"Your brother-in-law's whisky business?"

"The very same. The next installment on the loan is due in a few days. Just because I'm related to the fellow, I've no intention of showing leniency if the payment is late."

"Of course not," Peyton said. "I know enough about you to understand that family loyalty won't rank above a contractual obligation."

A tall gentleman hailed them on his way out of the clubroom.

"Peyton!" he said. "I didn't realize you were here."

"Good to see you," Peyton said. He turned to Dexter. "Hart, you know Mr. Young, don't you? Founding member of the Mayfair Gentlemen's Chess Club."

Dexter nodded.

"Are you playing at Durrants tonight, Peyton?" the gentleman asked. "Simpkins has a new opening gambit he wants to try out on you. He says it guarantees checkmate in six moves."

"It probably does," Peyton replied, "but only if his opponent is either in his cups or has sustained a blow to the head. I suppose I could use it as a reference for my book. I could have a chapter at the end entitled 'checkmate for dimwits' and dedicate it to Simpkins."

The gentleman laughed and took his leave. Peyton finished his drink and glanced at the longcase clock by the door.

"I'd better be going."

"You're writing a book?" Dexter asked.

"On chess strategy," Peyton replied. "I want to focus on the mid-part of the game. Too many books cover the opening gambits and the endgame. But the real skill is in bringing your pieces together after the first few moves, once you've begun to understand your opponent's style, and in preparation for the final stages of the game."

"I wish you luck."

Peyton laughed. "*You'll* need more luck than I, dealing with your in-laws."

"Luck won't come into it," Dexter said. "Alderley is a weak opponent. His weakness lies in his transparency. He might have fooled me once, but I won't make the same mistake again."

"You might enjoy your visit," Peyton said. "You're paying enough to rent the place, so you should reap the benefit and *live* there."

Peyton set his glass down and followed in

Mr. Young's wake.

Dexter lifted his glass to his lips. The prospect of a week in Alderley's company—not to mention Elizabeth's, would drive most men to drink. But a small part of him whispered that there was one element of his forthcoming visit he did not regret. And that was seeing his wife again.

More than anything, he wanted to see her smile.

Chapter Sixteen

A CLOUD OF dust rose up as two footmen lifted the sheets off the drawing room furniture. Meggie couldn't contain the tickle in her nose, and she let out a sneeze.

The housekeeper rushed to her side. "Perhaps you should wait elsewhere, ma'am," she said. "You've been working nonstop since the master's letter arrived, and it's high time you took a break."

"But there's so much to do," Meggie protested.

"Mr. Billings has already engaged four members of staff, and your father doesn't arrive until Saturday."

"You need help here," Meggie said.

"It wouldn't do for the master to return home to find his wife has a cough," the housekeeper said. She placed a gentle hand on Meggie's arm. "My dear, nobody will think any less of you for wanting to rest. The lady of the manor shouldn't be expected to work harder than her staff. Why not take a turn outside? Some fresh air would bring that lovely bloom back to your cheeks."

Another puff of dust flew up as a footman uncovered a chair, and Meggie exited the drawing room and made her way to the breakfast room where Milly and Sarah were polishing a large, round table.

"You're doing well," Meggie said. "I've never seen so much dust in my life!"

"The house hasn't been tended to for years, ma'am," Milly said. "But, we'll have it bright and clean in no time."

Sarah frowned at Milly. "There's the windows to do next," she said. "They'll take hours."

"I can help," Meggie said. "But for now, Sarah, Mrs. Wells wants you in the drawing room."

Sarah dropped her dust cloth, bobbed a curtsey, and left.

At that moment, Meggie heard a gurgling sound, and Milly blushed, clutching her midriff. "Pardon my stomach."

"Haven't you eaten yet?" Meggie asked.

"No, ma'am."

"Then we must do something about that,"

Meggie said. "It's a beautiful day, and I fancy taking my luncheon outside."

"I was just about to suggest that myself," a male voice said.

Ralph stood in the doorway, holding a posy of wildflowers. "I found these and thought they'd brighten the place up," he said.

Milly squealed with delight and rushed toward him. He frowned, then relinquished the bouquet.

"Ralph, how lovely!" she cried. "Shall we see if Mrs. Brown has something to eat in the kitchen if the mistress will permit me to take my break now?"

"No, I should return to the horses," he said.

"Oh, very well."

Meggie's heart tightened at the disappointment in Milly's expression.

"Perhaps we could take luncheon together, outside, Milly?" she suggested. "I'd appreciate the company. We could have a picnic if you're up for a walk. I'm sure Mrs. Wells would give you the afternoon off."

"Oh, thank you!" Milly said. "I'd like that. It's perfect weather for a picnic, and I know just the spot."

"Ralph, will you join us?" Meggie asked. This was a perfect opportunity to bring the two young people together, for the groom could hardly resist a request from his mistress.

"It would be my pleasure, ma'am," he said.

Milly's face lit up with joy.

"Milly, go and ask Mrs. Brown to make up a basket for us while I fetch my bonnet," Meggie said. "Ralph, can you find something for us to sit on?"

"It would be my pleasure." He bowed and exited the room, followed closely by the lovestruck young maid. Meggie's heart leapt for joy at the thought of bringing two young lovers together.

Today was going to be a good day.

THE ONCE-BARE TREES showed spots of green as new shoots came to life all about her. Before long, the woodland floor would be a blaze of color, and the air would carry the sweet scent of spring flowers.

Beside the path ran a stream, where crystal-clear water danced over rocks and stones, forming soft music.

This was her home. For the rest of her life, she'd be free to wander through these woods any time she chose and lie among the carpet of bluebells.

And indulge in delights such as the treats Mrs. Brown provided. Her stomach rumbled at the smell of the freshly baked rolls in her basket.

"Let me carry that for you, Mrs. Hart."

Ralph reached for Meggie's basket, but she shook her head. "You've enough to carry as it is."

She gestured to the young woman who walked ahead of them through the trees. "Why don't you help Milly? Her basket's heavier than mine, and she'd enjoy your company. I should like her to be happy today."

"Whereas you wish to be miserable?"

Meggie laughed. "I am content by myself," she said. "I'd like today to be special for Milly. There's a lot of work for her to do—even more, when my husband arrives."

"And for you, Mrs. Hart."

"Ah, but today's excursion is not about me, Ralph. It's about Milly." Meggie met his gaze. "She's a pretty girl, is she not?"

"I suppose she's prettier than old Mrs. Brown."

"Ralph!" she chided. "I may not be a lady, but even I know that's a very ungallant thing to say to the young woman you intend to court."

He frowned and opened his mouth to speak, but before he could say anything, an excited cry rose up ahead.

"We're here! Look!"

Meggie caught a glimpse of a larger expanse of water, and she heard a rushing, thundering sound. Sparkles of light reflected the sun, dancing on the surface. She picked up the pace, and the trees thinned out into a clearing.

The stream widened out to form a lake. Light shimmered across the surface as the water rippled and moved with the current. Beyond, she glimpsed the source of the sound. A waterfall plunged into the lake. Droplets of water filled the air, catching the sunlight to form a rainbow.

"It's beautiful!" Meggie cried. "What a perfect spot for a picnic."

"The best place is over there," Milly said, pointing to a large, flat rock near the water's edge. "It'll give us a good view of the waterfall, but is far enough away that you don't get caught by the spray."

"Then we'll eat there," Meggie said. "Ralph, would you set out the blankets?"

"Of course." He sounded sullen but did as she asked, then they unpacked the baskets.

"Ooh look!" Milly cried. "Mrs. Brown's included some of her rock cakes. They're my favorite! Did you ask her to bake some, Ralph?"

"I know you like them," he said.

She picked one up. "I'm so hungry. I could eat it whole."

"Don't eat too many, or you'll be plumper than Mrs. Brown," Ralph said. "I think she models her rock cakes on her own shape!"

"Nonsense!" Meggie said as Milly blushed. "Milly's in no danger of that, are you, Milly? And it wouldn't matter if she was."

"No, ma'am," Ralph said.

Meggie frowned at him. He gave her a smile, then nudged Milly affectionately. "Forgive me, Mills," he said. "You know you're the prettiest girl hereabouts, don't you?"

"Ralph, why don't you eat with Milly?" Meggie asked. "I'm not hungry yet, and I'd like to explore the woods before I eat."

"You should join us," he said.

"No, I'll eat later," Meggie replied. "After all, Milly's the reason you're here, isn't it?"

Ralph scrambled to his feet.

"Where are you going?" Milly asked.

"Forgive me," he said. "I've remembered I have to do something for Mr. Billings."

"Can't it wait?" Meggie asked. "We've walked all this way."

"I'm afraid not, ma'am," he said. "Mr. Billings was most insistent, and I wouldn't want to disappoint him. I'm anxious to please him—to show I'm capable of the responsibility of head groom."

Milly's disappointment showed on her face, but Meggie couldn't argue with Ralph's reasoning.

"Perhaps another time?" she suggested.

"Once I've completed my duties, I shall be at your disposal any time you wish," he said. "Enjoy your picnic, and don't worry about carrying the baskets back. Leave them here, and I can fetch them later."

He bowed and disappeared through the trees.

Milly let out a sigh. "Why does he always do that?"

"Perhaps I pushed him a little too hard," Meggie said. "But, we can still enjoy our picnic."

"I should go back," the maid said. "Mrs. Wells will be expecting me."

"Nonsense!" Meggie said. "I say you can have the afternoon off."

"I suppose..." Milly hesitated.

"Don't worry about Ralph," Meggie said. "I am by no means discouraged. The head groom needs a wife—he shouldn't live alone in that cottage. And you're perfect for him."

"Do you think so?" Milly asked, rummaging in the basket. She pulled out a stoneware bottle. "Ooh—Mrs. Brown's lemonade!"

"Then let us enjoy our picnic," Meggie said, "and, for the moment, think no more of men."

By the time they'd finished eating, the air had grown even warmer. Meggie lay back, drinking in the sound of the babbling waterfall.

Where else could she come so close to paradise? With a haven such as this at her disposal, she could weather any storm her father's visit might bring.

Milly tidied away the picnic items, then yawned and stretched. "When I get an afternoon off, I pray for good weather. There's so much to do here!"

"Such as?"

"I love to swim in the lake," Milly replied, "though Sarah's too scared of the water. It's warm enough today—why don't you try it?" Almost as soon as she spoke, she blushed and lowered her gaze. "Begging your pardon, ma'am, I forgot my place. I shouldn't be speaking as if you're my friend. Mrs. Wells has already warned me against it."

Was this what Meggie's newfound status had done? Alienated her from people she'd typically choose as friends?

"Nonsense, Milly," she said. "I don't see why we can't be friends—out here, at least, where it doesn't matter what a few stuffy old lords and ladies think."

"Then you'll come for a swim?" Milly asked. "I can help you undress."

"You mean we should remove our clothes?"

"We can swim in our undergarments," Milly said. "They'll dry quick enough if we lay them out on the rock. I've done it before."

The water did look inviting—clear and deep in the center—and Meggie had fond memories of swimming in the river at Blackwood Heath.

But she hesitated. What would her husband think?

"Perhaps I shouldn't," she said. "It's not what

the mistress of the house should do."

"Oh, ma'am!" Milly cried. "Don't you think it'll cheer you up? Everyone says I'm a feather-brained fool, but I can see you're not entirely happy. A little swim doesn't do nobody any harm."

"I suppose not…"

"We'll be out and dry in no time. Nobody will be any the wiser. It can be our little secret. Ralph has gone, and the master isn't here."

Meggie couldn't resist the eager expression on the young maid's face. Milly had been so disappointed by Ralph's rebuff that Meggie didn't have the heart to refuse her invitation.

"Oh, very well," she said. "Let's see who makes it into the water first."

While Meggie fumbled with her gown's laces, she heard a splash as Milly beat her into the water. Stripped to her undergarments, she picked her way across the rocks to the waterfall. Then, taking a deep breath, she clasped her hands together, as if in prayer, and launched herself off the rocks.

The water hit her body like a knife, the cold giving a sharp contrast to the warm spring air. She opened her eyes and thrust out her arms to propel her body toward the bottom of the lake, relishing the feel of the water pulling through her hair. Then, with a kick of her legs, she swam toward the surface where the sunlight shone through the water.

She surfaced and saw Millie's head bobbing a few feet away.

"You swim so well!" the maid cried. "Can you teach me to dive like that?"

She flicked water at Meggie, and, laughing, Meggie splashed back. The two of them continued, splashing each other and squealing with laughter. It was as if Meggie was, once more, the carefree child she had once been before she'd been forced to grow up.

Milly moved to splash her again.

"Oh no, you don't!" Meggie laughed and dived underwater. This time, she was going to make it to the bottom and collect one of the stones as a trophy. She kicked out with her legs and brushed her hands over the bed of the lake until she found a small, round stone that fitted her palm perfectly. Curling her fingers round it, she swam back up.

She heard a scream, muffled through the water, and kicked out harder until she resurfaced.

"Milly! Are you all right?"

"Oh, ma'am! I'm so sorry!"

Meggie caught sight of the maid, shivering at the water's edge, her face pale with terror.

"What's wrong?" She swam forward until her feet got a purchase on the rocks, then she stood up, the water reaching her waist.

"What the bloody hell do you think you're

doing!" a deep male voice roared.

Meggie looked up and saw two men beside the lake. Ralph stood, arms folded, his eyes on her, a hungry expression in his gaze.

His companion stood half a head taller. Body ramrod straight, hands curled into fists, his face was pale with anger, his brow furrowed, eyes dark.

His expression was one of pure fury—as if he was ready to commit murder.

It was her husband.

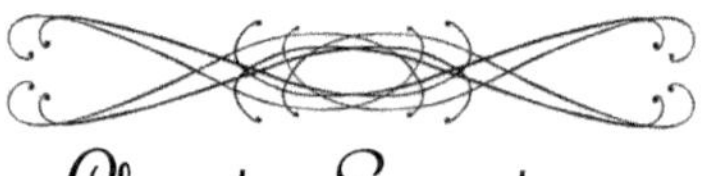

Chapter Seventeen

"WHERE THE DEVIL is my wife?"

The journey to Hampshire had only served to darken Dexter's mood. Two days cooped up in a box, with the prospect of that bastard Alderley's company for a week, was enough to turn even the sunniest disposition sour.

The steward scraped a bow. "I don't know, sir." The woman standing next to him—Mrs. Wells, if Dexter recalled the name correctly—seemed to possess a little more backbone. Though she dipped into a curtsey, she looked Dexter square in the eye.

"The mistress is taking a walk," she said.

"On her own?"

"Milly's attending her."

"Good," he said. "It wouldn't do to have her

roaming about the place alone."

"No, sir, it wouldn't." Her voice held a note of a disappointed nanny. "Had the mistress known the exact time of your arrival, I'm sure she'd have been waiting to greet you."

The housekeeper was right. Even if his wife had known the time of his arrival, was it any wonder she wasn't eagerly waiting for him with a smile? What had he done to deserve it?

"Perhaps young Ralph knows where she is," Mrs. Wells said.

Jealousy flared within him. "Who the devil is *Ralph?*"

"The groom, sir." the steward said. Dexter glared at him, and he seemed to shrink further. "He's young but very talented."

Talented?

That's what Dexter was afraid of.

"With the horses," the steward continued. "He was ostler at the Queen's Head. I trust I did no wrong in hiring him."

"Fetch him at once."

"But sir, you've had a long journey. Wouldn't you want to…"

"Do as I bid, Mr. Billings," Dexter said, "or this will be your last day in my employ."

"Of course." The steward scuttled off. The staff lacked discipline if they deemed it acceptable to question his orders. Perhaps it was as well that he'd come now before they acquired too many bad habits.

"May we return to our duties inside?" the housekeeper asked. "There's much to do before Lord Alderley arrives."

"Yes, yes." Dexter waved dismissively at her, and she slipped back inside, followed by the rest of the staff.

Shortly after, the steward returned, accompanied by a strikingly handsome young man with blonde hair, bright blue eyes, and the kind of face that some women might describe as *dangerous*. Were he rich or titled, he'd have presented Dexter with some pretty stiff competition for the attention of London's courtesans.

But his looks came with an air of arrogance. No doubt, he could claim responsibility for several broken hearts.

The steward nudged him, and he dipped into a bow.

"Ralph, is it?" Dexter asked.

The youth nodded.

"I believe you know where my wife is?"

"She's taking a walk. She'll be back soon if you'd care to wait—she usually returns about this time."

Who was this young jackanapes that he knew so much about her habits?

"Take me to her," Dexter said.

"I don't know if that would be..."

"Did I ask for your advice or give you an

order?" Dexter barked. "Lead the way."

The groom hesitated, and the steward prodded him again.

"Very good, sir," he said, his smile slipping. He pointed to a line of trees. "It's this way."

DEXTER HAD TO admit that the grounds of the Molineux estate were remarkably pretty—if one liked that sort of thing. Save for the ornamental garden, much of the grounds had been left to the care of Mother Nature. An uneducated country girl such as his wife would find much to like here compared to the harsh lines of London.

He heard a shriek, and his stomach tightened. Almost immediately, it was followed by splashing and high-pitched female laughter.

The path widened out into a clearing, with a lake in the center. On the opposite side, by the water's edge, a picnic had been set out beside a large, flat rock, with what appeared to be a lady's gown draped over it.

A young woman stood by the edge of the water, bent double with laughter. She turned and caught sight of him and screamed.

Then a vision emerged from the surface of the lake.

A goddess covered in water glistened in the

sunlight. Though clothed, she might as well have been naked. White, lacy undergarments clung to her skin, leaving little to the imagination—a body ripe with curves, ready for the taking—soft, round breasts, made to fit his hands. The water had rendered the material translucent to reveal two peaks.

"Bloody hell!"

The groom stood transfixed. Dexter could swear he saw a bulge in the man's breeches.

Dexter's manhood had hardened the moment she'd risen from the water, and now it strained against his breeches. She raised her arms, and the action lifted her breasts into a deliciously full shape, as if in offering.

A low growl from the groom brought Dexter to his senses.

His wife was romping around, practically naked to be ogled at by the servants!

"What the bloody hell do you think you're doing!" he roared.

She screamed and covered her breasts with her arms.

"H-husband!" she cried. "I didn't think you'd arrive today."

"That much is obvious," he said. "Get out of the water at once! I'll not have you parading around like a bloody slattern. I ought to have you horsewhipped for this!"

The groom stood still.

"Ralph, take the girl back. I'll deal with my wife," Dexter said. "Quickly!" he added when the young man hesitated. "The sooner you're gone, the better."

His wife shivered.

"Is that your dress over there?" He pointed toward the garment on the rock.

She nodded.

"Then, for goodness sake, take those wet clothes off and put the fucking thing on!" He gestured with his cane, and she shrank back, her eyes widening in fear.

Ye gods, did she think he was going to *hit* her? He lowered his arm and softened his voice. "Do as I say, please, Margaret."

She stepped out of the water and approached the dress.

"Well?" he demanded, "what are you waiting for?"

"Shall I remove my undergarments while you watch?" she asked.

Good lord no—that was not a good idea, not when that groom looked like he was about to spend at any moment.

It was a small spark of defiance and spirit, but it flickered out as he moved toward her.

"Use the blankets," he said. "For pity's sake, cover yourself up! Ralph, see to it that the rest of the mess is cleared up. But for now, we need to get my wife home before she catches a chill."

"Are…are we in trouble?" the maid asked.

"Yes," Dexter said through his teeth. "You're in a lot of trouble. What the devil do you think you were doing?"

"I saw no harm in it," his wife said.

"That's not helping your case, Margaret."

"It was my idea!" the maid cried.

"And what possessed you to encourage your mistress to behave like a slut?" Dexter demanded.

"I-I thought it would make her happy. She needed cheering up."

The reply pricked at his conscience. But whatever the reason, there was no excuse for such behavior. What would the servants think of their mistress if she carried on like this? Not to mention Alderley.

That spiteful man was coming tomorrow, together with his snob of a daughter. They'd tear Margaret to pieces. She must learn—quickly—that it was not acceptable to mingle with the servants.

And given how little time he had to teach her before Alderley's arrival, she'd have to learn the hard way.

AS SOON AS they reached the main house, Meggie's husband ordered Ralph to take Milly inside. Then he grasped Meggie's arm and pulled her close.

"Get yourself changed," he hissed, "then wait in your chamber. I'll deal with the servant first."

"What do you mean—deal with her?" she asked, her stomach tightening in fear.

"You can't expect such a deed to go unpunished."

"But it wasn't her fault!" she cried. "I was the one in the water.

"At her suggestion, if I recall her confession correctly."

"Her confession?" she asked. "Am I on trial?"

"Perhaps," he replied. "After all, as my wife and mistress of this house, you must abide by certain rules, many of which you broke today."

Who was he—her jailer? Did he think he could order her about within minutes of returning?

"Pardon me for not knowing all the rules," she said.

His mouth twitched, almost as if he were going to smile before his lips thinned again.

"My dear," he said, "a woman of even *your* level of intelligence should understand that the mistress of the house shouldn't go swimming naked with the scullery maid! Do not insult *my* intelligence by feigning ignorance."

How many insults could he throw at her in a single sentence?

"If I'm the one who broke the rules, punish me instead," Meggie said. "Milly doesn't deserve it."

He shook his head. "I'm afraid it's not so simple."

"What are you going to do with her?"

"I haven't decided yet," he said, "but it should serve as a reminder not to do it again. One or two strokes should suffice."

Meggie's blood chilled. "You mean to have her *thrashed*?"

"Perhaps."

She grasped his hand. "Please!" she cried. "You cannot! She meant no harm, and it's not her fault if I didn't behave as you expect me to. You can't punish her for that."

"I can," he said. "And I will. She should know both her place and yours."

"No!" she cried. "Dexter, please!"

At her mention of his name, his eyes narrowed, then he looked away.

"I'm sorry, my dear, my mind is made up."

"Why must you be so cruel?"

"It's not out of cruelty," he said, "but of necessity. I don't expect you to understand."

"Then explain it to me."

"You're the mistress of the house," he said. The anger had gone from his voice, and now he sounded as if he were at Mrs. Preston's school, explaining the laws of mathematics. "You cannot form friendships with the staff. They're your subordinates, not your equals, and the distinction must be maintained, so they respect you as their mistress. If you don't have their respect, the estate cannot be run properly. They won't look to you to rule them when the need arises, and the estate will descend into chaos."

"What if I have no wish to rule them?"

"It's the world we live in, my dear," he said. "Sometimes, we must do what is required, even if it's not to our liking. Therein lies our strength of character. As master and mistress of the house, our responsibility is to tend to the people here. To do that, we must maintain the distinction of rank."

"What about kindness?" she asked.

"We can rule with kindness, but the boundaries of propriety must always be observed. Transgressions, however minor, must be dealt with swiftly and efficiently, to ensure that order is restored."

He squeezed her hand and spoke more softly. "It will give me no pleasure to administer the girl's punishment, but it must be done."

"Then punish me instead," she said. "If I am to be mistress and tend to the people here, then let me do this for Milly."

He shook his head. "I cannot agree with that. Besides, I believe a worse punishment awaits you."

Meggie's stomach plummeted as if she'd swallowed a stone. "W-what do you mean?"

"Your punishment will be to know what happened to another because of your transgression." He lifted his hand as if to caress her face, then lowered it again, and curled it into a fist.

"I shan't force you to watch," he said. "I'll let you know when it's done."

"Hiding it behind closed doors doesn't mean it's not happening," she said.

He sighed. "Let us say no more on the matter. There is much you need to learn about life, Margaret."

"And there's much you have to learn about compassion, *husband*."

He frowned at her address, then sighed. "Do not believe that where compassion—or love—is not displayed, it's because it does not exist. Perhaps one day, you'll realize that." He released her arm. "Go and find Mrs. Wells, and ask her to tend to you," he said. "Whatever you think of me, I have no wish to see you catch a chill. You've endured enough."

Clutching the blanket round her, she retreated inside the house, turning at the door to look back at him. He stood still, hands clenched, watching her, regret in his eyes.

Chapter Eighteen

DEXTER STARED AT his reflection while his valet selected a jacket and held it up.

"This one, sir?"

He nodded and held his arms out while the servant slipped the jacket on, smoothed down the sleeves' material, and brushed a speck of dust from the cuff.

"Do you require anything else, sir?"

"No, James, you're dismissed."

"Very good." James bowed and left.

Dexter adjusted his cravat—the damned man always tied it too tight—and exited the dressing room. He turned left and followed the corridor until he reached the door to the mistress's bedchamber.

He lifted his hand and knocked smartly on the door.

Silence.

Perhaps she was asleep.

Or had the foolish woman run away?

He pushed the door open.

The room was empty. Elegantly furnished, it bore all the trappings of a lady's chamber, but no sign of occupancy.

"Mrs. Wells!" he roared.

He heard a scurry of footsteps, and, at length, the housekeeper appeared at the end of the corridor.

"Can I help you, sir?"

"This is the lady's chamber, is it not?"

"It is."

"Then, why is my wife not here?"

"She asked to be moved elsewhere."

"Show me."

The housekeeper dipped into a curtsey and, with a jangle of keys, turned and led him to the back wing of the house. She stopped beside a door and pushed it open.

The room must be less than half the size of the chamber he'd just left. At the far end, beside a tiny window, was a single bed, and, besides a small fireplace, freshly laid, was a straight-backed chair and a footstool.

Despite the drab appearance of the room, it looked lived in and cared for. Earthenware pots covered almost every surface, filled with wild grasses and flowers. A quilt covered the otherwise unremarkable bed, which was decorated with embroidered flowers. A stack of books lay on the table beside the bed, together with a small chess set.

A dress was draped over the back of the chair, and he recognized the garment he'd seen on the rock beside the lake.

"*This* is her chamber?" he asked.

"It is, sir."

"What the devil were you thinking of putting her in here, Mrs. Wells?"

"She insisted," the housekeeper replied.

"But it's so damned small!"

"I dare say it's what she's been used to most of her life." The housekeeper gestured to the window. "There's a fine prospect over the woods and..." she hesitated, "...your wife was anxious about the expense involved in maintaining a full suite of rooms."

She glanced at him, and he could swear he caught a glimpse of accusation in her eyes.

"I've given her no cause to be anxious," he said, "at least not concerning money."

"Would you mind if I spoke out of turn?" she asked.

"I daresay you will, whether I mind or not," he replied.

"Very well," she said. "That young servant might have deserved her punishment, but your wife has suffered as a result. I'd ask you to treat her with kindness. I know she must learn the ways of a lady, but it's hard for her. Not only doesn't she know what's required, but she also doesn't *understand* it, either."

"You think I don't know that?"

"She was abandoned by her father, hidden away like a dirty secret—then as good as abandoned by her husband. She's had nobody to teach her how to behave like a lady—nobody to give her any regard, let alone love."

She folded her arms as if to scold him. Hell— she *was* scolding him!

"Has my wife been tattling?"

"No," she said, "but her background is common knowledge hereabouts. Gossip spreads below stairs as well as above it, sir."

"Where is she now, Mrs. Wells?"

"You'll find her in the parlor. Do you know the way?"

Yes, he did. Despite only having visited the place once before signing the lease, he'd studied the layout and knew it well.

Unlike his wife.

What the devil was he to do with her?

He found her in the parlor. She sat in a chair by the window, a pair of stockings in her hands, a needle flying in and out. Her brow was furrowed with concentration. She tied a knot in the thread, cut the ends with her teeth, then set the stocking aside and lifted her head to look out of the window. The sunlight caught her hair, forming a soft halo.

He moved forward, and she stiffened.

"The deed is done," he said.

She rose to her feet and turned to stare at him, her expression unreadable. Then she dipped into a curtsey and moved past him. He caught her sleeve, and she flinched.

"Where are you going?" he asked.

"To tend to her."

"It's not your responsibility."

She pulled herself free. "It's my duty to care for her, despite what you say."

With the housekeeper's words echoing in his mind, he relented.

"Very well," he sighed. "I'll have someone take you to her."

"I can find my way."

He stepped aside and let her pass.

MEGGIE PUSHED THE door open and entered the small attic room. Milly lay on her stomach underneath a thin blanket on the bed. She appeared to be asleep but stirred as Meggie sat in the chair beside the bed.

She took Milly's hand.

"Are you in pain?" she asked.

Milly mumbled incoherently and shook her head. Meggie drew back the blanket. Someone had placed a cloth on her back.

She lifted the cloth. Two red, parallel lines stretched across Milly's back. They had not cut the skin, but Meggie winced at the sight. No hand brandishing a whip could ever be called gentle, but at least the punishment hadn't been administered with savagery. The lash marks glistened with a sticky salve, and Meggie wrinkled her nose at the scent of chamomile and lavender.

Someone had tended to her.

A pile of bandages lay on the table beside the bed, together with three vials. Meggie picked up one and read the label.

Laudanum.

Which explained why the maidservant wasn't crying in pain.

"Milly, I'm so sorry," Meggie whispered. She stroked the maidservant's hand. The skin of Milly's fingers was already thickened with callouses, despite her youth. In her short life, the maid had already done more hard labor than Meggie would ever do.

"You did nothing wrong, ma'am," Milly whispered. Thin, bony fingers wrapped around Meggie's wrist. Meggie settled into the chair and stroked the back of Milly's hand.

"I'm here now," she said. "I'll take care of you like I should have done from the moment I arrived."

"Thank you, ma'am."

The response pricked at Meggie's conscience. She'd been the cause of Milly's suffering, yet the maidservant was *thanking* her.

As the light began to fade, the door opened, and a footman appeared.

"Begging your pardon, ma'am, but dinner is served."

"Could you bring mine up here?" she asked.

"The master's expecting you in the dining room."

"Tell him I'm not hungry."

"The master was most particular about you joining him." He shifted uncomfortably from one foot to the other. "He said he had no wish to be kept waiting."

"Go," a soft voice said from the bed. "I'll be all right."

Meggie placed a soft kiss on Milly's hand, then followed the footman out of the attic and down the stairs.

"Shall I fetch Sarah to help you dress for dinner?" the footman asked.

"No," she replied firmly. "If my husband is demanding to see me as soon as possible, then he must be obeyed. If he dislikes my apparel, then he can blame his impatience."

Dexter might have explained the reasoning for his actions. He might have ordered someone to dress Milly's wounds. But Meggie couldn't forgive him.

She found him in the dining room, seated at one end of the table. He rose as she entered and arched an eyebrow as he looked her up and down. Hair still wet, loose tendrils on her face, she looked the antithesis of the elegant lady he'd wanted for a wife, but she cared not. She tilted her chin and stared at him as if in challenge.

His gaze settled on her, the blue of his eyes like a deep, cold ocean. They regarded each other across the table.

For a moment, she thought she saw a glimmer of admiration in his eyes. Then he gestured toward her chair.

"Please, sit," he said. "Then, we can dine, at last."

At last…

A footman approached with a tureen. Meggie ladled soup into the bowl in front of her, waited until he served her husband, and then began eating.

"Did you find everything to your satisfaction when you visited the attic, my dear?"

She looked up to find him staring directly at her.

"She's sleeping," she said.

"I thought as much," he replied. "Laudanum is very effective when needed."

"Yes, husband," Meggie said, sipping her

soup. "And there was much need of it today."

He frowned but did not respond. When he finished his soup, he set his spoon down, and the footman rushed forward to clear his place.

"May I ask whether the maidservant…"

"Milly," Meggie interrupted. "Her name's Milly. You should at least remember the name of the girl you thrashed."

"It wasn't my hand on the whip."

"No, you left that for others to ease your conscience."

He flinched and picked up his wineglass. "I don't regret my decision," he said. "She would have known that her behavior warranted such a punishment. Worse, in fact. Any master worth his salt would be within his rights to have her dismissed immediately."

"Then why don't you?" she cried.

"Because I'm not a monster," he said quietly. "I'm not so devoid of feeling that I cannot see how much it hurts you to see another suffer as a result of your actions."

"Nobody should suffer for the crimes of another," Meggie said.

"But they often do."

"Did you see the marks on her back?" Meggie asked. "She's barely out of childhood, yet she was lashed as if she were a man!"

"That cannot be right," he said. "I told Billings to ensure that…" he trailed off and drained his glass, motioning to the footman to refill it.

"How long will she have to lie on her stomach?" Meggie cried. "The skin on her might be ruined! The pain—the humiliation..." She shook her head, blinking back the tears. "You cannot possibly know how she suffers."

"I do know, Margaret," he said. "Believe me, I know."

"How can you? You have no understanding of the feelings of others!"

He slammed his glass on the table. "Do *not* presume to know what I do, or do not, understand," he said through gritted teeth. "I know that with each lash, it's like your body's on fire. You tell yourself you'll survive by counting the strokes, that the pain will reach a point where it cannot get worse. But it *does* get worse. Then you pray that the skin won't break—and when it does, it's like your whole body is being sliced open with knives. After the tenth lash, you pray for oblivion, for the relief it will give you from the pain. But it does not come, so you bite your tongue and taste the blood, hoping that it lessens the pain on your back. Then you hear the laughter—the triumph of the hand on the whip—when you realize that you've been reduced to mere flesh for the entertainment of others."

He closed his eyes, as if reliving a memory, then opened them again. Their color had deepened to that of a midnight sky.

"Only then," he said, "do you realize there's only one place where you can find sanctuary. In that moment, you pray for death."

Before she could respond, the footman returned with the entrée. Her husband smoothed his expression into the emotionless mask he usually wore. He remained silent for the rest of the meal, speaking only to the servants as they milled about, clearing the plates.

As soon as the meal was over, she drew back her chair and stood.

"Will you excuse me?" she asked. "I'm tired and wish to go."

"Of course," he replied. "You do not need to ask permission."

She opened her mouth to make a retort but stopped herself. Though his expression was impassive, she saw the pain in his eyes.

He nodded to the footman, who rushed toward the door and held it open. As she walked through, she heard his voice.

"Good night, my dear."

Before retiring, Meggie climbed up to the attic room. Milly's expression had softened, and she slept peacefully. As Meggie left, she almost bumped into Sarah.

"Oh, ma'am!" Sarah bobbed a curtsey. "Begging your pardon, I didn't expect to see you here."

"Have you come to tend to Milly?"

"Yes, ma'am," Sarah replied. "Master's orders. He said I was to come straight here after seeing to your room."

"My room?"

"Yes, ma'am. He was most particular."

What transgressions had Meggie committed in her room which her husband had ordered Sarah to rectify?

Sarah bobbed another curtsey, and Meggie retired to her bedchamber.

A fire burned brightly in her room. Meggie had always lit it herself, using the logs sparingly, but someone had placed a full complement of logs on the fire, which hissed and crackled, illuminating the room with a comforting glow. The flowers, which had begun to droop, had been replaced with fresh ones, and the scent of spring blooms filled the air.

Meggie pulled off her gown and undergarments, then searched for her nightshift.

It was missing.

She sighed in frustration. It wasn't the most elegant garment, but it was hers, and he had no right to take it from her.

She drew back the bedsheet.

A warming pan had been placed in the center of the bed and her nightgown neatly folded on top. She picked it up and held it against her face, absorbing the warmth. Then she put it on and slipped inside the bed. Heat penetrated her feet, and, for the first time, her toes weren't numb with cold.

Her husband was capable of kindness, even if he were incapable of expressing it overtly.

As she was drifting off to sleep, she heard footsteps. Recognizing her husband's confident gait, she sat up. The footsteps slowed, and a shadow appeared under the crack at the bottom of her door. She waited, holding her breath, and watched the door handle. It seemed to shift, the candlelight reflecting off the brass, but then the shadow moved, and the footsteps faded away.

She sank back into the pillows and rolled onto her side. At first, relief washed over her. After today, the thought of intimacy with the stern, forbidding man she'd married terrified her. But a voice in her mind whispered of the pleasures he'd given her—of how he'd made her body shatter with ecstasy.

She closed her eyes to shut out her disappointment. Had he tired of her already?

Or was he waiting for their guests to arrive so that he could resume his affair with Elizabeth?

Tears stung her eyes, but this time they were not tears of pain or anger. But of rejection. He might not hate her, but he saw her as nothing more than a charity case he'd been burdened with.

His gesture had not been one of kindness but

of pity.

Chapter Nineteen

WHERE THE DEVIL was she now? It was almost eight o'clock, and there was no sign of her. Was she sleeping late to avoid him?

Dexter pushed aside the plate of eggs, untouched. Last night's outburst had killed his appetite. What on earth had possessed him to speak of the thrashing Alderley had administered on his nine-year-old back? To reveal his pain—his weakness—to her?

He wanted to see her smile, but, by God, he didn't want her pity.

After she had left the dinner table last night, he'd taken a half dozen brandies, then stumbled upstairs to her room, the memory of her near-naked body in the lake fueling his ardor.

Then regret had conquered lust. He had no right to inflict himself on her. The church and the law might decree that he could do whatever he wanted to her, but a higher power existed. That of common decency. Of kindness. And more than anything, he wanted to treat her kindly.

But first, he needed to ensure she learned how to be a lady, which included punctuality in the breakfast room.

He pushed back his chair, left the room, and waved down a passing footman.

"Would you ask Mrs. Wells to rouse my wife?"

"The mistress is already up, sir," the footman said.

"Has she breakfasted?"

"About an hour ago."

"Then, where the bloody hell is she!"

The footman flinched. "You'll find her in the morning room, sir."

The morning room was situated on the opposite end of the house. As Dexter approached it, he heard female voices, followed by laughter.

He pushed open the door and entered.

A ladder stretched from floor to ceiling beside the windows. At its foot stood a young woman in a maid's uniform. But his eye was drawn to the woman standing halfway up the ladder.

His wife clung to the ladder with one hand while she polished the window with the other. At this angle, her delectable behind was in full view, which left little to the imagination.

He drew in a sharp breath as he hardened in his breeches.

The laughter stopped. The maid turned and caught sight of him.

"Mistress!" she cried. "The master's here!"

The ladder wobbled. His wife dropped the cloth and clutched the ladder as she turned to face him.

"Sarah, go to the scullery," she said, panic in her voice.

"But, mistress, you need help to…"

"Now!" she cried. "Must I repeat myself?"

The maid bobbed a curtsey then fled, her pace increasing as she passed Dexter in the doorway.

He approached the ladder and held out his hand.

"Let me help you down."

"I can manage," she replied, "or do you think me incapable in this, as in everything else?"

He sighed and shook his head. "I don't offer my hand out of a belief of your weakness, Margaret," he said. "I offer it for *my* sake, for I've no wish to see you fall. Indulge me if you will."

She took his hand. A crackle of need rushed through him, and he squeezed her fingers. Her breath hitched, then she tightened her grip and climbed down.

"Why did you dismiss the maid so abruptly?" he asked. She colored and looked away, withdrawing her hand. "It's time she took a break," she said. "We've been working since breakfast."

She bit her lip—the same gesture she'd made when she lied about the bruise on her wrist on their wedding day.

"Margaret," he said softly. "Did we not promise to be truthful to each other?"

"Very well," she said. "I sent her away because I didn't want her to be punished."

"Why would I punish her?"

She gestured around the room. "There's so much work to do," she said. "It'll only get done if I help."

"And you think that would make me angry?"

She tipped her chin and gave him that familiar look of defiance. "I'm not afraid of hard work," she said. "I've worked all my life and don't see why I have to languish in a chair while others clean the house. If that breaks your rules, then so be it. But punish *me*. Not the servants. I can weather it."

A stray curl had come loose over her forehead. He lifted his hand to catch it, and she flinched.

Good lord—she really did think him a monster!

"I'd never lay a finger on you," he said quietly. He brushed aside the curl, then traced the outline of her face with his fingertip until he reached her lips. He brushed his thumb against her mouth. She closed her eyes and sighed, and he felt her warm breath against his hand.

What had she said?

I can weather it.

Had she been beaten before? By Alderley? Dexter understood a victim's shame all too well. He'd suffered it as a child and had vowed never to feel it again. Was it shame that had prevented her from telling the truth about the bruise on her wrist?

"Open your eyes, Margaret," he whispered.

She did so, and he was met with the full force of her gaze. Intelligence and insight sparked behind her eyes. He placed his hand on her cheek and caressed her skin.

"I would never hurt you," he said. "I may be a little…strict…on matters of decorum, but I have your best interests at heart. And, mine, too, of course."

"Of course."

"Perhaps it would help if we found a little common ground which we've both walked on," he said. "Despite our difference in rank, I believe we've had similar childhoods."

He dipped his head to kiss her. Her eyes widened, and he withdrew.

"We could begin by your telling me what you've been doing with your days here," he said.

"I've been trying to prepare the house."

"I know," he replied, Mrs. Wells's admonishment ringing in his hears. "It pleases me to see how hard you're working."

"I've also helped Mrs. Brown in the kitchens," she said. "She's been making bread for my father's visit." She cast him a wary glance, as if concerned she'd committed another transgression.

"Would you show me how?" he asked.

Her eyes widened.

"I have some skills in bread-making." he continued. "Shall we try it together this morning before I see the estate?"

She nodded. "Very well."

"Then let us attend Mrs. Brown."

Half an hour later, Dexter stood at the kitchen table with his wife, kneading a ball of dough. He had no idea what had possessed him to suggest it. A whim, perhaps, fueled by the memory of happier childhood times. Mrs. Brown had stared at him, open-mouthed when he asked her to fetch the flour, then she'd shaken her head, muttering about the eccentricities of the *nouveaux riches*, set out the ingredients and left them to it.

He folded the dough and kneaded with his hands, relishing the once-familiar sensation as it became more pliant, the more he worked it. His wife watched him, surprise in her expression. He buried his fingers in the dough, relishing the silken texture—as silken as her flesh. As he massaged it, he imagined his hands on those soft, round breasts which peeked out of the top of her dress—what it would be like to run his tongue across the top of that creamy white flesh and dip it into the valley between. He flicked his tongue out to wet his lips. She mirrored the gesture, and he wanted her.

Did she know what she was doing to him? Or was she unaware that she had the power to render him hard with a single glance? He inhaled deeply, then swallowed to cool his ardor. The image of her legs open, begging him to take her, was clouding his mind.

She wiped her brow and left a smear of flour across her forehead.

"Here," he said. "Let me." He lifted his hand to brush away the flour. Her eyes widened as their bodies touched, and his manhood strained against her stomach.

Any moment, he'd toss up her skirts and take her over the kitchen table. But it wouldn't do for the servants to encounter their master rutting in the kitchen. He didn't give a damn about his reputation—but he did care about hers.

With a sigh, he wiped the flour from her forehead and returned to the other side of the table, and continued working on the dough.

Disappointment shone in her eyes, and she lowered her gaze and resumed her kneading.

"How did you acquire such skills?" she asked.

"In making bread?"

"When I was a child, my best friend—John Farrow—taught me how to make bread at his father's bakery."

"I didn't expect…" she hesitated.

"You didn't expect me to exhibit prowess in a kitchen?" he asked. "I grew up in poverty, Margaret, in the village surrounding the Alderley estate. Our backgrounds are the same."

"Except, I'm a bastard."

Irritated, he reached over and took her hand. "Margaret, how many times must I tell you not to take such words upon yourself? Your origins are of no consequence." He gestured about the kitchen. "You're the mistress of this house and of the estate which surrounds it. That makes you a person of consequence. And you must behave as such, no matter how much you miss your life before you came here. We can never go back. We can only look forward."

She wiped her hands on her apron and sighed. "I can't help it if I miss my former life," she said. "I never wanted to be mistress of a big house." She lowered her gaze. "I didn't want to marry."

He took her hand. "I know," he said. "I never wanted to marry a…" he hesitated. "I mean…you were just as reluctant as I."

A tear splashed onto her cheek, and he cursed himself.

He'd meant to give comfort, but, instead, had only reminded her that he'd wanted to marry another—the woman arriving tomorrow, who would be their guest for the next seven nights.

Chapter Twenty

"THE CARRIAGE IS here, ma'am."

Meggie set aside her mending. "Thank you, Sarah," she said. "I'll be down directly. I wish to fetch my shawl first—it's turned rather cold."

"You must come now," the maid replied. "The master said he wasn't to be kept waiting."

"Very well."

Better to weather the cold than her husband's disappointment. Since the tender moment they'd shared in the kitchen, he had returned to his cold, detached self, spending his time with the steward.

Though she longed to defy him, she did not have the strength to deal with both him and her father.

Not to mention the Honorable Elizabeth.

She only needed to survive the next seven

days, then she could wave the guests goodbye.

And, most likely, her husband, when he returned to London and forgot about her.

Sarah joined the line of servants waiting to greet their guests. Meggie's husband stood by the door. He motioned for her to stand beside him.

What was she—a gun dog?

"It's about time," he said. "They're almost here."

Halfway down the drive, a coach-and-four approached, laden with trunks and steered by a single driver who cracked his whip to urge the horses on. Two liveried footmen stood at the back of the coach, clinging on as it swayed to and fro, and a thin, young woman sat beside them, clutching onto one of the trunks.

It was the same carriage Meggie had been forced into when Alderley had ripped her from her old life.

The carriage drew to a halt, and one of the footmen rushed to the door, opened it, then retreated with a deep bow.

A man emerged from inside, dressed in a dark red jacket with cream-colored breeches and polished black boots. He puffed out his chest, then turned and held out his hand.

A woman stepped out of the carriage, and Meggie's stomach churned.

Elizabeth was even more beautiful than she remembered. Golden curls were piled on her head in an extravagant fashion, most likely administered by the slim young woman sitting atop the trunk. Her fur-trimmed cloak was fashioned from dark purple velvet. Beneath it, she wore a bright blue dress and embroidered slippers.

Meggie's husband drew in a sharp breath, then he glanced at Meggie and muttered a curse.

Did he have to make his desire for Elizabeth so obvious?

He bowed to Meggie's father.

"Lord Alderley, a pleasure to welcome you to my home."

Alderley nodded. "Hart."

"And the Honorable Elizabeth," her husband continued. "I am..." he glanced at Meggie, "...that is, my wife and I are delighted you could come."

Elizabeth held out her hand, and he lifted it to his lips.

"I wouldn't miss this for the world, Dexter," she said. "It's a pleasant surprise to see you looking so well." She lifted her brows, cocked her head to one side, and waited.

"And you're looking as beautiful as ever, Miss Alderley."

"Come, come, Dexter, darling," she chided. "Must you address me so formally, when we're such *very* old friends?"

She threw a spiteful glance at Meggie.

"And my dear sister!" she cried, "oh, forgive me, I should say *half*-sister. Marion, isn't it? Or Margaret?" She wrinkled her nose. "Yes, Margaret! So difficult to remember. But then, when one's origins are so—*complex*—a lady can be forgiven for her confusion, can she not?"

"My dear," Meggie's husband prompted, "aren't you going to greet our guests?"

"Perhaps she doesn't know how," Elizabeth said, her smile broadening. Meggie dipped into a curtsey, lost her balance, and fell against her husband. He took her arm in a firm grip, and she lowered her head, her cheeks burning.

Elizabeth let out a laugh. "Dexter, perhaps you should lead us inside before your wife is further discomposed..." she nodded toward him, expectantly. "If you'd be so obliging?"

He released Meggie and held his arm out to Elizabeth, who took it as if it belonged to her.

"I hope you'll show me the sights, Dexter, darling," Elizabeth said. "Both inside and outside."

"I'd be happy to oblige," he replied. "But first, let us take tea in the parlor. I have it on good authority my cook makes the best fruit cake."

"Fruit cake?" Elizabeth cried with an excess of enthusiasm. "Dexter, you spoil me, for that's my favorite, as well, you know. Come, take me inside immediately."

He led the way, leaving Meggie standing

alone.

No, not alone. The imposing form of Lord Alderley towered over her.

She curtseyed again, this time maintaining her balance.

"Father."

He rolled his eyes and gestured toward the door with his cane.

"Lead the way, child," he said. "What are you waiting for?"

Meggie followed her husband and Elizabeth inside. Never had she felt so out of place—a base-born peasant among three members of society.

How was she going to survive tea with them, let alone a whole week?

MEGGIE POURED THE tea and handed a cup to Elizabeth, who frowned, then took it.

"A little overfilled, but I can manage," she said. "I daresay you have much to learn."

"Would you like a slice of cake?" Meggie asked.

"Oh, good Lord, no!" Elizabeth laughed. "A lady cannot be expected to *eat* it—not when supper is imminent. Madame Deliet would despair of me if I necessitated the purchase of another gown."

Dexter took a slice of cake. "Elizabeth, I'll wager you visit Madame Deliet every week, regardless of whether your size increases."

"But, if I recall, Dexter, you prefer a slimmer form," Elizabeth said. "When we last visited Madame Deliet together, you said it was evidence of self-restraint, and therefore the mark of a true lady."

She smoothed down the front of her dress, as if to demonstrate her gamine frame, then cast her glance over Meggie's rounder, curvier figure.

"Madame asked after you, Dexter," Elizabeth continued. "She was most put out when I told her you'd married, for you'd promised to employ her services for your bride's gown."

"I'm sure your regular visits are enough to offset any disappointment Madame harbors as a result of my no longer patronizing her," Dexter said, "whatever they may cost your father."

"A lady must maintain her wardrobe," Elizabeth said. "Isn't that so, Margaret?"

"I-I don't know," Meggie stammered.

Elizabeth's lip curled into a smile, which could be interpreted as a sneer.

"Of course, how foolish of me to assume!" she laughed. "Who is your modiste?"

"My *what*?" Meggie asked.

What the devil was a modiste?

"My wife has not yet had the opportunity to engage a modiste," Dexter said.

"Then I recommend she does so at once," Elizabeth said. "Madame Deliet is somewhat discerning over her customers, but I daresay she'd be willing to accommodate her on my recommendation."

"At considerable expense to myself, Miss Alderley."

"My dear Dexter, it would be an investment, not an expense," Elizabeth said. "I'm sure Madame would be prepared to travel here to see your wife. She's very particular about who is seen going into and out of her establishment, given her clientele' exclusivity. I can write on your behalf."

"That's not necessary," Dexter said.

"Nonsense!" came the reply. "There's much to be gained from giving your wife the appearance of a lady."

"That may be," he replied, "but I'm perfectly capable of engaging a modiste for her."

Was Meggie invisible, that they saw fit to discuss her without acknowledging or asking for her opinion?

"Well, at the very least, you must engage a proper lady's maid," Elizabeth continued.

"Whatever for?" Dexter asked.

"Good lord, Dexter!" Elizabeth laughed. She turned her attention to Meggie. "Margaret, my dear," she said, speaking as if Meggie was a child. "You need a proper French maid."

"Why would I need a French maid?"

Elizabeth gestured toward the cascade of curls, adorning her head. "Only a French maid knows how to treat a lady's hair properly. Whoever you've engaged to tend to your hair, my dear…" She shook her head and sighed. "…At the very least, she should be dismissed, though I'd also recommend a thrashing."

Meggie froze at the stripes' memory along Milly's back, though healing, still pained the young maid. Did Elizabeth know Meggie didn't have a lady's maid? Was this her way of saying that Meggie deserved to be thrashed?

"Mistress Elizabeth…" she began. Dexter raised his eyebrows at her form of address but said nothing.

"Take it from one who knows and wishes to help," Elizabeth interrupted. "Whoever styled your hair lacks skill and, I daresay, intended to insult, rather than serve, her mistress." She turned to Meggie's husband. "Dexter, an errant servant must be dismissed. If the mistress is incapable, then the master must direct."

"My dear Miss Alderley," he said, "you set too much store on looks."

"As do you, if I recall," she replied. "You once told me that the scarlet gown I wore to Lady Strathdean's card party rendered me goddess-like, and that had I been a plain-faced little miss…" she glanced at Meggie, "…you'd never have given me the time of day."

"Miss Alderley…"

"You must take my counsel on the matter of a modiste," Elizabeth said.

"Madame Deliet is not the only modiste in town," Dexter replied. "Madame Dupont has an excellent reputation and is perhaps more suited to a woman such as my wife. The Duchess of Westbury patronizes her."

"That plump little commoner!" Elizabeth scoffed. "How the devil did *she* snare a duke?"

"She's an amiable woman," Dexter said, "and Westbury's an excellent man.

Alderley let out a snort. "Duchess she may be," he said, "but she's a commoner by birth."

"As am I," Dexter said.

Alderley opened his mouth, then closed it again.

Meggie took a mouthful of fruitcake. Did her husband only value a woman who was dressed in extravagant finery, with a body as thin as a railing?

A woman such as my wife.

What had he meant? That she was the commoner he regretted marrying, compared to the lady he'd wanted?

Tea concluded, Dexter directed their guests to their rooms to rest before dinner, and Meggie fled to her chamber. How would she even begin to make herself look presentable for tonight? But Elizabeth would, most likely, taunt her however she looked.

The woman loathed Meggie and wanted to bed her husband.

The question was—did he want to be bedded?

"CURSE IT!" MEGGIE exclaimed as the pin pricked her finger for the fourth time. Why could the damned things not stay in?

She pulled the remaining pins out of her hair, and it fell round her face in loose, limp tresses. Her hair refused to be curled into elegance—it possessed a will of its own.

She had seen little need to engage a maid. The notion of having another at her beck and call, performing tasks she could undertake herself, was neither right nor fair. But Mrs. Wells had explained that the lady's maid position was highly sought after and that a maid did not only dress her mistress or style her hair. She was a respected confidante—a friend, even.

Elizabeth's maid was unlikely to be treated as such. Meggie had passed the girl on her way to her chamber, and her heart had stung at the way she'd bobbed into a curtsey and mumbled her apology before scuttling off as if she feared Meggie would have her beaten for being seen abovestairs.

She grasped her hair, brushed it out again, and twisted it behind her head, then, holding it in place with her left hand, she picked up a pin with her right and drove it in, wincing at the stabbing sensation. She picked up another and another until there must have been at least a dozen pins in her hair.

Meggie lowered her hands and studied her reflection. Not as elegant as Elizabeth, but a ribbon or two might conceal the imperfections. She reached for a ribbon, and a pin fell out, causing part of her hair to tumble down.

With a cry of frustration, she pulled out the remaining pins, then buried her face in her hands, closing her eyes to stem the tears which threatened to spill onto her dress.

Would she forever be an outsider here? Might she never have a single friend in this world in which she'd been thrust?

"Why can't they leave me alone?" she cried.

A hand touched her shoulder, and she jumped with fright. She jerked her head up and opened her eyes. In the mirror's reflection, she saw her husband standing behind her, one hand placed on her shoulder, long, lean fingers brushing against her neck. His fingertips caressed her collarbone.

"Hush…"

She blinked, and a single tear beaded and

splashed onto her cheek. She wiped it away, ashamed that he witnessed her distress.

"Here," he whispered. "Let me."

He picked up the hairbrush, then ran it through her hair with long, smooth strokes. His mouth curled into a smile, then he lifted his gaze to hers.

For the first time since she'd laid eyes on him, the smile reached his eyes. They crinkled slightly at the edges, and their blue color resembled sapphires. As they continued to stare at each other, a light sparkled in his eyes, and an invisible knife pierced her heart.

With his gentle hands caressing her, and a smile to melt the harshest of frosts, he was in danger of capturing her heart.

He resumed his attention on her hair and curled it into a coil, sliding the pins in place with expert fingers as if the task were second nature to him. Then he pinned a ribbon in place and placed both hands on her shoulders to admire his handiwork.

"There!" he said. "That wasn't so difficult, was it?"

She shook her head. "I could never learn to do that."

"You can apply yourself to anything if you have the inclination," he replied. "Any task can be perfected with experience and practice."

"How were you able to perfect the art of

styling a woman's hair?" she asked.

She could swear she saw a faint flush on his cheeks.

The knife twisted in her heart. The answer was obvious.

"You have performed the task for Elizabeth," she said, "and, perhaps, your other mistresses."

His smile slipped, and he broke eye contact.

"But, I never did this," he whispered.

A warm hand caressed the back of her neck. Tender fingers traced a path along her collarbone, stroking, caressing. Then he began to massage her shoulders. The tips of his fingers ran along the line of her muscles, coaxing her to relax.

"Have you…" she began.

"Hush, wife," he whispered. He bent his head, and she felt his breath hot against her skin. He nuzzled her neck, and a warm fire radiated through her body.

"Is that better?" he asked, his voice a warm, soft burr.

Overwhelmed by a sensation she could not fathom as his fingers continued to administer to her, she tipped her head back.

"Meggie?"

A small cry erupted from her throat at his use of her name. She tipped her head further back and looked into her husband's eyes. But she didn't see the hunger she'd expected. Instead, she saw tenderness.

He lowered his mouth to hers.

"Meggie," he whispered, his breath warm against her lips. "My own Meggie."

She had only to move a fraction, and their lips would meet. His mouth curled into a knowing smile, and the hunger returned to his eyes. He knew she wanted him.

She pulled herself free. How could she give herself to him when his lover was, at this moment, preparing to taunt Meggie at the dinner table over her many shortcomings?

"Thank you for your assistance, husband," she said, forcing the emotion out of her voice. "You should tend to our guests. I shall see you at eight."

He frowned but nodded and left her chamber as silently as he came. She could swear she almost saw hurt in his expression. But he was incapable of such feeling.

She needed to steel herself for the ordeal to come—a formal dinner with guests who would relish every opportunity to point out her inferiority.

She could weather insults from the Alderleys, for she cared little for their good opinion. But, as for her husband—the man she was in danger of falling in love with...

She could not bear to have her heart broken.

Not again.

Chapter Twenty-One

AFTER JAMES HELPED him into his dinner jacket, Dexter dismissed the valet. He stood in front of the cheval mirror and stared at his reflection.

He'd traveled an almost impossible distance to reach his present position—from poverty, through hard work and determination, to become the head of one of the leading banks in London.

Where he'd once been thrashed like an urchin and spat at in the dirt, people now looked up as he walked into a room. They might not like him, but they respected him enough to value what he had to say.

He compared his reflection to that of his wife. Her discomfort was evident for all to see—including Alderley and Elizabeth.

Dexter wasn't so foolish as to be blind to Elizabeth's games. She'd meant to insult Margaret, and each arrow had met its target. But before he called out Elizabeth's behavior, he must first find out what Alderley and his daughter were playing at. Was Elizabeth a queen—a powerful piece intended to entrap him? By believing they could behave as they pleased, they were playing into his hands.

He glanced at his pocket watch—ten to eight. The last thing he wanted was for Margaret to be on her own with those two vultures. At all costs, he must arrive in the drawing room first. If Elizabeth could insult Margaret in his presence, doubtless, she'd unleash the full force of her spite if he were not in the room.

He entered the drawing room to find his father-in-law pouring himself a glass of Madeira.

"Help yourself, Alderley," he said. "Though you need no encouragement."

Alderley flinched, and his lips thinned, but he didn't rise to the bait.

He must want something from Dexter—and want it badly. Perhaps he could repay the man for his daughter's insults to Margaret by indulging in a little game—see how far he could push the old bastard.

"You've chosen well," he said, nodding toward the row of decanters on the side-table. "You've picked the finest in my collection.

Doubtless, it's not something you've been able to afford recently."

Alderley frowned but did not respond.

"Now we've concluded the niceties," Dexter said, "might you indulge me by explaining why you invited yourself here? I hardly think it came from a desire to further family relations, or whatever story you presented to my wife."

Alderley drained his glass and reached for the decanter. "That's always been the problem with you, Hart," he said, refilling his glass, "a distinct lack of understanding of social traditions."

Dexter filled himself a glass, then reclined in a chair.

"Come, come, Father," he said, smiling to himself as Alderley flinched involuntarily at his address, "I doubt you were driven here by *social tradition*. I'd respect you more if you paid me the compliment of telling the truth. I'll find out eventually, and it would save a lot of awkwardness if you were just to tell me now."

Alderley drained his glass again and set it down with force.

The old bastard was rattled. Good. An opponent was more likely to make a wrong move when ruled by emotions rather than reason.

"Very well," Alderley said. "I find myself in need of funds."

Of course!

"You already have a loan," Dexter said. "A

not insubstantial one, for which the interest is due next quarter day and the principal is, I believe, due to be redeemed in two years. Are you looking for an extension?" He smiled at his adversary. "I'd be happy to consider an extension of one year, provided you continue to service the interest on time. My business partner arrives in a few days, and I can instruct him to make the arrangements."

"I don't want an extension."

"You cannot expect my bank to grant a further loan," Dexter said. "You have nothing else to pledge as security, and, if I may be frank, no banker of sound mind would be willing to grant you an unsecured loan given the extent of your debts."

"I wasn't referring to a loan," Alderley said. "We're family. It's not unheard of for a son to subsidize his father."

Dexter almost choked on his drink.

God's blood! Did the man believe he'd be disposed to *give* him the money?

The expression on Alderley's face confirmed it. A mixture of self-loathing and desperation— self-loathing at having to come cap in hand to a man he despised, and desperation at his mounting debts, most likely caused by Elizabeth's extravagances.

Was that why Elizabeth had accompanied her father? To persuade him to part with his cash if she parted her thighs?

The woman in question swept into the room, and he flushed at the notion of her whoring herself. Two months ago, he'd have relished the prospect.

But not now—not when he'd caught a glimpse of goodness in a woman, in the shape of his little wife.

Not long after, Margaret entered the room and glanced at Dexter, then Elizabeth and back to Dexter. Most men would bask in the knowledge that his wife believed she had a rival. But not him.

And Margaret didn't have a rival. Elizabeth might be an exotic bird of paradise, with her brightly colored silks and elegant hairstyle. But, next to her, the diminutive little woman dressed in a plain gown of white muslin surpassed her in beauty, as the sun surpassed a candle. He longed to run his hands through his wife's hair once more, to toss aside that delicate lace cap, rip out the pins, and bury his hands in her tresses.

Margaret's beauty came from within. And she was rendered even more desirable by the fact that she had no idea quite how lovely she was.

And Dexter was the only one in the room who recognized it.

He held out his arm. "Margaret, my dear, now you have joined us, shall we lead our guests into dinner?"

Elizabeth's face fell into a frown. But Margaret smiled at him and placed her hand on his elbow. He squeezed her fingers, then led the party into the dining room.

As the final course was placed before him—Mrs. Brown's lemon sorbet—Dexter's wife had begun to lose her hunted expression. Save for a remark about the proper use of a fish knife—for which Dexter had responded by saying that table manners could be taught, but nothing could redeem a character that was rotten to the core. Elizabeth had largely left Margaret alone, directing most of her remarks and compliments to Dexter.

"Elizabeth, my dear," Alderley said as the meal drew to a close, "Perhaps you should retire. You've had a tiring day, and if you're to rise early tomorrow, you must take your rest."

"Of course, Papa," Elizabeth said. "I'm looking forward to our ride tomorrow, Dexter. Will your wife be joining us?" She cast a sneer in Margaret's direction, but Margaret appeared immune to the insult, most likely due to the quantity of wine she'd imbibed.

"I'd love that," Margaret said. "Ralph's been giving me lessons. He says I'm most proficient in the saddle."

Ralph? The arrogant young groom?

"I'm sure this *Ralph* is an obliging fellow," Elizabeth said. "I love a good hard ride. What say you, Dexter?"

"Ralph is our head groom," Dexter growled, "and the most natural person to teach my wife how to ride."

Elizabeth sipped her wine. "Does Margaret possess a riding habit? I would lend her one of mine, though I doubt she'd be able to button it up. Madame Deliet is renowned for her close fits."

Madame bloody Deliet again. Why did Elizabeth insist on dropping that woman into the conversation?

Elizabeth rose to her feet, and the men followed suit.

"If you'll forgive me, I shall retire," she said, glancing at her father. "Dexter, thank you for a wonderful dinner. I'll see you in the morning."

She swept out of the room, and Margaret visibly relaxed.

"Join me for a brandy, Alderley?" Dexter asked. "I've a bottle in the library."

"I'd be delighted," came the reply, "if I may be excused for a few minutes."

It came as no surprise that Alderley needed the privy—the man had imbibed two bottles of wine tonight. It was a wonder he was still standing.

Dexter rose. "Margaret, we'll join you later in the drawing room."

"As you wish," she replied.

Dexter made his way to the library and poured himself a drink. By the time he'd finished it, Alderley was nowhere to be seen. Perhaps the old fool had passed out while taking a piss. That would give the gossips something to laugh at.

But it wouldn't do to let the sly old bastard wander about the house unaccompanied. Who knew what he was up to?

He set his glass aside and went in search of him. Raised voices came from the drawing room.

"I won't! You can't make me!"

Margaret's voice.

"Ungrateful little bastard!" Dexter recognized Alderley's harsh tones. "All you have to do is ask him. One simple question. After everything I've done—you selfish little brat!"

"Why don't you ask him yourself?"

A pause, then she let out a mirthless laugh. "Oh, I see. You asked, and he refused. What on earth makes you think *I'll* succeed?"

"Because you're his wife," came the reply. "Women can be put to use."

"Haven't you used me enough?" she cried. "And what—you expect me to whore the money from him? You'll find yourself disappointed, *Father*. As the Honorable Elizabeth so eloquently put it on my wedding day, a husband expects his wife to spread her legs for free."

Alderley let out an exclamation, but Dexter barely heard it. Anger pulsed in his ears at the crude expression. What else had that poisonous witch said to Margaret?

"You *will* ask him," Alderley said, coldly, "or it'll be the worse for you. Remember what I said about the school."

"You've threatened me enough," she replied. "There's nothing more you can do."

"Isn't there? I can turn your precious Mrs. Preston and her grubby little brats out on the street. All because you're a coward—too afraid to ask your husband for a little money."

"Five hundred guineas is a lot of money," she said. "I may fear my husband, but I'd rather ask him to give the money to Mrs. Preston's school than to you."

"You ungrateful little bastard!" Alderley's voice had risen in pitch, "When I think of everything I've done for you!"

Fearing for his wife's safety, Dexter broke into a run.

"Everything you've done?" she cried. "You sold me to your enemy to pay off your debts, with no regard for my safety or happiness. And as such, I no longer belong to you—I am the property of Dexter Hart."

Dexter reached the drawing room and burst through the door.

"What the devil's going on here?" he roared.

His wife and Alderley stood in the center of the room. Alderley's face was a bright shade of puce, and he looked as if he was going to have a heart attack at any moment. Beside him, Margaret's face was ashen. Her eyes widened as Dexter approached her.

"My daughter and I were having a private conversation," Alderley said.

"A wife should not have secrets from her husband," Dexter replied. "I'm sure there was nothing you said to her, which I shouldn't be a party to."

"Dexter," Margret pleaded, "I…"

"Margaret, I think you should retire," Dexter said. She flinched at the sharpness in his voice, but he needed her out of the room so he could deal with Alderley himself.

He took her hand, squeezed it, and then bent his head, placing his mouth near her ear.

"Trust me," he whispered. She glanced at her father, then back to Dexter, and nodded. The trust in her eyes was almost his undoing. How could she place such faith in him—merely because he'd asked her to?

He waited until she exited the room before addressing his father-in-law.

"You're to leave my wife alone from now on," he said, his voice flat and even. "And if I hear of any harm coming to the school at Blackwood

Heath, I'll deal with the perpetrators in such a manner that they will regret their actions until they draw their last breath."

Alderley paled with anger but at least had the good sense not to argue.

"Is what I have said in any way unclear?" Dexter demanded.

"No."

"And I trust you'll abide by your promise not to molest my wife further?"

"I promised, didn't I?" Alderley snapped. "I'm a man of honor and will abide by my words."

"Good," Dexter said. "Then I suggest we retire and forget this conversation took place. We can at least be civil to each other for the remainder of your stay. But once you're gone, any request to set foot on my property again should come through *me*, and not my wife."

"Very well," Alderley said. Not bothering to bow, he swept past Dexter and disappeared down the corridor.

Ye gods! The Alderleys had not been here a full day, and they had already disrupted his marriage.

He made his way to his wife's chamber at the back of the house. There was no sign of life inside, not even the flicker of light under the door. He turned the handle and pushed the door open.

The curtains were drawn, and a shaft of

moonlight stretched across the room.

She was in bed, her face illuminated in the moonlight. She looked like a woodland sprite—too pure for the mortal world.

She had already fallen asleep—though whether from wine or exhaustion, he didn't know. Her dress was thrown over the chair's back by the dressing table, together with one stocking. The other lay at his feet on the floor. He picked it up and brought it to his lips. As if she sensed him, she sighed, then rolled onto her side.

He hadn't the heart to wake her. She'd had enough of an ordeal for one day, to be woken by the man she professed to fear.

Her confession had unsettled him. A stern man he might be, but he always believed himself to be fair. True, he relished the notion that his rivals feared him. Fear was often enough to garner victory before the battle began. It prevented opponents from besting him and servants and employees from swindling him.

But when it came to Meggie—he didn't want her fear.

He wanted her trust.

And her love.

Chapter Twenty-Two

MEGGIE ADJUSTED HER jacket and climbed down the stairs. Elizabeth would, most likely, look down her long, elegant nose at her attire, but Meggie would never understand the need to wear a different dress for each hour of the day.

The modistes—or whatever they were called—must have been fooling their customers for decades. By cutting gowns and jackets to a slightly different style and fashioning jaunty little hats trimmed with feathers, they'd got away with charging double the price by labeling the ensemble a 'riding habit.'

She made her way to the stables and found Ralph adjusting the harness of the gray mare. He lifted his golden head and smiled.

"Mistress Margaret, you look lovelier each

day."

"It's not my appearance I'm concerned with," Meggie replied, "but whether I'll fall flat on my face in front of my husband and our guests. They look down on me enough as it is."

"Then they're fools," Ralph said. "Here, let me help you up."

She took his hand, grasped the saddle with the other, and placed a foot in the stirrup, as he'd shown her. Then she launched herself off the ground. He clasped her waist, and for a moment, she felt him squeeze her thigh.

Then he took the reins and led her across the courtyard where two riders waited. Dexter sat astride an enormous black stallion. His charcoal-gray jacket fitted his form perfectly, complement-ed by black lapels and hat to match the horse's pelt. His breeches left nothing to the imagination, hugging his thighs, and his muscles rippled as he steered his mount toward her.

Next to him, Elizabeth sat atop the steward's gelding. She wore a habit of bright blue velvet, a military-style jacket with black trim, and a hat topped with an enormous bright blue feather that curled around the brim. Her habit's color emphasized her eyes, and her hair shone in the light of the morning sun.

They looked the perfect couple.

Elizabeth took one look at Meggie in her plain gray jacket and dress, and her mouth curled into a smile of triumph. She surpassed Meggie in beauty and elegance. And she knew it.

"Ah, sister dearest," she said. "I was beginning to worry you might never join us. I trust the ride won't be too taxing for you."

"I'll manage," Meggie replied.

Dexter's lip curled into a smile. "You sit well in the saddle, my dear," he said.

Elizabeth's mouth creased into a scowl. "That she does, Dexter, darling, but *I* intend to do more than just sit this morning. I've been looking forward to a good, hard ride with you, but fear my sister is unable to maintain our pace."

Ralph came around the corner, astride a brown gelding, and Dexter's smile disappeared.

"Is that one of the coach horses?"

"Aye, it is, master. He takes a saddle well."

"And you saw fit to accompany us this morning?"

Meggie recognized the flare of anger in her husband's voice, but Ralph seemed oblivious.

"Begging your pardon, sir, I'm here to accompany the mistress."

"Well, really!" Elizabeth wrinkled her nose. "Dexter, darling, surely you won't permit this hobbledehoy to join us? This estate's turning into a haven for riff-raff."

Meggie curled her hands round the reins, and the mare shifted beneath her as if sensing her distress.

"Pay no heed to her," Ralph whispered. "She's nothing compared to you."

Dexter shot Elizabeth a look of annoyance, then directed his irritation at Ralph.

"We can survive without your assistance," he said. "The nag can take his exercise later, surely?"

"I want him to stay," Meggie said.

Elizabeth cleared her throat, and Dexter rode toward Meggie until their mounts were almost touching.

"Does my wife contradict me?"

Meggie squared her shoulders and met his gaze.

"I do," she said. "I'm inexperienced in the saddle and wouldn't wish you to trouble yourself with tending to me when your *guest* is in such need of attention."

He narrowed his eyes but said nothing.

"In fact," she said, "I insist Ralph accompany me. While I've been alone, he's taught me how to ride and knows my limitations. You've never seen me in the saddle."

"I find myself admonished," he said. "If my wife wishes another to accompany her, then I shall oblige."

Meggie caught a glimpse of pleasure on Ralph's face. Pleasure—mixed with triumph.

They set off at a leisurely pace, following the path through the forest. But before they reached the lake, they veered to the left and out into a field. Elizabeth urged her mount forward.

"What say you, Dexter?" she asked. "How about a wager to brighten a dull day?"

"What do you have in mind, Miss Alderley?"

She lifted a gloved hand to her forehead to shield her eyes from the sun and scanned the horizon.

"There!" She pointed ahead. "That large oak. Ten guineas say I make it there and back first!"

He glanced at Meggie. "I don't think it's wise…"

Meggie waved her riding crop at him. "Go," she said. "I'll be all right."

"Then," Elizabeth said, "with your *wife's* permission…"

She gave the gelding a hearty kick on the flank, and the animal raced ahead. Dexter spurred his mount on, less savagely, in her wake.

How on earth could a woman move at such a pace, riding side-saddle, and not lose her seat?

Elizabeth's mount reached the opposite edge of the field, and she spurred it toward the perimeter hedge. The animal launched itself into the air and cleared the hedge, shortly followed by Dexter on his stallion.

"That's the last we'll see of them," Ralph said. "I'm sorry, I should have known this would happen."

"It doesn't matter," Meggie said brightly. "At least now, I feel no pressure to ride harder than

I'm able to."

"You have the makings of a very accomplished rider," Ralph said, drawing his mount close. "Very accomplished indeed."

"Were it not for your guidance, I'd have no skill at all."

"Oh no," he replied. "You have a natural ability most women lack. But I look forward to giving you many more lessons in the art of riding if that is what you wish."

"You know it is," she said.

"Then let us enjoy our lesson unencumbered by those who would look down on us." He steered his mount in the opposite direction, and Meggie followed.

She'd been dreading today and the prospect of being sneered at by the Alderleys. Seeing her husband riding with his former lover tore at her heart. But with her friend at her side, she might salvage some pleasure from the excursion.

An hour later, there was no sign of Dexter or Elizabeth. Meggie's thighs ached with the ride, but Ralph was so kind and generous with his praise, she hadn't the heart to tell him she wanted to return to the house.

"This is the furthest we've ridden," she said, hoping he would take the hint.

"I thought the time had come to test the extent of your stamina," he said. "If you'll oblige me a little longer, I know somewhere we can rest."

Shortly after, a small building with a thatched roof came into view. Though it looked sound, it had a desolate appearance. A climbing rose bush surrounded the front door but had not been well-tended—not like the roses Mrs. Preston had been so particular about at her cottage in Blackwood Heath.

"Who lives here?" Meggie asked.

"I do." He pointed ahead with his riding crop. "Can you see the roof of the main house? Behind the trees? We've come full circle."

"Well, that's a relief," Meggie said. "I don't know how much longer I can keep my seat."

He dismounted and held out his hands. "Down you come," he said. "You'll be unsteady after such a long ride. Just relax into my arms."

She took his hands, and he pulled her off the saddle. As soon as she landed, her ankle gave way, and she pitched forward. He caught her in his arms and held her close.

"Steady, Meggie!" he laughed. She ought to admonish him for the familiar address, but she was done with propriety for one day.

"Can you walk?" he asked.

She tested her foot. "My ankle's a little stiff, but I don't think I've sprained it."

"Good." He took the reins of her mount. "Let me tether the horses, then we'll get you inside."

"Shouldn't we return to the main house?"

"We'll do that when you've rested," he said. "Unless the groom's cottage is insufficiently grand for you?"

"Hardly that," she laughed. "It's twice the size of the house I grew up in."

"Excellent!" he said. "Now, if you're willing to let yourself inside while I see to the horses, you'll find some of Mrs. Brown's lemonade in the kitchen—and some of her fruitcake."

Though she knew it was improper, where was the harm in going inside? Here, she could pretend that she'd never been elevated to a status where she was expected to look down on others.

Inside, the cottage was tidy, but it lacked the little touches that turned a place into a home. The kitchen furniture was purely functional—a small wooden table with four chairs and a cracked sink containing a single, dirty pan. It was the home of a single man. Meggie smiled at the thought of the inevitable transformation that would take place when Ralph married Milly. She would do everything she could to help the couple. She could furnish the place with curtains for a splash of color and stock the kitchen with new pans.

A stoneware bottle sat by the sink, and Meggie opened it and sniffed the contents. Lemons—sweet and sharp. She looked about and found two cups, then filled each one, placed them on the table, and waited.

When Ralph entered the kitchen, his eyes widened as he saw the cups on the table.

"It's not for you to serve me," he said.

She waved aside his protest. "Today, I'm a friend, not your mistress."

"Then let us drink to friendship." He lifted his cup, touched hers, then drained the contents.

"You have a charming cottage here," Meggie said.

"It serves a purpose."

"It should do more than that," she said. "It needs a woman's touch to make it a home."

"And you're the woman to do it?"

"There's much I can do, Ralph, for when you decide to take a wife."

"Is there?" His voice lowered, and he leaned over the table and took her hand. "What can you do for me?"

"Well..." she hesitated, "...for you and Milly."

"Milly?"

"You're going to marry her, aren't you?"

He wrinkled his nose. "That little milkmaid?"

"You must know she's sweet on you."

He shrugged his shoulders. "That's not suffi-cient reason to marry her."

"But you want a wife, surely?"

"Whatever for?"

"Companionship."

"I can find companionship anywhere," he said. "All I need for that is a willing pair of arms and a woman eager to warm my bed."

She recoiled at his words. "Respectability, then," she said.

"My pardon," he said, smiling. "I spoke out of turn. Of course, I'll marry, and doubtless, Milly shall be my choice. But you must admit that by keeping her guessing, I stand to gain from it by increasing her desire."

"That seems rather underhanded," Meggie said.

"It's a game all women play." He moved to take the seat next to her. His thigh bumped against her leg, and she stiffened.

"You're not adverse to a little game-playing yourself," he said.

"I don't know what you mean."

"Even now, you seek to tempt me to increase my desire." He placed his hand on her thigh. "Don't you realize there's no need to play games with me?"

His eyes darkened, and he drew close. She stiffened in fear and forced a laugh.

"You jest, Ralph!" she said. "Perhaps you seek to understand the best way to court a young woman so that I might tell you whether Milly would approve?"

"To hell with Milly," he said. "It's you I want."

She tried to stand, but he grasped her wrist. "Have you not been teasing me with your smiles, little Meggie?"

"No…"

"Yes," he said, his voice hoarse. "Why else would you wish to spend so much time alone with me? And if your husband's rutting that haughty creature, why shouldn't you indulge in a little tumble?"

She wrenched herself free and stepped back. "You should be saying this to Milly. She's the one who wants you, not I."

"You think I care for her when I could have you?"

"No, Ralph!" she cried. "You don't want me! You want a wife—a respectable wife, a family, children…"

He let out a laugh.

"You of all people should understand that a man can sire brats without the need for marriage vows, many of whom go on to do very well for themselves."

She backed away, but he was too quick for her, and he grasped her arm.

"What right have you to deny me?" he demanded. "You've thrown yourself at me at every opportunity—had me dancing to your tune ever since you arrived. Well, now it's time to pay the piper."

She struggled, but he tightened his grip, and

he forced her onto the kitchen table.

"That's it, my little filly," he said. "Time for your next riding lesson. I'll show you what it's like to be mounted and ridden hard."

He jammed his knee between her legs, and she let out a scream. She struggled in his grip, but he was too heavy, his weight pinning her down on the kitchen table.

He clamped his hand over her mouth, and she bit down, hard.

"Bitch!"

Pain exploded in her cheek as he slapped her. She kicked out and rammed her knee into his groin, and he grunted in pain and loosened his grip.

A splintering crash exploded in the air, followed by a roar of fury.

"Stop that at once!"

Ralph relaxed his grip, and Meggie saw two large hands grasp him by the shoulders and throw him across the room as if he were a rag-doll. He landed in a crumpled heap on the floor.

A huge demon stood before her. Hands clenched, his anger radiated off his body. Fire raged in his eyes, and his face was white with fury.

Dexter.

Chapter Twenty-Three

WHERE THE DEVIL was she?

The skin on the back of Dexter's neck tightened as if foreshadowing a storm.

After escorting Elizabeth back to the main house, he'd gone to the stables in search of his wife. But she'd not returned.

Neither had that bloody groom.

He steered his mount back to the field where Elizabeth had challenged him. The foolish woman had forgotten that a real man never feigned weakness to let a woman best him. He'd beaten her easily to the oak tree, and now she had to persuade her father to part with ten guineas. Doubtless, she'd offer to spread her legs for Dexter instead of paying the debt, and he'd enjoy spurning her.

But, for now, he was faced with the more

critical task of finding his wife.

He picked up a trail at the edge of the field—two sets of hoofprints leading to the groom's cottage. His stomach tightened as he spotted two horses waiting patiently by the door.

What the devil was she playing at?

A scream came from inside.

He dismounted and burst through the door in time to see his wife on her back across the kitchen table, the groom on top of her.

He rushed forward, roaring, and threw the man off her.

Margaret sat up, her face pale save for a darkening bruise on her cheek.

The groom struggled to his feet, and Dexter pulled out his riding crop.

"Stay where you are!" he roared. "What the devil were you doing with my wife?"

"Isn't it obvious?" came the reply. "You can't blame a man for taking what's on offer. And she's no better than I."

"You take that back, you bastard!" Dexter roared, raising his crop.

The groom gave a sly smile. "I think *she's* the bastard," he said. "If you'd rather her whoring were not gossiped about, perhaps we can come to an arrangement."

Cold determination replaced hot fury. Dexter curled his hand into a fist behind his back.

"Perhaps something can be arranged," he

said. The groom gave a smile of triumph. Out of the corner of his eye, Dexter saw his wife's stricken expression.

He stepped toward the groom, the action disguising the movement in his arm, then he punched him square in the face.

The groom fell back, red liquid dribbling from his nose, then collapsed on the floor.

"*That* was for insulting your mistress." Dexter pulled off his necktie and bound the unconscious man's wrists, then secured him to a chair to be on the safe side.

He held his hand out to Margaret. "Come here, my dear."

She took his hand, and he led her outside.

"Did he touch you?" he asked.

"N-no." She touched her cheek and winced.

"We'll need to get Mrs. Wells to see to that," he said.

"Are you angry?" she asked, her voice wavering.

"Of course I'm bloody angry!" he said. "I should have known what was going on."

"You think I encouraged him?"

"Dear God, no, Margaret," he said. "I only mean that he saw you as easy prey. It's not your fault that you were naïve enough to mistake his advances for friendship." He sighed. "It's *my* fault. It was too much to expect you to become a lady overnight."

She turned away and approached her mount.

"No, Meggie," he said softly. "You'll ride with me. I'll send Billings to deal with the horses and..." he hesitated, "...that young man. Rest assured, you'll never have to see him again."

He pulled her into his arms, and her body shook. Brave little soul, she was fighting back the tears.

"My sweet, Meggie," he said. "I'll do anything I can to make up for what's happened. I should never have sent you here alone and friendless. But you're not alone now."

He placed his hands on her waist and lifted her onto his horse. Then he mounted behind her and set off for the house.

"OH, MISTRESS—YOUR FACE!"

"That's enough of that, Sarah," Mrs. Wells scolded. "Use the poultice."

Meggie winced as Sarah placed a cloth on her face, which carried the aroma of lavender.

"Shh..." the housekeeper soothed. "Stay still. It'll help with the bruising."

The kitchen door opened, and Milly rushed in. "What's happened? I heard the master attacked Ralph."

"Hush your nonsense, girl!" Mrs. Wells admonished. "Look at what your precious Ralph did to the mistress?"

Milly's eyes widened, and she shook her head. "He wouldn't hurt anyone," she said. "He wouldn't…"

"Foolish child!" the housekeeper said. "If you've nothing useful to say, then return to your duties. Or do you want to be dismissed also?"

"Ralph…" Milly whispered.

"I always thought he was a bad lot," Mrs. Wells said, "but you were so sweet on him, you wouldn't listen to reason. He fooled you, just like he fooled the mistress."

She turned to Meggie. "Begging your pardon, ma'am, you weren't to blame, but he always did think too highly of himself. If you want my opinion, he deserves everything the master intends to do to him."

"What does my husband intend to do?" Meggie asked.

Shortly after returning to the house, he'd carried her to the kitchen, roaring for Mrs. Wells to tend to her. The feel of his strong arms around her gave her a sense of safety and security she'd never experienced before—almost as if he genuinely cared for her. He'd set her down on a chair, placed a delicate hand on her shoulder, and told her to remain there while he dealt with everything.

"You're in no fit state to worry about what

the master intends to do," the housekeeper said. "I always said he'd asked too much of you to take over the mantle of the lady of the manor when you have so little experience."

Why did they—her husband, Mrs. Wells, the rest of the staff—all think her so incapable?

What better chance did she have than now, to prove that she could weather her position?

"Where's my husband, Mrs. Wells?" she asked.

"He's in the study, but he won't want to be disturbed."

"Let me be the judge of that." Meggie rose to her feet and made her way to her husband's study. Raised voices came from within, and she pushed open the door.

Two men stood facing the large mahogany desk—Ralph, and Mr. Billings, the steward. Ralph had a pathetic air about him. Shoulders slumped, face swollen where Dexter had struck him, he looked every part the defeated bully.

Dexter's eyes widened as she entered. "I told you not to leave the kitchen."

"I wish to voice an opinion in respect of the groom's punishment," she said.

His mouth twitched into a smile, and she crossed the floor to join him at his desk. He rose from his chair and motioned to her to sit.

"Very well," he said. "Give us your counsel."

"You're not going to let this *woman* dictate

my fate?" Ralph sneered.

"I'll thank you to show my wife more respect," Dexter growled.

Meggie placed a hand on her husband's arm.

"Let us not distress ourselves any more over the groom's behavior," she said. She looked up and met Ralph's gaze, conquering her fear. At length, he colored and looked away.

"I would have you leave this establishment, never to return," she said. "Mr. Billings can pay your wages up to today. I would not have you accuse us of being uncharitable."

"And where would I go, *mistress*?"

"I care not," she said, "as long as poor Milly nor I set eyes on you again."

Ralph's eyes flared with a final burst of defiance.

"Your wife has you fooled, sir," he said to Dexter. "She's been mooning over me ever since she arrived and couldn't wait to spread her legs."

"That's enough!" Dexter snapped.

"Mark my words, she'll betray you," Ralph continued. "I can see it in your eyes—you don't trust her."

Dexter addressed the steward. "Billings, get him out of my sight. Do *not* pay him—he doesn't deserve my wife's generosity. Instruct the gamekeeper to shoot him if he's seen within ten miles of this estate. Then send Mrs. Wells here when you're done."

"Very good." The steward grabbed Ralph by the arm and marched him out of the room.

Dexter reached for the decanter on his desk and half-filled a beveled glass with brown liquid. Then he pushed it into Meggie's hand.

"Drink this."

She tipped the glass up and swallowed a mouthful of liquid. Fire burst on her tongue, and she spluttered as the liquid burned in her throat.

Her arm shook as she set the glass down, and he covered her hand with his.

"May I ask you a question, Margaret?"

"I-I didn't offer myself to him."

He shook his head and smiled. "I know," he said. "No, I want to ask you to do something for me."

Her heart fluttered. It had taken all her courage to face the man who'd tried to violate her. What else must she do?

He squeezed her hand. "Would you oblige me by moving your belongings to the lady's chamber?"

"For propriety?"

"No, my dear," he said. "For me."

He patted her hand. "I confess I took the liberty of asking Mrs. Wells to arrange it—but don't take that as an assumption on my part. The decision is yours."

He lifted his brows, and she saw the plea in his eyes.

"You'd accept if I refused?" she asked.

"I would." He lifted the glass to her lips. "Finish it," he said. "The brandy will settle your nerves. Then you must rest. You've had an ordeal."

"What about our guests?"

"I think you deserve a reprieve from the Alderleys. I'll tell them you're indisposed."

"I can face them," she said.

"I wish to spare you their company, nevertheless," he said. "I would not have you any more distressed." He hesitated, then swallowed, as if steeling himself.

"I'm not a man of tender words, Margaret," he said. "But I pledged to honor, cherish, and keep you. However reluctant I was at the time, I meant every word. You can trust me to abide by my vows."

He lifted his hand to her face, his eyes narrowing as if he felt her pain. "It would please me very much if you were to grant my request."

Someone knocked on the door, and he called out.

"Come in!"

Mrs. Wells entered the room.

"Ah, good lady," he said. "Please escort my wife to…" he focused his gaze on Meggie, hope in his eyes.

"To the lady's chamber, please, Mrs. Wells," she said. He smiled at her again, and the tenderness in his deep blue eyes touched her heart.

This brooding, enigmatic man she'd been forced to marry—he concealed a heart beneath the hard, outer shell. And she was in great danger of falling in love.

As she reached the door, she turned to face him.

"Dexter?"

His eyes widened at the familiar address, then he smiled.

"Why didn't you believe him..." she hesitated. "...Ralph?"

"Because you're my wife."

"It's more than that," she said. "You're a man of reason, not emotion. Blind faith alone wouldn't convince you. What was it?"

"If you must know, it was the look on his face," he said. "I recognized it from years ago—from when a fortune-hunter seduced my sister."

"Your sister?

"My sister Daisy."

"What happened to her?"

He cast a glance at Mrs. Wells, who looked away as if averting her eyes and her ears.

"She was seduced," he said. "She believed herself in love and paid the price. The bastard who ruined her thought he could coerce me into giving him a thousand guineas."

"A thousand!" she cried. "Who was he?"

"One of Alderley's servants," he said. "I confronted Alderley about it, and it earned me this." He fingered the scar across his chin.

His gaze seemed to cloud over. Then he blinked and focused on Meggie once more. "He threatened to spread rumors about Daisy being a light skirt if I didn't pay him. My fortunes were increasing, and he saw me as a source of income."

"And you agreed?"

"No," he said, his mouth set firm. "I didn't. A man who succumbs to blackmail is a fool. He shows himself to be weak-minded for not facing the consequences of his sins. *I* am not such a man."

"What about Daisy?" Meggie asked.

Hurt rippled across his expression. "She wouldn't have been happy in a coerced marriage, however much she wanted it."

"A marriage like ours?"

He sighed. "The circumstances that brought us together were different," he said. "And Daisy is happier now than she would have been, had I yielded to her seducer."

"How so?"

"An old friend of mine offered for her. I believe they are fond of each other."

"You believe? Don't you see them?"

The tenderness in his eyes disappeared. "I should see to our guests," he said, "lest they feel neglected."

His reluctance to continue the conversation was understandable. But she had to know one thing—to determine whether she could, as he claimed, trust him completely.

"Dexter?"

"What is it?"

"When your sister was ruined…" His jaw gave a tic, and he narrowed his eyes. Summoning her courage, she continued. "Was she with child?"

"No," he said. "Thank the Almighty I was spared *that* indignation. Her husband's a good man, but even he has his limits. No man should suffer the indignation of having a wife who bore another man's bastard."

He drew out his pocket watch and opened it. "Now, run along, my dear. I have much to do, and I want you well-rested before you face our guests again. Mrs. Wells, I trust you'll be able to conceal the mark on my wife's face before she joins us for supper."

"Of course, sir," the housekeeper said. "Come, mistress, let's get you settled upstairs."

Meggie let herself be led away, her heart aching in the knowledge that she'd never be able to trust her husband completely.

Not with the truth about her past.

Chapter Twenty-Four

WHEN MEGGIE WOKE, she didn't recognize her surroundings, and a wave of panic rose within her.

She was in an enormous bed with a thick, carved wooden post at each corner and a vast canopy overhead. The only familiar object she could see was the vase of wildflowers she'd picked the day before, next to a silver tray bearing an empty glass.

Of course!

Mrs. Wells had moved her belongings to the lady's chamber.

She stretched and looked about her. The room wasn't as imposing as it had been the first time she'd seen it. Someone had replaced the dark furnishings with warmer, sunnier colors, and the remnants of a fire glowed in the fireplace.

She swung her legs over the edge of the bed and stood, her feet sinking into the thick pile of the rug, then padded over to the window.

The garden stretched before her. Neatly clipped shrubs formed a regimental line, alongside a hedge of purple flowers. Beyond, a lake rippled in the sunlight, a myriad of colors dancing along the water's surface.

It all seemed smaller, less imposing than before. Had so much changed in so little time?

Or was it *she* who'd changed?

The sun was low on the horizon, casting long, silent shadows. How long had she slept?

She returned to the bed and brushed her fingertips over the flowers in the vase. Then she picked up the glass from the tray and sniffed it.

Laudanum.

Mrs. Wells had insisted she take a drink of milk before her rest as if she were an ailing child—and she'd slipped a spoonful of the sleeping draught in it. When Meggie had protested, the housekeeper responded, saying it was the master's orders.

She glanced at the clock on the mantelshelf. There were at least four hours until dinner. The laudanum hadn't completely worn off. If she closed her eyes, she'd fall asleep again. But she wanted her wits about her before she faced the Alderleys again, and the most effective remedy for an addled mind was fresh air.

She'd noticed a large, ornate armoire through the dressing room door when Mrs. Wells had helped her into her shift. Sure enough, her clothes had been moved there—presumably on Dexter's orders. She ought to have been annoyed at her husband taking control of her belongings, but it stemmed from a wish to care for her.

And she'd never felt genuinely cared for in her life, until now.

What would he do when their guests left? Would he stay with her so they could become better acquainted? Or would he abandon her for London? Though solitude brought peace, Meggie found the idea of not having her husband by her side increasingly unappealing. Even when silent, he radiated strength. And his solidity fueled her courage.

In short, she would miss him.

Perhaps she could persuade him to stay a little longer. Not cajole him as the fawning ladies of London undoubtedly did—but by showing him how useful she could be as a wife, and mistress of the house, might he consider her company worth keeping?

She selected a gown and slipped it on. The first step might be to employ a lady's maid. It would make dressing much easier, and she could resolve her conscience knowing she'd be giving a young woman employment. And though Meggie was loath to act upon any suggestion of

Elizabeth's, a French maid would help improve her command of the language.

She slipped out of the chamber with, for the first time, a sense of hope.

As she wandered through the main part of the house, she caught sight of Alderley languishing in the morning room, his nose in a brandy glass. She stepped back and watched him through a crack in the door. Decorum might dictate that she attend him as hostess, but she had no wish to spend any more time alone with her father.

Or her sister.

As if she read Meggie's mind, Elizabeth's sharp tones sliced through the silence. Alderley must have heard the voice, too, for he rolled his eyes, then drained his glass.

Meggie smiled to herself. At least she didn't have to *live* with the woman. Alderley resented the expenses he'd incurred paying for Meggie's upkeep, but they would have paled in insignificance compared to Elizabeth's extravagances.

Perhaps he should be thanking Meggie for her status. Bastards should be applauded for being cheaper to maintain than legitimate offspring.

She covered her mouth to stifle a giggle, then shrank back as Alderley rose from his seat. The last thing she wanted was to be discovered spying on him. He approached the door and pushed it shut, no doubt to muffle Elizabeth's caustic tones.

Meggie drew her shawl around her and made

her way to the main doors, smiling at the waiting footman who bowed as she approached him.

She stopped as she heard another voice—her husband's voice.

"Hush, Elizabeth! Your father will hear us, not to mention my wife."

"I thought you said she was asleep," Elizabeth's voice said, "and safely out of the way."

Heat rose in Meggie's cheeks.

The footman opened the main doors, and Meggie shook her head. "Thank you, no," she said. She glanced in the direction of the voices. "It's time you had your tea."

"I'm not to be relieved for another five minutes, ma'am."

"The door will be no worse for being unattended for a minute or two," she said. "Go to the kitchen, and tell Mrs. Brown I said you could have an extra slice of her shortbread."

"Thank you, ma'am." With a bow, he left.

The voices came from the direction of Dexter's study—the very room in which he'd promised she could trust him.

"Do you want your father to overhear, Elizabeth?"

"Oh, Papa!" Elizabeth scoffed. "He always does what I tell him."

"Then he's not a real man."

"That he's not." Elizabeth's voice lowered to a seductive purr. "Not like you. Perhaps that's why I find you so attractive, Dexter darling. You're all man—every single part of you. Including…"

"Stop it!"

"Oh, come on, Dexter!" Elizabeth scoffed. "You never protested before. In fact, *you* pursued *me*."

"Those days are gone."

"Pshah, nonsense! You just need a little reminder—of all those times you screamed my name! I could have given myself to any number of men, but I've saved myself for you, darling. Only you…"

Meggie heard a scuffle, followed by high-pitched laughter. "That's it, Dex, darling! I knew you were hard for me."

"I'm no such thing."

"Do you remember when you told me how wet I was for you? That I could spend at the mere touch of your hand?" Her voice lowered to a coaxing, seductive purr. "Would you like to test that assertion now?"

"Elizabeth, I'm married."

"To the wrong sister," Elizabeth said. "My fool of a father thought he could deceive us both by giving you that little slut instead."

Meggie flinched at the insult. Though she was prepared for Elizabeth's incivility to her face, the insult seemed all the more acute when issued behind her back.

"What's done is done," Dexter said. "We must both make the best of it."

"Which is why we should continue where we left off. You owe me that, at least."

"I owe you nothing."

"I think you do, Dexter. I saved myself for you."

He barked with laughter.

"I'm still a maiden," she said, "which is more than can be said for the doxy you married."

"Elizabeth, you let me take you in every manner possible while preserving your virginity. Physically that makes you a maiden—but an innocent? I think not." His voice rose in anger. "Look at you—even now, on your knees, desperate to service my cock."

Meggie moved toward the door, which was half-open. Her husband stood in the center of the room, arms folded, his back to her. Elizabeth knelt at his feet, face upturned, desire glittering in her eyes. She reached forward and grasped his hips.

Meggie drew in a sharp breath, and Elizabeth's gaze slid sideways and focused on her. A slow smile spread across her lips. She parted them and flicked out her tongue, running it along her bottom lip.

"Surely you've not forgotten the pleasures I've given you in this very position, Dexter, darling?" she said. "I offer you such pleasure now, such that you might cry my name and say you love me again."

"I did not…"

"Everyone knows that you regret being shackled to that little by-blow," she said. "Who even knows if she's Papa's? Any rutting footman could have sired her."

"Perhaps," he said, "but she's my wife, and I'm resolved to make the best of it."

With her gaze fixed on Meggie, Elizabeth's smile broadened. "That we must, my poor darling."

Meggie could bear it no longer. She withdrew, then turned and broke into a run, almost colliding with the footman who'd just arrived to tend to the door.

"Take care, ma'am!"

"Forgive me, I-I must get out…"

He pulled open the door, and she ran outside, almost tripping as she took the steps two at a time.

DEXTER GAZED AT the creature kneeling at his feet.

How could he have ever thought her desirable? Spiteful desperation exuded from every pore of her corrupted body. What possessed her to believe that she could conquer him by insulting his sweet little wife, then offering herself like a twopenny harlot?

He'd wondered how far she was prepared to go to degrade herself. But she had surpassed the depths to which even a common a prostitute would plumb.

Bile rose in his throat, and he reached for her. The triumph in her eyes magnified, and she parted her lips. Then he grasped her shoulders and pushed her back.

She fell to the ground and parted her legs.

"You always loved a little roughness to your bedsport, darling," she said. "I'm glad you've rekindled the taste for it."

"Get up," he snarled. "You're making a fool of yourself. You're worse than your father."

"Dexter darling, I…"

"I said, get up!" he roared. She flinched at the force in his voice. He grasped her wrist, then yanked her to her feet.

"The sooner you and your father are out of my house, the better."

"You can't mean that," she gasped.

"I mean every word!" he snarled. "Shall I tell your father what a harlot his *honorable* daughter is?"

"I'll tell him you violated me!"

"Who do you think he'll believe, Elizabeth? The son-in-law who can foreclose on his debts and turn him out on the street at a whim, or the daughter who bled his coffers dry to satisfy her greed?" He pushed her to the door.

"Tell him and be damned," he said. "I care nothing for his opinion of me. But I rather think you care a great deal what he thinks of you. If he believes you sullied, whether willing or not, he'll marry you off to the first man who'll take you. And I hear Viscount de Blanchard is prowling the marriage mart."

Her eyes widened in fear, and he gave her a cold smile at the notion of her being in the power of that fat, sweaty lecher. Her face paled. Were she any other woman, he would have pitied her.

"What must I do?" she asked.

"Pack your belongings and instruct your father to do likewise."

"What explanation shall I give him?"

"I care not," he said. "All that matters is that you're both out of my house within the hour."

"But…"

"Mr. Billings! Mrs. Wells!" he roared. Elizabeth colored and scuttled out of the study. He followed in her wake and hailed the footman waiting beside the main doors.

"You there! What's your name?"

"Stephen, sir."

"Stephen, our guests are leaving," he said. "Fetch Mrs. Wells, and send Sarah to the mistress's chamber to let her know."

The servant glanced toward the doors, then hesitated.

"Are you hard of hearing, Stephen?"

"N-no, sir, but the mistress has gone."

"Gone where?"

"Outside, sir. She left a moment ago. She seemed indisposed."

"Indisposed?"

"Yes, sir, she…" The servant hesitated, uncertainty in his expression.

"Spit it out," Dexter growled. "I don't have all day."

"She was in a hurry, sir. She was running from the direction of the study…"

"The study?"

"Yes, sir. About a minute before you arrived with Miss Alderley. I-I believe she may have heard voices."

The footman's expression told him exactly whose voices Meggie had heard.

Shit.

"Where did you say she went?" he asked.

"I-I don't know, sir. She ran down the steps as if a pack of dogs was after her."

A pack of dogs, indeed. They were all bloody dogs—himself included.

"Shall I help you find her, sir?"

"No," Dexter said. "You can assist Mrs. Wells in ridding me of my guests. I'll find my wife."

"Very good, sir."

Did he imagine it, or did he sense disapproval in the footman's voice?

But he could hardly blame the man. Disapproval was an understatement compared to Dexter's opinion of himself.

Where had she gone?

Hoofbeats crunched on the gravel outside. That was impressive. Billings must have worked a miracle to prepare the Alderley carriage so quickly.

But there was no carriage. Instead, a single horse stood before the front door, its rider already dismounting.

It was Oliver Peyton.

"Good lord!" Dexter exclaimed.

"Don't sound so surprised," Peyton said. "I'm here on your instruction."

"So much has happened, I quite forgot."

"That's unlike you!" Peyton laughed. "Perhaps you've been distracted by something far pleasanter than the running of a bank. Didn't I say, your adorable little wife…"

"Forgive me, Peyton," Dexter said. "I have an urgent errand to see to. I trust you'll make yourself at home in the interim."

"Can I help?"

"If you can dispatch two unwelcome guests, find my wife, and hire a full complement of staff, then I daresay you can," Dexter said. "Failing that, I'd suggest you let Stephen here show you to my study where you can indulge in a dialogue with my brandy until I return."

Leaving his friend open-mouthed at the threshold, he sprinted off toward the forest.

If he knew his wife at all, there was one place she would go.

As Dexter emerged from the woods, he saw a solitary figure sitting beside the waterfall at the edge of the forest lake, dangling her legs in the water.

"Margaret."

She stiffened but did not attempt to look up as he approached. Her body vibrated with tension, but she continued to stare at the water as if by not seeing him, she could will him to disappear.

He bent down and reached for the ankle of his boot and yanked at it. It hardly budged. How the devil did his valet manage to take the damn things off? He tried again and almost lost his balance. Out of the corner of his eye, he saw her turn her head to observe him. He pulled it a third time, and it came off, but he lost his balance and toppled onto his back.

"Shit."

Aware of her eyes on him, he removed the

second boot—much easier now he was positioned like an upended turtle—then pulled his stockings off. Then he stood up, brushed himself down, and sat beside her. He dipped his feet into the water and drew in a sharp breath.

Bloody hell, that was cold!

The corner of her mouth twitched in a smile.

"Margaret," he said.

The smile disappeared.

He took her hand. "Meggie?"

"What do you want?"

"Forgiveness."

She sighed. "What purpose would it serve? Will it absolve you of your sins such that you consider yourself at liberty to commit them once more?"

He lifted her hand to his lips. She didn't resist, but, if anything, that pierced his heart even more. She believed the worst of him, yet she was resigned to his attentions. Overcome with shame, he released her hand. He had no right to touch her—or even look her in the eyes.

"I cannot begin to think what you imagine I've done," he said, "and I have no right to expect you to believe me now."

She made no move. But she didn't slap him—neither did she push him into the lake.

Which he saw as a good sign.

"But," he continued, "I will explain what you witnessed if you have no objection."

He waited for her response, but she said nothing. The silence stretched, forming an uncomfortable void which he felt compelled to fill with words.

Was this what his rivals felt when he adopted the same tactics in the boardroom? Stony silence was the most effective method of coercing a man into saying what he intended to keep to himself.

Once again, he was reminded of how different his wife was from every other woman he'd met.

"I confess that Elizabeth and I were lovers before you and I married," he began, "but on my honor, I have remained faithful to you…"

"No," she said.

A needle pricked at his heart. Was he too late?

"Meggie, forgive me."

She turned to face him. "No, Dexter," she said. "If you wish to tell me what happened, you must look at me. Only then will I be able to decide whether you're speaking the truth."

He lifted his gaze to hers, and his body shivered with discomfort. He always believed that he could meet anyone's gaze—intimidate them by looking into their eyes until they looked away. But, at this moment, his wife's opinion was the only thing that mattered. To look into her eyes and see her disappointment—and her innocence—staring into his tainted soul…

It was going to be one of the most challenging acts of his life. Yet, if he was to deserve her, he had to do it.

He offered his hand. "May I?"

She nodded, and he took her little hand in his, caressing her palm with his thumb.

"On my life, Meggie, I swear I've been true to you. I have a past—we both do—but what matters is now. You are the only woman I want, Meggie. Now and forever."

"But what I saw, what I heard..." She shook her head. "You cannot deny that."

"No, I can't," he said. "When Elizabeth heard you were indisposed, she accosted me, and..." He hesitated, his cheeks warming with shame, but he owed her the truth. "She offered herself. I wanted to see how far she would humiliate herself to get what she wanted, how far her jealousy and her greed would take her."

He shook his head. "It was wrong of me, I know, but it served a purpose, for she has shown her true colors."

"*I* never doubted her true nature," she said.

"I know, my love," he replied. "Rest assured that from now on, you'll never have to see her again—either of them."

She lifted her brows in question.

"I sent them packing," he said. "They may be your blood relations, but blood means nothing without respect or love. With luck, by the time we return to the house, they'll be gone."

"Return to the house?"

"Will you come back with me?"

"Is that an order?"

"No," he said. "It's a request. You're free to do whatever you want, Meggie."

He lifted his hand to the bruise on her face. Her eyes narrowed, but she did not flinch.

"My poor little lamb," he said. "What hurt you've suffered—all because of me!"

"My face will heal."

"Ah, but your heart." He caressed her face with his fingertips, then lowered his hand to her breast. Her heartbeat thrummed faintly against his palm.

"Sometimes it's the invisible injuries that give rise to the most lasting damage," he said. "I would not have you suffer a broken heart."

"Dexter…" She reached up, and he caught her hand and lifted it to his lips. With his other hand, he caressed her breast, and her nostrils flared. A taut little bud beaded against his palm.

"Dexter…"

He withdrew his hand. "Forgive me. I have no right."

She curled her fingers round his hand, and he closed his eyes to temper his hope.

"Will you come home with me, Meggie?"

"Yes," she whispered.

He pulled her into an embrace and placed a

kiss on her forehead.

"I promise, Meggie, that I'll do everything in my power to regain your trust."

She said nothing.

He couldn't expect her to trust him overnight, but the almost indistinguishable nod against his chest told him that he'd made the first step.

Chapter Twenty-Five

"I'LL BE DAMNED—YOU'VE had an eventful few days, haven't you, Hart?"

Oliver Peyton held his glass out for a refill, and Dexter obliged.

"How goes it at the bank, Peyton?"

"I can spot your evasion tactics a mile off," Oliver laughed. "All's well. We have two new clients—a viscount and a baronet."

Dexter wrinkled his nose.

"They're not to be sneered at," Oliver said, "especially the baronet. He's a wealthy merchant who's brought with him a substantial fortune."

"Then you've done well. Perhaps I should send you straight back to London to continue the good work."

"You've evicted enough guests for today, methinks."

"Alderley's only reaping his rewards," Dexter said.

"Talking of rewards," Oliver said, "shall we resume our match? I can set up the board after dinner."

"I hardly think tonight's the time for chess."

"That's only because I have you cornered. Come on, Hart—there are fifty guineas at stake. You wouldn't begrudge me the opportunity to finally beat you at chess, would you? Besides, this has the makings of an epic game. It's perfect for my book."

"My wife will be joining us," Dexter said. "I doubt she'll be interested in our game."

"My, my, you have changed! The parson's noose has done you good if you've gained the inclination to be considerate." Oliver rose to his feet. "And here's the lady in question."

Margaret stood in the doorway, discomfort in her expression as she looked from Oliver to Dexter and back again. But Oliver, with his easy charm and grace, approached her and issued a deep bow.

"Charmed, Mrs. Hart," he said. "I'm delighted to see you looking so well. I had feared for your well-being after you were shackled to this reprobate..." He gestured toward Dexter, then lowered his voice to a conspiratorial whisper, "...but I believe that, despite appearances to the contrary, a flesh-and-blood heart might lurk inside that overly broad chest of his. What say you?"

She gave him a shy smile and held out her hand, and Oliver lifted it to his lips.

Dexter rose to his feet.

"That's enough, Peyton," he said. "Despite your manifest charms, I fear my wife is immune to them."

"Not completely," she said.

"Nevertheless." Dexter offered his arm. "Shall we dine?"

She flashed him a quick smile, and he squeezed her hand in encouragement.

You're looking well.

And she was. Mrs. Wells had worked a miracle, concealing the bruise on her face, and the Alderleys' departure had restored her confidence.

IT WAS PLAIN to see that Oliver Peyton was smitten with Dexter's wife.

But the man posed no threat. He reminded Dexter of himself a few weeks before, when he'd visited Harold and Anne Pelham and had felt like an outsider among a loving couple. But tonight, Dexter was part of the couple, and Oliver the outsider.

Dexter's wife rose to her feet, and the two

men followed suit.

"I'll leave you gentlemen to your brandy."

"No, let us accompany you," Dexter said.

"But custom dictates…"

"I think we can dispense with formalities tonight," Dexter said. "I would not have you lonely."

They retired to the drawing room. Oliver crossed the floor to the chessboard and set out the pieces.

"Can't that wait until tomorrow?" Dexter suggested, glancing at his wife.

"Do not desist on my account," she said. "I'd like to watch."

"Very well," Dexter said. "Do you remember what I showed you—about how pieces move?"

She smiled, and he swore he saw mischief in her eyes.

Oliver needed no further encouragement. He was clearly eager to win his fifty guineas. He set out the pieces, moving them in a position to resume their game.

Dexter studied the board. As he'd remembered from when they'd reached this point before, his white pieces were surrounded by Oliver's black ones. Any move he made would result in losing a significant piece, and Oliver had already taken both his castles and one bishop.

"I have you stumped!" Oliver said. "What shall I spend my fifty guineas on?"

"How about some humility?" Dexter growled.

Oliver chuckled. "You should concede the game now, rather than wait for me to move in for the kill. At least then, you save face by telling yourself you might have had a chance."

Dexter gritted his teeth in frustration. A slim hand was placed on his shoulder, and a gentle fingertip caressed the skin of his neck.

"Husband, might I make a suggestion?"

"Go ahead," he said. "The game is lost."

"Why not move your queen?"

"Where to?"

"There." She pointed across the board. "You'll place the king in check."

"No, that won't work," Dexter said. "His knight can take my queen. I've lost enough pieces as it is."

"Very well." She withdrew and took a chair beside the fireplace.

Oliver followed suit. "Perhaps you're right, Hart," he said. "We'll conclude our game another time. Your poor wife won't want to witness the endgame unless she's a patron of blood sports." He nodded toward the pianoforte in the corner of the room. "Do you play, Mrs. Hart?"

She colored and shook her head. "I'm afraid not."

"Accomplishment is overrated," Dexter said, noticing her stricken expression. "I find there are other qualities to be valued in a wife."

A smile danced in her eyes. Perhaps she might trust him after all.

Perhaps she might not be averse to him visiting her chamber tonight.

DEXTER LISTENED AT the chamber door, hearing soft footsteps and the rustle of linen. He closed his eyes and imagined his wife, slipping her naked body between the sheets. He hardened almost immediately, catching his breath.

When silence fell, he opened the door.

The room was dark save for a solitary candle. His wife lay in the bed, the sheet drawn up to her chin, staring at the canopy.

"Meggie."

She sat up, eyes widening.

"Dexter?"

"May I join you?"

"Yes," she whispered. "I had hoped..." She averted her gaze.

His heart leapt. She wanted him!

"So had I," he said. "I've been hoping and wishing for so long. Will you grant my wish, Meggie?"

She drew the sheet aside, revealing her body. His mouth watered at her shapely form. He unbuttoned his breeches and let them fall to the floor. His manhood sprang in eagerness to bury itself inside her.

Her eyes widened, then she smiled—an invitation.

Tonight, he would claim her as his—truly his. For she was giving herself freely.

MEGGIE WOKE AND blinked in the sunlight. She'd forgotten to draw the curtains, and the window of the lady's chamber looked full east, catching the light of the dawn. She rolled onto her side, and a pair of warm, strong arms caught her and held her body against a broad chest.

She closed her eyes, reliving the night before when her husband had taken her to heights of pleasure she never believed existed. He had touched every inch of her skin until her whole body blazed with need. With gentle commands and tender words of praise, he'd coaxed her into submission, then, when she could bear the wait no longer, he eased himself into her.

When he'd cried her name, her heart burst with love and pride. This beautiful man, who revealed so little of himself, who the world thought was cold and hard—he was not. He trusted her enough to bare his soul.

And he was hers. All hers.

"Mmm…" his voice rumbled in her ear.

"If only I could wake up every day like this." He shifted his body, and she felt him, hard and hot, against her back.

"How shall I bid you good morning?" he murmured, his voice still laden with sleep. "Shall we break our fast in bed?"

He cupped a breast, and her nipple beaded against his palm.

"My wife shares my appetite."

"Dexter, I'm not hungry, I…oh!" she cried out as he dipped his hand between her thighs.

"I beg to differ," he said, his voice deepening. "My wife is ravenous."

She shifted her thighs to accommodate him, and he murmured his approval and moved his fingertips along her flesh. Deep inside her, pleasure flared, and she tilted her head back.

He slipped his finger inside her, and her body rippled with pleasure. He captured her cries with his mouth, plunging his tongue in, devouring her. When her climax subsided, she relaxed into his arms, and he sighed, his breath warming the skin of her neck.

"I wish I could stay here forever."

Her stomach flipped at his words. London was calling to him. His eyes had lit up with eagerness last night when Mr. Peyton discussed the bank. Now the Alderleys had gone, Dexter had no reason to remain in the country.

"Forgive me, Meggie," he said, "for disrupting your life yet again, so soon after everything you've endured."

"You're leaving for London," she said, flattening her tone to temper her emotion.

She freed herself from his embrace.

"Aren't you pleased?" he asked. "It's sooner than I'd planned, but I think you're ready."

"For what?"

"There's much to do," he continued. "You'll find yourself under scrutiny, and though you're beautiful to me in the dowdiest of gowns, I trust you'll permit me a little indulgence."

"Indulgence?"

"As soon as we arrive in London, I'll secure an appointment with the best modiste in town."

"I'm going with you?"

"Of course!" he said. "Do you think I want you anywhere else but at my side?"

"But I thought…"

"You thought I wanted you tucked away out of sight?" He shook his head. "My love, I sent you here to protect you. Despite the outward appearance of finery, London society is somewhat savage, and I had no wish to see you devoured by the creatures that inhabit it. But I've come to realize that my little wife is stronger than she looks and can deal with anything."

He lifted her hand to his lips, his eyes glistening with pride. "I will be by your side to fight for you."

As if ashamed he'd revealed his feelings, he patted her hand and rose from the bed.

"We should dress for breakfast, or Peyton will begin to wonder what we're doing." He shot her a mischievous grin. "But, given how you screamed my name last night, he'll be a simpleton if he doesn't know."

He moved across the floor, his naked body exuding the casual, easy grace of a panther. Then he turned his back, and she let out a cry.

A crisscross pattern of scars covered the flesh.

"Dexter—your back!"

He picked up his shirt and slipped it on.

"Forgive me," he said. "It's been so long. I sometimes forget they are there."

"Do they trouble you?"

"Sometimes in the cold weather, they itch a little. The only trouble they give me is knowing that the man who administered them was never brought to justice. I had to seek my own retribution."

"Who was he?" she asked.

He sighed and averted his gaze. "Can't you guess?"

Her wrist ached in memory of Alderley's vice-like grip, the day he'd instructed his brutish footmen to discipline her.

"My father," she whispered.

He nodded.

"Why didn't you tell me?"

"Few people know." He narrowed his eyes as if in pain.

She reached out and caught his hand. "Will you tell me now?"

The bed shifted under his weight as he sat on it. "There's little to tell," he said. "It happened when I was nine years old when we lived in the shadow of the Alderley estate. My sister Lilah was caught up in a scrape involving Alderley's son and his friend. They caught her playing in the woods and tormented her. She came home, crying, bruised, and scratched. She's always been a tough little fighter—more than a match for two boys. But I couldn't let it rest. Our parents had died, and Lilah was my responsibility. I demanded an audience with Lord Alderley."

He shook his head. "I was naïve enough to believe we lived in a fair world and that men in authority understood the difference between right and wrong."

"What happened?" she asked.

"Alderley accused me of spreading lies about his son and had me thrashed." He closed his eyes, furrowing his brow. "Twenty lashes, and I remember every one. They say the pain can be borne, provided the skin doesn't break. Alderley broke the skin on the second lash. After that, all I saw was blood. I thought that if I focused on the blood at my feet, I could forget the pain. But I failed. I was weak—and for months afterward, all my dreams were filled with blood and fire."

She squeezed his hand. "I'm so sorry."

He covered her hand with his own and caressed it, then met her gaze. Her heart almost broke at the vulnerability in his expression.

"Even now, I cannot bear the sight of blood," he said. "The slightest drop and I find myself unable to breathe."

"Then, when you cut your hand, the day after our wedding…"

"It took all my strength not to pass out," he said. "But you were there, with your soft voice and kind hands, despite how afraid you must have been that day."

He lifted his lips into a smile, and his eyes sparkled. "I think, even then, I was already beginning to fall in love with you."

She took his face in her hands and pulled him to her for a kiss.

"Thank you for trusting me enough to tell me," she said. "It must have been hard for you."

"No, not hard," he whispered. "I find it the easiest thing in the world to trust you, Meggie.

He held his palm up, his fingers splayed out.

"Take my hand."

She took it, and he interlocked his fingers with hers. He tightened the grip until his fingertips dug into her hand, and she did likewise.

"Let us pledge, here and now," he said, "that there shall be no more secrets from each other. As a mark of our faith—and love."

She nodded, and he captured her mouth in a kiss. Then he rose from the bed.

"You have no idea how much it means to me, Meggie, to have someone in this world I can trust completely."

He blew her a kiss and disappeared through the adjoining door to his chamber. Not long after, she heard the murmur of voices as his valet helped him dress.

He trusted her—he loved her!

But the thrill in knowing that he did, was tempered by the fear that he'd discover her secret—the secret she dared not tell him.

Chapter Twenty-Six

A LIGHT BREEZE rippled in the trees as Dexter strolled alongside the Serpentine, his wife on his arm. Though he received the occasional haughty stare, many of the couples they passed were civil enough to exchange a word or two.

Each time someone drew near, his wife's hand tightened its grip on his arm. Though he took pleasure knowing she viewed him as a source of strength, he also knew that she needed to learn to weather London independently.

And a public excursion was the best way to achieve that.

"How are you bearing up, my dear?" he asked.

"It's not as bad as I feared," she said. "Some of the people are quite friendly. I particularly liked the tall lady with the red hair."

"Countess Stiles," Dexter said. "The earl was the first of the upper ton to bank with me."

"She's the most beautiful woman I've ever seen," she continued. "I couldn't begin to compare to her in a ballroom."

"Nonsense!" he said. "You'll outshine them all in your new gowns."

She blushed. "You've been far too generous, Dexter," she said. "First the school, then the gowns…" She shook her head. "As for the pin money, I have no idea what I'm supposed to do with it."

That morning, he'd taken her to Madame Dupont's and ordered three day dresses, three evening gowns, and a riding habit. Silencing his wife's protests over the expense, he'd explained to the modiste that every whim should be catered to. Madame Dupont, with her easy charm and maternal nature, took Meggie under her wing, and soon, his little wife's shyness had disappeared. The two women spent the morning chatting as if they were old friends, while Madame's assistants took Meggie's measurements. They were to return for a fitting in a week, and Dexter found himself looking forward to the simple pleasure of spending a morning in a shop with his wife.

His former self would have laughed at him for being a milksop. But he lifted her hand to his lips, not caring whether the other occupants of the park saw what a happy man he was.

"Your pin money is yours to spend as you wish," he said.

"But I have everything I want. Can't *you* keep it, then I'll ask if I want money?"

"You shouldn't have to ask," he said. "But if you prefer, I can set it aside for you."

"I'd like that," she said. "After all, you're a banker, so it makes sense for you to employ your skills at home. Perhaps you'll grant me a little interest each quarter day."

She smiled up at him, mischief twinkling in her eyes.

Yes, he was a very happy man, indeed.

A familiar couple appeared ahead—a diminutive lady, holding a small dog in her arms, blonde curls peeking out from beneath her bonnet, together with a tall man dressed in a smart light brown jacket and cream-colored breeches.

"Ah, the Pelhams," Dexter said. "The very people I want you to meet. Mr. Pelham is a business associate. He's responsible for that rather fine brandy we've been enjoying."

His wife blushed, and his manhood twitched at the memory. Last night he'd brought a glass of brandy to bed and proceeded to shake droplets of the fiery liquid over his wife's naked body before lapping them up with his tongue.

"I must ask Pelham to supply me with another bottle," he said casually. "We'll have exhausted our supplies in a week or so."

"Dexter..." Her voice spoke of discomfort, but he could see she was aroused.

The Pelhams drew near, and she tightened her hold on him.

"Hart!" Pelham cried. "I knew it was you! I'd heard you were in town. Anne and I have been eager to call on you."

"Then why haven't you?" Dexter asked.

Anne Pelham glanced at Meggie, who appeared distressed.

"I thought it best if we give your lovely wife time to familiarize herself with London," she said. "It can be a rather hostile environment if one doesn't know who one's friends are."

"May I introduce my wife, Margaret," Dexter said. He turned to Meggie. "My dear, this is Mr. and Mrs. Pelham."

"A pleasure to meet you at last," Mrs. Pelham said. "I was most sorry I missed you when I first called—just before you left for the country."

Dexter's wife stiffened, and Dexter recalled Charles's account of the day Meggie had hidden behind the curtains to avoid visitors.

But Anne Pelham's nature was capable of coaxing the most terrified mouse out of its nest. She offered her arm to Meggie.

"Shall we?" she asked. "If you would permit it, Mrs. Hart, I'd love to show you my favorite parts of the park. I've made it my mission to seek out those hidden little spots that are shunned by those who come to the park merely to show themselves off to the world. I suspect you're a woman after my own heart."

Meggie looked at Dexter and raised her eyebrows in question, and he smiled encouragement. Anne Pelham was just the sort of woman to put her at ease.

Meggie took the proffered arm, and the women set off ahead of the men.

"Fate has chosen well for you, my friend," Pelham said. "I almost didn't recognize you today. You were actually *smiling*."

"I've been known to smile," Dexter said.

Pelham scratched his chin in an exaggerated gesture. "Now let me see…" he hesitated, as if in concentration. "Ah, yes! December the fourth 1822. Your lip twitched a little. I believe it was reported in the Times." He grinned. "Then there was the momentous occasion in the Spring of 1823. An unconfirmed report of both corners of your mouth lifting. That report, I believe, made it as far as the Dundee Courier."

"That's enough, Pelham," Dexter said.

His friend laughed. "I jest because it pleases me to see your content. I rather suspect you've discovered the secret which few are party to?"

"Which is?"

"That a man can fall in love with his wife."

"I want her to be happy here," Dexter said.

"She has no friends to speak of."

"She's found one friend at least. My Anne seems quite taken with her," Pelham said. "There's your sisters, also, and of course, she'll have children to occupy herself with."

"Children?"

Pelham grinned. "You have the look of a well-served husband, and she, the satisfied wife. I'll wager you'll soon be announcing a new arrival. As it is..." he lowered his voice, "...Anne informed me this morning that I'm to be a father again. And take it from me, there's nothing more glorious than a woman with child."

"Congratulations," Dexter said.

"I look forward to the day when I can rename my business Pelham and Sons. Perhaps the same will happen to you."

Hart and Sons...

Dexter watched his wife, taking in her delicate curves concealed beneath her skirts. Might she be carrying his son, even now? At that moment, she turned her head and laughed at something Anne Pelham said, her face illuminated with mirth. How might she look when she gave him a child?

The two women seemed as thick as thieves, and it was more than Dexter could have hoped for. He found himself regretting his estrangement from Daisy. Of all his sisters, she was the most like his wife in temperament.

As Pelham rattled on, Dexter watched his wife. All of a sudden, she stiffened. Hardly noticeable, but he'd learned to spot the signs of distress. He quickened the pace and caught up with her. Anne Pelham was describing her lapdog, most likely in an attempt to foist one of the smelly, yappy little creatures onto Meggie. But though Meggie nodded and responded, her attention was diverted. She was staring across the Serpentine.

A solitary man stood on the bank opposite, leaning against a tree, hands thrust into his pockets. He stared across the water toward the two women. His features were concealed in the shadow of the brim of his hat, but Dexter could make out a sly smile on his lips.

"Mrs. Pelham, I trust you'll not bully my wife into taking one of your dogs," he said.

Meggie jumped at his voice, and her gaze darted from Dexter to the man opposite the river.

"My dear?" he prompted.

"N-no, of course not," she said.

"Mr. Hart, I must protest," Mrs. Pelham said. "A lady needs a companion when her husband is absent, and who better than a dog? He is, after all, a better proposition for maintaining a happy marriage than a lover. Besides, I've already issued an invitation to take tea with me tomorrow and meet Lady Guinevere's litter. You wouldn't have me be so ungracious as to rescind my invitation, would you?"

Margaret colored and fixed her gaze on the ground.

"My dear," Dexter said, "I have no objection if you'd like a dog or if you wished to visit Mrs. Pelham tomorrow."

"Thank you." She glanced across the water, then smiled, relief in her eyes. Dexter followed her gaze.

The man had gone.

Who was he, and why had he discomposed her so?

Chapter Twenty-Seven

AFTER SPENDING THE afternoon with Mrs. Pelham, who insisted she call her Anne, Meggie returned with a small bundle of fur in her arms. One puppy had stood out from the rest of the litter. Smaller and more subdued than its siblings, the little creature had lifted its gaze to her, a silent plea in its soft brown eyes.

And her heart was lost.

"Welcome home, ma'am," the footman said, taking her shawl.

"Thank you, Charles."

"We have a visitor," he continued. "I took the liberty of placing him in the parlor."

Him...

Her chest tightened, and she almost dropped the puppy as a wave of apprehension rippled through her.

"Here, ma'am, let me help you." The footman reached for the dog. "Shall I find a basket for him while you see to your guest? I'm sure Mrs. Draper will be able to find a blanket or two."

"My guest?" she squeaked, panic rising.

"I told him the master was not at home, ma'am, and he said he already knew that. He's come to see you."

Meggie swallowed her fear. If she must face her past, then at least Dexter wasn't here to witness it. But could the servants be trusted not to gossip?

She pushed open the parlor door. A solitary figure occupied the wing-backed chair in a dark corner of the room. As she entered, he stood and turned.

A wave of relief rushed through her.

It wasn't *him*.

He might be clad in a gentleman's clothes, but he did not wear them well. He seemed to fidget in his suit as if he found it distasteful. But his most distinguishing feature was the black silk mask covering the upper portion of his face. Thick, dark hair framed his face, and she could discern two brown eyes behind the mask. She'd always thought brown eyes conveyed warmth, but a frost lingered in this man's eyes. His mouth was set in a frown, made all the more acute for being the only visible feature, save his eyes.

"Who are you?" she asked.

He clicked his heels together in the manner of a soldier standing to attention.

"I suppose I'm your brother-in-law."

"I don't understand."

"Major Devon Hart, at your service." His voice held a note of sarcasm.

"My husband never mentioned a brother," she said.

He curled his mouth into a sneer. "Why am I not surprised?"

"Do you mean to insult my husband or me with that remark?" she asked.

"Neither."

"Would you like tea, Major Hart?"

"Not particularly."

"Then why are you here?"

He shrugged his shoulders. "Dexter said I had to pay my respects to his bride."

"And you chose to do so at a time when he was out?"

"Exactly."

"May I ask why?"

"I can't prevent you from *asking*."

What a strange man he was! No wonder Dexter hadn't mentioned him.

"The last thing I want is to be visited out of a sense of duty," she said. "If you'd rather be elsewhere, I'll gladly relieve you of any obligation you feel toward me."

"Don't worry," he replied. "I doubt you'll

want me to visit again."

"Why not?"

"Because of this."

He reached behind his head and lowered the mask, and she let out a low cry.

One side of his face was beautiful—strong, chiseled features, a square jaw, straight nose, and deep, chocolate-brown eyes that looked almost liquid in the light. But the other side...

A thick, jagged scar bisected one cheek, narrowly missing his right eye from just above the chin to his temple. The flesh around it was puckered where the wound had healed, distorting his features.

Were it not for the scar, he'd have been one of the most handsome men she'd ever seen.

He stood, stiff and erect, facing her head-on as if challenging her to scream or throw him out. What must he have endured to learn such stoicism? How many insults would have been hurled in his direction in a world where appearance meant everything?

She blinked, and tears stung her eyes. His expression hardened.

"I don't want your pity, madam."

"What happened?"

"I was injured in a fight."

"In a battle?"

"A street brawl, near the docks," he said. "I encountered a group of men assaulting a prostitute and intervened. One of them slashed me with a broken gin bottle." He gave a hollow laugh. "Nothing honorable, I'm afraid."

"There's honor in saving a life."

"And what if I told you I'd gone there in search of a street whore?"

She flinched at the bitterness in his voice. "Does it matter?" she asked. "You put yourself in danger to help someone in need. That makes you a hero, whether it happened at Waterloo or in a brothel."

She held out her hand. "You must stay for tea," she said. "I usually take it at this hour, and I have so few friends that any new acquaintance is welcome."

He stared at her hand as if trying to discern whether it was an illusion.

"Please?"

He nodded and took her hand. His skin was dry and rough—evidence, perhaps, of soldiering.

When he released her, she rang the bell for tea, then gestured for him to sit.

He picked up a book from the table beside the chair and read the cover.

"*Mo Chridhe*," he said. His lips lifted into a smile. "Lilah's poems. Are you reading them?"

"I am," she said. "They're extraordinary. I struggle to comprehend some of the words, but when you hear them in your head, it's like they sing to you. I can't wait to meet your sister. She must be very clever to write such work."

"Little Lilah? Don't tell her that, or you'll never hear the end of it! Once you get her talking, the day is done, for she'll never stop. But, she does write pretty verse." He smiled, his focus shifting as if remembering happier times. "We used to exchange verses when we were children."

"You write poetry also?" Meggie asked. "I had no idea what a talented family I've married into. You should be the talk of the town."

The scowl resumed. "I'm nothing," he said.

"I refuse to believe that," she replied. "If you value yourself, then others will see your worth. I've only known you a few minutes, yet I can see there's more to you than you care to reveal. In that way, you're very much like my husband."

"Like Dex?"

"Exactly," she said. "He would have the world believe that he doesn't care. And, in the world he inhabits most of the time, there's no room for emotion. But when he comes home to me..." she smiled to herself, "...then, he reveals his heart."

"Well!" he said. "You're the last woman I'd have expected Dex to choose."

For the second time, she found herself wanting to ask him whether he meant to insult her or her husband.

He rolled his eyes and sighed. "I meant no insult," he said. "I don't make pretty speeches.

After all, what right do I have to understand beauty?"

"As much right as anyone else," she said. "Perhaps—if it's not too bold to suggest it—you might permit me to inspect your scar? I might be able to do something for it."

His smile disappeared. "You find me repulsive? Do you offer your services in order to lessen the discomfort you feel when looking at me? I have the remedy for that, madam." He reached for his mask, and she caught his hand.

"No, she said. "I only offer my help in order to lessen *your* pain. It matters not what others feel."

He let out a bark of laughter.

"What's so funny?" she asked.

"I never would have believed that the most heartless of all the Harts would find such a compassionate mate," he said. "Did he court you with gentle words? I wish I'd been there to see it!"

"It wasn't his decision," she said, her cheeks warming. "He was tricked into a marriage he didn't want. Did you not hear the gossip?"

"Where gossip's concerned, I'm more the subject than a participant," he said. He took her hand. "Forgive the incivility of a bitter old soldier. For all that Dex is an arse, he has one defining characteristic."

"Which is?"

"Loyalty," he said. "Stay true to him, and

he'll remain by your side until he draws his last breath."

He kissed her hand. "But, on no account must you tell my brother I've said that. He'd be unbearable if he knew."

"Knew what?" a new voice said.

Dexter stood in the doorway.

As soon as Dexter spoke, his brother turned to face him. It had been a long time since he'd seen Devon unmasked. The scar on his face was more extensive than he'd remembered.

Guilt needled at him. In a world where appearance ranked above loyalty, he'd abandoned the care of his brother in the pursuit of his goal to ally himself and Delilah with the nobility.

But what had caused him to stop short in astonishment was the fact that his younger brother was smiling. The man who'd not smiled or laughed in years.

Devon lifted his mask and set it in place.

"There's no need to do that, brother," Dexter said.

Devon ignored him. "Good day, sister," he said. "I'll leave you in your husband's care."

"Don't go on my account," Dexter said.

"You can't order me about," Devon replied.

"Not like you did with Daisy, or how you tried and failed with Lilah. There's only Thea left, now. Will you ruin her life as well?"

"Dev…"

"Save your breath," Devon said. "I'm not interested. But let me say this, you've driven all of us away. Don't make the same mistake with your wife."

He bowed to Meggie. "Ma'am."

After Devon had left, Dexter took his wife's hands. "I trust he did nothing to upset you."

"No," she said. "I like him. I should like to know him better, and…" she hesitated, "…the rest of your family."

"You'll see Dorothea when she returns from visiting Delilah in Scotland," he said. "Lilah herself, I expect, at some point in the future."

"And Daisy?"

"I'm afraid that's out of the question."

As if to lessen the blow of his outburst, he gave her a lopsided grin. "Let us speak of better things. What the devil is that furball sitting in cook's vegetable basket in the front hallway?"

"I saw Anne Pelham today."

"And she furnished you with a little friend. Does he have a name?"

"Titan," she said. "I thought it appropriate given his size."

He let out a laugh, lifted her hand, and kissed it. The pug was the smallest dog he'd ever seen.

"An excellent name!" he said. "Come, let us help him to settle in before dinner."

His brother might still hate him, but he'd spoken the truth. Dexter had let his family down, but he had been given the opportunity to atone by caring for his wife. And he was right on another matter. Dexter would be loyal to anyone who stayed true.

And he knew of nobody more honest than his wife.

Chapter Twenty-Eight

"TITAN!"

The puppy turned its head to stare at Meggie, then resumed sniffing the bush. She tugged at the leash, and he whined in protest.

"Don't give me those eyes," she scolded. "They won't melt my heart *this* time."

The animal whirled his tail. She could never be angry with him for long—not even when she'd found one of Dexter's neckties in his basket, ripped to shreds.

Titan had taken a liking to Dexter, following him everywhere when he was at home. She smiled to herself at how her husband had finally relented and let Titan sit on his lap. But he refused to carry the dog when they walked together in the park, arguing that was one step removed from donning Meggie's evening gown and adorning himself in pearls.

Her gown had arrived that morning from Mrs. Dupont's. Pale orange silk with crimson trimmings and matching headdress, it was the most elegant thing she'd ever owned. Dexter had insisted she try it on, then lifted the skirt and made love to her.

She hadn't imagined how deliciously decadent it would feel, indulging in pleasure, fully clothed. And now, each time she wore the dress, she'd be reminded of the feel of him inside her. Afterward, he'd lowered her skirts, set her on her feet, and called for Francine to assist her as if nothing had happened. Meggie had stood demurely while her maid helped her out of the dress, seemingly ignoring the fact that the faint aroma of arousal lingered in the chamber.

She had never imagined he'd be so attentive in the bedroom—or that she would come to crave his attention.

A gust of wind whipped her handkerchief out of her fingers, and she raced ahead to catch it, the dog trotting after her. It landed on the grass, and as she stooped to pick it up, a pair of booted feet appeared. The smell of cologne tickled her nostrils, and a hand grasped the handkerchief and handed it to her.

"Thank you, sir," she said.

"The pleasure's all mine, Megs."

She looked up into a familiar pair of gray

eyes, and her heart somersaulted in her chest.

"Georgie!"

So, it *had* been him in the park the other day.

Fate had been kind to him. Instead of a footman's livery, he wore a tailored suit. In the years since she'd seen him, he'd grown more muscular, his athletic form evident beneath the material of his finely cut jacket. He had always been handsome. Today, he was nothing short of breathtaking.

But she was no longer the lovesick young girl who had believed his honeyed promises.

"Why are you here?" she asked.

"Is that how you greet an old friend, Megs? Or must I address you as Mrs. Hart, now you've risen from the gutter?"

"An old friend?" she cried. "You seduced me, then disappeared without so much as a backward glance! Did you come to London in search of easy prey?"

"No, Megs," he said. "Unlike you, I've not fucked my way to the top."

She flinched at his crude expression.

"I was Lord Blessingham's valet," he said.

"Was?"

"The old codger died on me, but I'll find another position soon. I don't suppose your husband is looking for a new valet?"

"No," she said, "he's very happy with the present incumbent."

"Is he happy with *you*, Megs?"

Her skin crawled at his familiar address, recalling the memory of the last time he'd used it.

"I hear he's a changed man," he continued. "Your influence, when on your back, is to be commended. Perhaps it can be utilized in other ways."

"What do you mean?"

"Is he a generous husband? Of course, he'll expect to bed his wife for free, but I'm sure with a little inventiveness, he'd part with a little extra cash. A whore can charge what she likes if she's prepared to degrade herself."

She grimaced, though his turn of phrase was oddly familiar. Where had she heard it before?

"A man of my stature has considerable expenses to maintain his upkeep while he seeks a new position," he continued. "I'm merely asking for a little help."

"I cannot secure you another position," she said, "and my husband is unlikely to recommend a man of whom he knows nothing."

"Perhaps I should acquaint myself with Mr. Hart to further his knowledge of me." He smiled, revealing even white teeth, and his tongue flicked out, moistening his lower lip.

Her stomach rippled with apprehension. "Georgie, please," she said. "He wouldn't welcome an acquaintance."

"Then, I must seek recompense."

"I don't understand."

He let out a laugh. "My poor foolish lover, you never did understand. Yet, look at you now! I've worked hard to achieve my current status. All you did was prostitute yourself into a wealthy man's bed."

"I did no such thing!"

"I care not," he said. "What matters is that you have the means and incentive to help me. What say you to a small stipend to keep me afloat until I no longer need it?"

She shook her head. "I can't…"

He gripped her arm. "Yes, you can, Megs. Hart's wealthy enough to buy half of London. His social status is rising, despite his origins. I wouldn't think he'd relish the prospect of his wife's whoring being made public knowledge. Is that incentive enough?"

She tried to pull free, but he tightened his grip.

"My husband knows I was with another man," she said. "Say what you wish, and be damned!"

He let out a laugh. "There it is!" he cried. "The language of the gutter. Once a scrubby bastard, always a scrubby bastard, eh?" His smile disappeared. "Is poor, trusting Dexter familiar with the old adage that bastards beget bastards?"

"Let me go," she said. "You're hurting me."

"Not until I have an answer," he said. "Does

he know that his wife bore another man's child?"

Her stomach shriveled into a knot, and she swallowed as a wave of nausea rippled through her.

"Of course, I'll never know whether the child was mine or not," he said. "Who knows how many men you spread your legs for? What became of the brat? Did you sell it as your father sold you? How much does a bastard fetch these days?"

She drew her hand back to strike him, and he caught her wrist.

"Careful, lover," he said. "My face is an asset in my profession. You wouldn't want to incur further expense by marking it."

Titan whined at her feet and strained on the lead. Georgie aimed a kick at the little dog, and she jerked the leash away.

"Don't touch him!" she cried.

"Are you prepared to be reasonable?"

"What do you want?"

"A mere trifle compared to your husband's wealth. Shall we say a thousand pounds?"

A thousand!

"Georgie, I cannot!" she cried. "I don't have such a sum."

"You can pay me in regular installments, say, fifty pounds a week? Surely your beloved gives you pin money?"

"Nowhere near as much."

"Then you'd better get creative in the bed-room, my dear, and find ways to encourage his generosity. How much do you have now?"

She reached into her reticule and pulled out a sheaf of notes. "Twenty pounds."

He snatched the notes and pocketed them. "That will have to do," he said. "I'm prepared to remain silent if you return next week with the next installment."

"I can't ask my husband for fifty pounds," she said. "He'll wonder what I want it for."

"That's *your* problem," he said, "and it'll be eighty pounds, given that your first payment was thirty short. Of course, if you're able to procure the full thousand, then I'll consider our business concluded."

"I say! Mrs. Hart!" a voice called. Meggie turned and saw Oliver Peyton striding along the path.

"I thought it was you," he said. He glanced at Georgie, curiosity in his eyes. "Who's this fellow?"

Georgie bowed. "George Hanson, at your service, sir," he said. "I was assisting this—lady—here, in a matter concerning the training of her dog. Is that not right, Mrs. Hart?"

Meggie glanced at Oliver and felt her cheeks warm under his scrutiny.

"Yes, that's right," she said. "Thank you, Mr. Hanson."

"The pleasure was all mine," Georgie said. "I must be going. But I look forward to meeting you and your dog next week as arranged."

He issued a bow and disappeared along the path.

"May I escort you home, Mrs. Hart?" Peyton asked. "You look unwell."

"No, I'll be fine, thank you," she said. "I wouldn't want to put you to any trouble."

"It's no trouble."

"Nevertheless, I insist."

Before he could protest, she picked Titan up and, cradling him in her arms, strode out of the park. Only when she arrived home and handed her dog over to Charles did her heart stop fluttering.

The prospect of meeting the man who'd ruined her, each week, was too much to be borne—and it carried the risk of her being seen. But how could she persuade her husband to part with a thousand pounds?

THE AFTERNOON STRETCHED into evening, and Dexter hadn't returned home yet. Alone, with nothing but her imagination for company, Meggie grew restless. What was Georgie planning? Would he carry out his threat if she didn't give him the money? And would Mr. Peyton tell Dexter he'd seen her with a man?

At length, her fears got the better of her, and she made her way into Dexter's study where he kept her pin money. She knew she only had to ask for it, but what if he asked what she wanted it for? She'd struggle to lie convincingly, especially to a man such as Dexter, whose striking blue gaze could penetrate her soul.

Her heart thudded as she slid open the top drawer of his desk. Her husband valued trust and honesty above all, and she'd pledged her honesty several times. But she quaked at the thought of him discovering that she'd borne another man's child—he'd made his views abundantly clear on the matter.

A sheaf of notes was stacked neatly in the drawer. She picked it up and counted them. Just over ninety pounds. It wouldn't silence Georgie for good, but it was enough to buy his silence for a week.

She spotted an envelope in the drawer with directions penned in Dexter's bold, clear hand.

Mrs. John Farrow
London Lane
Croxleigh Green
Hertfordshire

The envelope was unsealed. With trembling

fingers, she opened it. A note was inside covered in Dexter's handwriting, together with five-pound notes.

While she suffered guilt from deceiving her husband, was he deceiving her also?

"Margaret?"

She squeaked at the voice and looked up.

Dexter stood in the doorway. He lowered his gaze to the envelope in her hand.

"That's a private letter," he said, his voice dangerously quiet.

"I haven't read it."

"I should bloody well hope not."

"I-I was looking for something," she said.

He folded his arms and waited. The silence stretched like an empty vat waiting to be filled.

"I needed my pin money," she blurted. At least that was the truth.

"What for?"

"Must I give a reason?"

"Of course not, but it doesn't explain why you have my private correspondence in your hand."

"I…" she broke off, unwilling to continue.

"Well?"

She dropped the letter in the drawer. "I was merely curious," she said.

"You were a little more than that." Disapproval lined his features, and she found herself irritated. He was accusing her of snooping, yet he had a secret of his own.

"Who's Mrs. Farrell?"

He narrowed his eyes. "So, you *have* read it."

"Only the direction," she said. "Why do you send her money?"

"If you suspect me of something, Margaret, pay me the courtesy of saying what it is."

Unwilling to voice her fears, she shook her head. "I-I don't know…"

"But I do," he said, anger flashing in his eyes. "What would you say if I told you that despite pledging my honesty to you, I was sending money to a mistress behind your back? Or, perhaps, that I had sired a by-blow and was funding the brat's education? Is that what you wish to hear?"

"No, of course not!" she cried.

"Good God, woman, what the devil do you take me for?"

He closed his eyes and wiped his brow. When he opened them again, the anger had been replaced by disappointment.

"Mrs. Farrow is my sister, Daisy," he said. "She doesn't have much, and I send her money from time to time. You're at liberty to read the letter if you require proof."

She picked up the letter, and he set his mouth into a hard line, then she set it down again. "No," she said. "I don't want proof."

"Then what do you want, Margaret?"

"Nothing. I-I'm sorry, Dexter, I shouldn't have assumed…"

"No," he said. "You shouldn't."

"Do you want to visit her?"

He sighed and shook his head. "She wouldn't welcome it."

"Not even now, you're married?"

"She doesn't know."

"But if you write…"

"I send her money," he said. "That's all. Daisy belongs to a different world, and long ago made it abundantly clear that she had no wish to reside in mine. I see no reason to burden her with tales of my life when I was responsible for ruining hers."

Meggie's heart ached to see the pain in his eyes. She approached him and took his hand. He stiffened, then relented, and she curled her fingers round his.

"You care for her," she said. "I can see it in your eyes."

"Margaret, I'm tired," he said. "I've had a busy day and have been looking forward to a quiet evening. Can't this wait?"

"No," she said, "it can't. I should have trusted you. You've been nothing but honest with me. I'm sorry, Dexter."

He drew her close. "I see I must work harder to gain your trust, my love," he said. "But whatever regrets I have over Daisy, she and I cannot return to how we were before."

"Yes, you can," she said. "I believe that if you had the opportunity to see your sister again, you would take it. Can we not visit her?"

He shook his head. "No."

"Why not?" she asked. "We could deliver your letter in person."

"And if she refuses to admit us?"

"Then at least we'll have tried," she said. "Won't you at least consider it, Dexter? As a favor to me?" She swallowed her guilt and continued. "What better way to gain my trust than to grant me this?"

He cursed under his breath, then caught her chin and tipped her head up until their eyes met.

"Is this what you really want?"

"Yes."

He leaned forward and brushed his lips against hers. "Then your wish is my command," he said. "I'll do anything you ask in order to prove I'm worthy of your trust."

He held her against his chest, and she relaxed into his embrace, feeling the steady thud of his heart against her body—a heart that beat for her.

Perhaps, by reuniting him with his sister, she might be able to lessen the guilt of her deception.

Chapter Twenty-Nine

A S THE CARRIAGE drew to a halt outside the squat, stone building, Dexter's wife gave him a smile of encouragement.

This was a bloody mistake. Daisy would turn him away at the door. Meggie would suffer the insult, and he'd be reminded of what a bastard he'd been to his sister when she needed him.

With luck, Daisy was out. But then, his tenacious little Meggie would most likely insist they remain at the Croxleigh Arms until she returned.

He didn't want to stay another night in that godforsaken inn. The walls were too thin, and though he cared little whether the landlord and the other guests heard his wife screaming in ecstasy as he pleasured her, he didn't want to subject Meggie to their stares.

Christ—was this what love did to a man?

Meggie had seemed out of sorts for the past few days—ever since he'd caught her in his study. He'd seen her staring out of the window, looking as if she were about to burst into tears—and for the past few meals, she'd not cleared her plate. Perhaps she still felt guilty over being caught with Daisy's letter. Given her upbringing and treatment at Alderley's hands, it was no wonder she suffered guilt at almost everything she did.

As for her poor appetite—he smiled to himself over the likely cause. Harold Pelham had told him that Anne had stopped eating the moment she quickened with their first child and that her moods were as interchangeable as a weathercock in a whirlwind.

He took Meggie's hand and led her to the front door of the cottage. The building next to it bore a sign written in clear, neat letters.

Jon Farrow
Bread and Biscuit Baker

Meggie squeezed his hand in a gesture of comfort. "I'm sure she'll be pleased to see you."

He knocked on the door, praying it would be met with silence, but he heard footsteps from within.

The door swung open to reveal a tall woman with black hair and brilliant blue eyes. Small creases lined her face, which was grayer than when he'd last seen her. But she was as beautiful as he remembered—a beauty to torture men's hearts, he'd said. But in the end, it was Daisy who'd been destroyed.

"Can I help you, sir?" she asked.

He took off his top hat. "Hello, Daisy."

Her eyes widened.

"I thought I said I never wanted to see you again!"

"Never is a long time."

"Not long enough for me." She glanced at Meggie. "So, you're married?"

"Yes," he said. "May I introduce you to…"

"Spare me," Daisy interrupted. "I've no wish to be looked down on by you or some fancy heiress."

"Can we at least continue this conversation inside?" Dexter asked. "I doubt the residents of Croxleigh Green wish to hear our grievances."

"Of course," she sneered. "We must maintain appearances. It matters not what's said or done, as long as it's behind closed doors. Come in, though I doubt my cottage is grand enough for you and your wife. But the sooner you tell me what you want, the sooner I can disappoint you and send you on your way."

He took Meggie's hand and followed his sister inside.

The parlor was neat and tidy, with a homely feel. Bright coverings adorned the furniture with matching curtains. Several children's drawings lined the walls. Meggie sat in a chair and took in her surroundings, her mouth curving into a smile as she looked at the pictures.

"You have a lovely home, Mrs. Farrow," she said.

"My apologies, it's not what you're used to," Daisy replied.

Dexter rolled his eyes—why did his sister have to be so bloody prickly?

Meggie gave a nervous smile. "Where I grew up, we had no parlor," she said. "My home consisted of two rooms, which I shared with three others."

"You never told me that, Margaret," Dexter said.

"You never asked," she replied. "When I was moved to Blackwood Heath, we had a small parlor, but it wasn't as comforting as your sister's."

"Why has Dexter brought you here?" Daisy asked. "Does he want to show you how far he's risen in the world?"

"You've hardly fallen, Daisy," he said. "John's a businessman, as am I. Therefore, we are equals."

"Equals!" she scoffed. "All you do is send money with impersonal little notes as if I were a dirty secret. Admit it, Dexter—you're ashamed of me, and you always have been. Which is why you strove to marry a woman like *her*."

She gestured toward Meggie. "How much did you get for this one?" she asked. "You once said you'd take no woman for less than thirty thousand and a title. A perfect heiress for my perfect brother—not like the sister who disgraced the family." She turned to Meggie. "I trust you were worth it, Mrs. Hart, for your sake. I know better than anyone what it's like to suffer Dexter's disappointment."

Dexter jumped to his feet.

"For heaven's sake!" he roared. "Say what you like about me, but I'll not let you insult my wife! If you must know, Margaret has no fortune, no title, and was brought up in disgrace. I was duped into marrying her in a game of cards! Does that give you satisfaction?"

Daisy folded her arms. Some of the fight had gone from her eyes.

"*You've* insulted your wife more than I," she said. "No woman wishes to be told that she was wagered in a game of cards, or that her husband was tricked into marrying her."

He glanced at Meggie, whose cheeks were flaming.

Christ! Why had he been so foolish! But Daisy always had the ability to get under his skin and drive him to act on impulse.

"Does my brother speak the truth?" Daisy asked.

Meggie nodded and gave a rueful smile. "I've learned enough of your brother to know that he always speaks the truth, often to the detriment of himself and everyone else."

The corner of Daisy's mouth twitched into a smile, and Dexter caught a glimpse of the sister he had lost.

"Then let me apologize on his behalf," she said.

Meggie returned the smile. "There's no need. There's something refreshing in brutal honesty. I have learned that your brother's rather..." she gave Dexter a saucy glance, "...*savage* exterior, conceals a good heart." She lowered her voice. "Of course, it's not a discovery I'm inclined to share with the rest of the world."

Daisy flicked her gaze from Meggie to Dexter. "Ha!" she cried, smiling. "I believe you may have met your match, Dex. Are you happy with her?"

"Very," Dexter replied. "I trust you're as happy as I am. How is John? Is he well?"

"He is," Daisy said, "but he misses his best friend."

"Oh!" Meggie cried. "The baker! So *that's* why you're so proficient at making bread."

Daisy folded her arms. "Don't tell me you're employed in your kitchen, brother."

Footsteps approached, and a man's face appeared at the door.

"I thought I heard voices." His eyes widened as he recognized Dexter.

"Good God!" he cried. "Dex!" He rushed forward, arms outstretched. Dexter rose to his feet, and his old friend drew him into an embrace and clapped him on the back.

"It's been too long, Dexter," he said. "Far too bloody long."

"Aye," Dexter said. John Farrow—the most loyal man on earth, and the only man worthy of Daisy. How he'd missed his old friend!

John released him and wiped his hands. "Begging your pardon," he said, glancing at Meggie. "Dex, aren't you going to introduce us?"

"John, this is my wife, Margaret," Dexter said. "Meggie, my dear, this is my old friend."

John bowed before Meggie and took her hand, bringing it to his lips. "A pleasure, ma'am."

"Margaret," Meggie said, shyly. "You must both call me Margaret. After all, I'm your sister, aren't I?"

John and Daisy exchanged glances, then he nodded.

"Will you stay for supper?" he asked. "I'm sure we have enough to stretch."

Daisy colored and looked away. Dexter recognized the shame of a woman struggling to make ends meet.

As usual, his compassionate little wife took the helm.

"How about we all dine at the Croxleigh Arms?" Meggie suggested.

"I don't know…" Daisy began, but Dexter interrupted her.

"Please, Daisy," he said. "Just one meal. Then, if you wish it, we won't impose on you again. My wife wanted so much to meet you, and I…I find I miss you."

"Very well," she said crossly. "I'll have to ask Mrs. Weatherby to keep an eye on Rosie, but I dare say she won't mind. But don't expect me to dress up in finery, brother. I cannot afford to indulge in silk."

Her words might be harsh, but her voice had softened. Perhaps, in time, he may find the sister he'd lost.

DEXTER STRETCHED OUT on his back and studied the ceiling. The Croxleigh Arms dated back to Tudor times. He considered the beams which crossed the ceiling, following the uneven, parallel lines.

The bed shifted, and his wife stretched and yawned. He captured her arms and pulled her on top of him. Her breasts pressed against his chest and her little buds peaked against his skin.

She squirmed and parted her thighs until he

felt her warm, sweet flesh against him.

"Meggie, you're a temptress," he said. "I vowed not to ravish you here, but, by God, woman, you're enough to tempt any man to sin."

She grinned and squeezed her thighs against him.

"Witch!" he hissed. "Do you want them to hear you scream my name?"

She pouted, and he thrust his hips upward. She squealed with laughter, and he rolled onto his side, taking her with him. She snuggled into him and placed her head on his chest. He ran his fingers through her hair, and she sighed.

"Much as I want to lie in this bed and make love to you all day, I fear we must rise," he said. "I'm anxious to return to London before dark, and I know you'll wish to see Daisy and John before we leave."

"They seem happy," she said, "and you should forgive yourself. You did what was best for her. It's plain to see they're very much in love."

"True," he said. "After her—ruination—I wanted no man to go near her. But John, it seemed, had loved her for years. I nearly beat the living hell out of him when I saw them together, but he was a determined man. He said that even if I broke every bone in his body, he'd not be deterred."

He sighed and stroked his wife's hair. "Were

it not for me, John might have courted Daisy, and that bastard Hanson'd have never seduced her."

Meggie's head shot up, a wild look in her eyes. "Hanson?"

"Yes, do you know him?"

"I-I've heard the name," she said. "Perhaps Daisy mentioned it at supper last night. Yes, I remember—that was it."

She wriggled out of his arms. "We should dress. I'd like to spend as much time with Daisy before we leave."

Not meeting his gaze, she climbed out of bed and padded over to the trunk. She pulled out a shift and inspected it. He crept up behind her.

"Here, let me." He reached for the garment, and she jumped at his touch. What the devil was wrong with her?

She turned and let him help her dress, chatting animatedly, her voice overly bright.

"I hope we'll see Rosie this morning," she said. "How old is she?"

"I'm ashamed to say I have no idea of my niece's age," he said. "About four, I think."

"And is she..." his wife hesitated, "... John's daughter?"

"Yes, thank Christ," Dexter said. "John might be smitten with Daisy, but not even he's so lacking in dignity that he'd accept another man's child—especially that bastard Hanson's."

He held out his shirt.

"My turn," he said. She snatched it from him.

Where had her smile gone?

"I trust you're up to James's standard," he said. "If you perform a better service, I'll have to advertise for another valet."

She stiffened.

"Are you well?"

Her throat bobbed as she swallowed. "Yes," she said. "I merely felt a little queasy. Too much wine last night, I expect." She gave him a watery smile and helped him with his shirt.

She was harboring a secret, and he knew what it was.

But he'd let her reveal the happy news in her own time.

Chapter Thirty

GEORGIE HANSON COUNTED the notes, then slipped them into his pocket, which he gave a satisfied pat.

"Very obliging, Megs," he said. "I'm glad we've rekindled our relationship."

Titan looked up at him, lips curled in a snarl. Meggie picked the pug up and cradled him in her arms.

"That concludes our business," she said.

"Oh, Megs!" He clutched his chest in mock hurt. "Leaving so soon? Would you abandon an old friend?"

"We were never friends," she said. "I was an innocent, and you a seducer."

"Oh, you wound me!"

"You knew what you were about," she said. "You flattered me into your bed, and I believed your lies."

"You said you loved me, Megs," he said. "That's the vocal equivalent of offering up your cunny."

She winced at the profanity. "You disgust me!"

In a blur of movement, he grasped her elbow and propelled her off the path.

"Let me go. You're hurting me!"

He brought his face close. "It takes two to fuck, Megs. Have you told Dexter that you love him? Perhaps I should ask him myself."

"You wouldn't dare!"

"Would you wager your marriage on it? I'll be writing to him to offer my services, and could ask him then."

"I've told you before, my husband has a valet."

"Poor James isn't so steady on his feet," he said, "He's forever running back and forth to Savile Row to add to his master's ever-expanding collection of cravats. What if he were to trip and break his ankle?"

He released her, and she stepped back and rubbed her arm.

"You see the harm that can arise from you not obliging me, Megs?" He shook his head. "Let's say one hundred next week, shall we?"

"One hundred? We agreed on fifty a week."

"I underestimated my needs."

She longed to slam her fist into his face and wipe off the self-satisfied grin, but she had no wish to draw attention to herself with so many people milling about the park.

"Very well," she sighed. "I'll find you another hundred."

"Of course, if you're disposed to present me with a thousand, then we can conclude our relationship."

"A thousand?" she asked. "But I've given you a hundred already—there's nine hundred left."

He tutted and wagged his finger at her. "Oh, Meggie, Meggie," he said. "You have it all wrong. As your beloved Dexter would say, think of the thousand as the capital sum, representing your debt to me. What you are paying me now merely represents the interest on that capital."

"That's not what…"

"Hush," he said, silencing her with a raised hand. "If you struggle to understand the concept of capital and interest, I could ask Dexter to explain it to you." He blew her a kiss. "In the meantime, I'll bid you adieu, and shall look forward to our next—*liaison*."

He curled his tongue round the final word and licked his lips. She fled, her cheeks flaming. He'd always had the ability to discompose her. When they were younger, his gallant attentions had caused butterflies in her stomach. But now, her skin crawled at the thought of him.

Before she reached the park gates, she caught a glimpse of Anne Pelham and her husband. The epitome of the loving couple, they walked arm-in-arm while Anne held her free hand over her belly. Mr. Pelham raised his hand in salute, but Meggie forged ahead, pretending not to see them. Anne Pelham was a dear friend, but she was unnervingly astute. She had recognized Meggie's distress the day she'd first spotted Georgie in the park and would unearth her secret in no time.

DEXTER WAS WAITING for Meggie as she arrived home.

"My dear, where have you been?" he asked, an edge to his voice.

"Must I obtain permission before venturing out?"

"Of course not," he said, "but we have a guest for dinner unless you've forgotten?"

Guilt needled at her, and she took his hand. "Forgive me," she said. "I'll be ready long before Mr. Peyton arrives. Might I ask a favor, first?"

"Anything."

"I-I wondered if you might oblige me with a little more pin money."

"Have you already spent what I've given you?"

She averted her gaze. "I want to send a little more to Daisy," she said, "and Mrs. Preston's always in need of new books at the school."

"You don't have to explain yourself, Meggie," he said. "Will fifty pounds suffice?"

"May I have a hundred?"

"Good Lord!" he exclaimed, laughing. "Don't tell me my frugal little wife is turning into an extravagance! I trust you don't intend to follow Elizabeth's example and bleed me dry as she has done her father."

She blinked back a tear, and he squeezed her hand.

"Meggie, my love," he said. "I jest."

She looked into his eyes and saw the longing.

"I-I could wear the orange silk dress tonight," she said.

His nostrils flared, and he drew in a sharp breath. She moved closer, and her body pulsed as she felt him. The longing had turned into need.

"It's time we put it to use again, husband. Together with the brandy."

He closed his eyes, and a low growl rumbled in his chest.

"Then, wife," he whispered, his voice a low rasp of need, "you shall have anything you wish."

Three sharp raps sounded on the door, the calling card of the housekeeper, and he withdrew.

"Bloody woman!" he said through gritted teeth. "Why does she always come at the most inopportune moment?"

"I suspect she wishes to discuss the menu," Meggie said.

"Then I'll leave you to it."

He approached the door and opened it. Mrs. Draper stood in the doorway and dipped into a curtsey.

"Mr. Hart, sir…"

"Yes, yes." He waved his hand at her. "My wife's all yours."

Meggie ushered the housekeeper in and listened to her prattle on about the venison stew. But she struggled to hear, for Georgie's words rang in her ears.

A whore can charge what she likes if she's prepared to degrade herself.

Tonight, she had prostituted herself to obtain money from her husband.

⇶✦⇷

"BLOODY HELL, PEYTON, must we continue this damned game?"

Meggie's husband sat at the chessboard, brandy glass in hand. The pieces were positioned exactly as they had been at Molineux Manor.

"Didn't you finish that game?" she asked.

"No, dear lady," Mr. Peyton said. "And I've upped the ante. The victor now stands to gain one thousand pounds from the loser. I cannot understand why your husband won't concede."

"Because to surrender is a weakness," Dexter said. "All games must be played out to the bitter end. If you don't have the stomach for the kill, then you've no right to play."

"Are you talking about chess, my friend, or life?"

"I'll leave that for you to decide, Peyton."

"Perhaps I might assist you?" Meggie asked.

Dexter folded his arms while he studied the board.

Mr. Peyton chuckled. "Look at the pieces as long as you like, Hart, but the game's over, and you know it."

"Be quiet!" Dexter growled.

"You see, Mrs. Hart?" Mr. Peyton said. "Your husband isn't entirely perfect, for he has one fatal flaw.

"Which is?" Meggie asked, not daring to look at the expression on Dexter's face.

"He's a sore loser."

Dexter shot to his feet and scraped his chair back.

"Very well," he said. "Consider the money a bonus for all your hard work this past twelve-month."

Mr. Peyton's smile slipped. "Bloody hell," he muttered. "Begging your pardon, ma'am." He nodded to Meggie.

"Is this how you save face, Hart, by saying you intended to give me the money anyway?"

"Perhaps," Dexter said.

"You see, Mrs. Hart?" Mr. Peyton laughed. "See how your husband snatches victory, even in defeat?"

Meggie took the seat Dexter had vacated and studied the chessboard.

"May I play?" she asked.

"You wish to take my place?" Dexter asked.

"Why not? If you're resigned to losing, then there's no harm in it."

"There's little point when you know so little about the game," he replied.

She smiled to herself. This was one secret she'd enjoy revealing.

"Very well," Dexter said. "Do what you can, provided my friend doesn't object."

"Would you use your wife to play on my gallantry in an attempt to win?" Mr. Peyton asked.

"I expect no special favors," Meggie said, "not because of my sex, or..." she glanced at her husband, "...my inferiority of birth."

To his credit, Mr. Peyton blushed. "Forgive me. I meant no disrespect."

She gestured to the pieces. "Then let us proceed."

She moved the white queen across the board.

"Check," she said.

Mr. Peyton shook his head, sympathy in his eyes. "I'm sorry," he said. "I'd like to be kind, but there's one thousand at stake."

"What did I say about not wanting any special concession?" Meggie asked.

"Very well," Mr. Peyton sighed. "Hart, your wife demands fair play." He picked up his knight, moved it to the queen's position, and knocked the queen sideways.

"Knight takes queen."

"Never mind, my dear," Dexter said. "Chess is a complicated game. You made a good effort. Shall I pour you a brandy?"

"No," she said.

"But you always have a brandy at this hour."

"I mean, no, *you* were in an impossible situation." She picked up a bishop and moved it one square along the diagonal.

"Checkmate."

Mr. Peyton leaned forward and studied the board.

"I'll be damned."

Meggie rose to her feet, and the men followed suit.

"I find I'm a little tired," she said. "Would you gentlemen excuse me?"

"Not without explaining what you just did," Mr. Peyton said. "Or did lady luck hand you the victory?"

"I think it was down to my lady wife, rather

than lady luck," Dexter said.

Meggie approached the door, aware of two pairs of eyes following her. When she turned, her husband and his friend both stared at her, lips parted.

"I wonder if you'd be obliging and close your mouths, gentlemen?" she asked. "I find myself reminded of the biology lessons I used to give at the school at Blackwood Heath."

If anything, they parted their lips further.

"Mrs. Preston had a book on wildlife," she explained. "To this day, I remember a beautiful illustration of wide-mouthed frogs."

She dipped a curtsey and exited the room before either man could answer.

As Meggie reached her chamber, she heard a door slam, followed by hurried footsteps, then her husband burst into her chamber.

"Dexter, I…"

He grasped her shoulders and crashed his mouth into hers. She parted her lips, and he slid his tongue in, claiming her. He groaned as he feasted on her, his strong hands holding her firm. Then he pushed her back until she fell onto the bed.

"God forgive me, Meggie, what you do to me!" He fumbled at his necktie and threw it onto the floor, then began to unbutton his shirt. "Oh, to hell with it!"

He fisted his hands in the shirt and ripped it

open, and buttons clattered to the floor. Then he reached for her skirts, and she grasped his wrists.

"Dexter, no."

Raw, primal lust flashed in his eyes, but he stopped.

"Is this not what you want?"

Dear lord, yes, she wanted him! The smoldering gazes he'd cast in her direction over dinner had sent shockwaves of desire through her. When he'd licked the sorbet spoon, devouring her with his eyes, she imagined the feel of his tongue on her flesh and squeezed her thighs together to ease the ache, praying that Mr. Peyton didn't notice her state of arousal.

"Do you want me because I've earned you a thousand pounds?" she asked. "If so, what does that make me?"

"A damned clever woman, "he said, "and the best wife a man could hope for." He reached for her skirts again.

"Do you think me a harlot?"

"God, no, Meggie," he said. "I've wanted to make love to you all evening. Had Peyton not been with us, I'd have swept that sorbet aside, spread you over the table, and feasted on you instead."

Her insides throbbed at the image of him crawling over the dining room table.

He sighed. "How did you know how to win the game?"

"I studied chess at the school," she said. "I learned the moves from one of the books there."

"But what you did tonight wasn't the mere execution of moves. There were very few pieces left, and you moved one of them right into the path of Peyton's knight."

"I sacrificed it," she said. "To force him to move his knight out of the way and weaken his defenses. I learned a long time ago that sacrifice was the key to victory. And, if necessary, you sacrifice your most powerful piece to gain a strategic advantage."

He reached for her hand and lifted it to his lips. His expression had softened into one of compassion—and love.

"Not all sacrifices are justified," he said. "I would never sacrifice my queen, for she is my strength, even though she doesn't know it." He cupped her face and placed a gentle kiss on her lips.

"You are my queen, Meggie," he whispered, "the one piece on my board, which I never wish to be without."

She blinked, and her eyes filmed over with moisture.

"I must yield the spoils to you," he said. "One thousand pounds. Peyton would never forgive me if I kept it for myself, given that it was you who secured the final victory."

One thousand pounds…

The answer to all her problems.

"I should like that," she said. "Would it be mine to spend how I wish?"

"It is a rather large sum."

"I'm thinking of patronizing a charity," she said. "Mrs. Pelham told me about some of her ventures—such as a shelter for disadvantaged widows."

How easily the lie slipped off her tongue! Was this what happened when one had a secret? A small lie was required to conceal it, then a second lie to hide the first—then lie after lie, until the perpetrator had forgotten the truth.

"How like you, to think of others!" Dexter said.

He traced a line across the front of her gown, then dipped his finger into the valley between her breasts.

"Now…where were we?"

She lay back and lifted her skirts. His smile broadened as she parted her legs, and he unbuttoned his breeches.

Her release came as soon as he entered inside her, the pleasure magnifying with each powerful thrust. At the moment of his dissolution, he cried out her name and collapsed on top of her, his movement growing weaker until he buried his head in her shoulder and grew still. Before he fell asleep, she heard a faint whisper.

"I love you, Meggie."

She cradled his head in her arms, fighting back the tears. She had won his heart, but at what cost? She'd deceived him and parted her legs for cash.

She was no better than a harlot, and if he ever discovered the truth, she'd lose his love forever.

Chapter Thirty-One

DEXTER LOOKED UP at the knock on the door.

"What is it?"

A timid-looking face appeared.

"Come in," he said. "I like to know my staff have bodies as well as heads."

The clerk shuffled in. "There's a gentleman to see you."

"Does he have an appointment?"

"N-no."

"Tell him to make one," Dexter said. "Can't you see I'm busy—what's your name?"

"Jenkins, sir. He said he has a large deposit to make and insists on seeing you personally."

"How large?"

"He wouldn't say, but he said the meeting would be to your advantage."

Dexter sighed. "Let him in."

Jenkins bowed and disappeared, closing the door behind him.

Imbecile! A few months ago, Dexter would have dismissed him on the spot. What the blazes was happening to him?

His wife, that's what. She'd taught him that there was no shame in a little kindness.

The door opened again, and a man stepped inside.

Dexter looked up. "You!" he cried.

He was more finely dressed than when Dexter had last seen him. He wore a gentleman's suit, not the livery of a footman of Alderley Hall. But he'd recognize that face anywhere—the finely chiseled lines and the cold gray eyes.

The man gestured to the chair opposite the desk. "May I?"

Without waiting for a reply, he drew back the chair and sat, leaning back and crossing his legs with a presence at nonchalance.

George Hanson.

George bloody Hanson, the reprobate who'd seduced Daisy, then abandoned her when he'd realized Dexter wasn't going to give him any money.

"What do you want, Hanson?"

"Didn't your man tell you? I wish to make a deposit."

"I hardly think *you* have sufficient funds to

make it worth my while," Dexter said. "I suggest you leave before I throw you out."

Hanson smiled, and Dexter's fists itched to smash that smug grin off his face. He rose to his feet and reached for the man's collar.

"Wait!" Hanson cried. "Will a thousand pounds be sufficient?"

"Where the devil did you get such a sum from?" Dexter sneered. "Did you steal it?"

"It was a most generous gift."

"Do you think I care?" Dexter asked. "After what you did to my sister? I wouldn't want your filthy money tainting my bank, however much you have."

"Your sister?" Hanson laughed. "This has nothing to do with your sister."

"Then, get out."

"I'm here about your wife."

Dexter froze. "My wife?"

Hanson folded his arms and gave him a triumphant smile. "Old habits die hard," he said. "She was a little too quick to give me what I wanted."

He picked up Dexter's inkpot—cut crystal set in gold.

"May I have this?" He slipped it into his pocket. "Most generous. I'll wager you'll be more inclined to give me what I want. Now you're rubbing shoulders with the high and mighty. For you have further to fall."

Dexter gritted his teeth, swallowing the red-hot ball of fury in his throat.

"What is my wife to you?"

"My lady patroness," Hanson said smoothly. "She opened her legs even faster than your sister."

"It was you?" Dexter asked. "Dear God! What possessed you to ruin her? Did you expect payment from her father as you did from me?"

"That old skinflint!" Hanson scoffed. "But I'm sure you're prepared to be generous. A man can disown his by-blow, but it's more difficult for a prominent banker to deny the existence of his wife."

"You think I didn't know that my wife lay with another man?"

"Men," Hanson said. "I wasn't the first. Doubtless, you suffered the same disappointment on your wedding night that I experienced when she offered herself to me. I'm sure we both know when we're bedding a virgin"

"You filthy bastard!" Dexter curled his hands into fists.

"Think about it, Hart," Hanson said. "What on earth possessed a miser such as Alderley to pay for her upkeep? A woman like her can make a fortune on her back."

Dexter reached out and grasped the man's collar. "Insult my wife again, and I'll kill you!"

"Did she tell you about her child?"

Dexter's blood froze. "You lie."

"Never told you that, did she?" Hanson grinned. "She said it was mine, but who knows? I heard she spread her legs for half the population of Blackwood Heath."

The spring snapped. With a roar, Dexter slammed his fist into Hanson's leering face. Then he grabbed him by his lapels and frog marched him out of the office and down the stairs.

The footman in the hall barely turned a hair as he opened the doors. Dexter propelled Hanson onto the street with a push, where he fell in a heap on the pavement.

"Come back here, Hanson, and I'll have you shot!"

"What about the money?"

"Keep the bloody money," Dexter said. "You've lied, seduced, and blackmailed your way to it. But it won't make you happy. Not for a man like you. For that, I pity you."

"And I, you," Hanson said. "For you'll never be happy. Not with *her*."

"Get rid of him," Dexter told the footman. "If he comes again, you're at liberty to use force."

"Very good, sir."

"And then, tell Mr. Peyton to see to things here. I'm leaving early."

"Shall I tell him where you've gone, sir?"

Dexter clenched his hands, but it did nothing to lessen the pain in his heart.

Neither did it obliterate the fact that Meggie had lied to him—had betrayed him.

"Tell him I've gone home," he said. "There's something I need to discuss with my wife."

Chapter Thirty-Two

WHEN MEGGIE RETURNED to the house, it was unusually quiet. There should have been more activity upstairs, yet none of the first-floor windows showed any signs of light.

Perhaps Dexter was working late at the bank or dining at his club.

Her feet ached. It would be good to sit after a long day's volunteering with Anne, and with Dexter out of the house, she could allow herself some liberties and take a footbath.

She smiled at the prospect of sitting in the kitchen with her feet in a tub of hot water, sprinkled with lavender, one of Mrs. Preston's remedies.

The door opened as she ascended the front steps, cradling Titan in her arms.

"Ah, Charles," she said. "Would you ask Mrs.

Draper to arrange a footbath? In the parlor this time, if my husband's out."

"The master's at home," the footman said. "He wishes to see you in the study."

"Very good," she said. "Tell him I'll see him once I've settled Titan in his basket."

"I'm to take you to him immediately, ma'am."

"Charles?" A ripple of apprehension threaded through her. "Is anything wrong?"

He gestured toward the study. "If you please."

The study door was ajar as if Dexter were listening for her return. A solitary candle flickered on the desk in the center of the room. He sat behind it, his face illuminated by the flame.

"Husband?"

He reached forward and picked up a beveled glass, the light catching the pattern etched into the crystal.

She moved closer. "Dexter?"

"Leave us, Charles," he said quietly. "Close the door behind you."

After the footman left, Dexter gestured toward the chair in front of the desk, and she sat.

"Are you going to tell me what's going on?"

"I want to discuss the money."

"Is this…" she hesitated, "…about Daisy?"

"No."

"Then what is it about?"

He lifted the glass slowly and took a sip. His silent control unnerved her more than his raised voice.

"I was rather hoping you'd tell me."

"Forgive me, Dexter. I don't know…"

He held up his hand, and her voice died in her throat.

"I had a visitor today," he said.

"At the bank?"

"A man with one thousand pounds to invest."

Icy fingers caressed the back of her neck. "Oh?"

"Is that not a coincidence? The same sum you obtained from me three nights ago?"

"I'm sure it's not an uncommon sum to invest."

"Are we going to continue this charade all evening?" he asked. "Please do not insult my intelligence by feigning ignorance. My visitor, as I'm sure you're aware, was a Mr. George Hanson."

She curled her fingers around the arms of the chair.

"Do you have nothing to say?"

"It's not what you think," she said.

He frowned. "What *do* I think?"

"That I've been unfaithful."

He remained motionless, staring at her as if trying to read her thoughts. Then he set the glass aside in a slow, deliberate gesture.

"Untruthful, at least," he said.

"I-I thought he'd gone."

"Gone?"

"He said that once he had the money, he wouldn't tell..." She broke off, her cheeks flaming.

"Let me guess," Dexter said. "He promised to leave you alone, and you believed him. Can't you see that if you pay a man like that to hide your sins, there's no guarantee he'll desist?"

"You knew when we married that I wasn't..."

"That you weren't a maiden? If I recall, I knew no such thing. I had to discover it for myself." He tapped his finger on the desk. "And now I find you continued to deceive me, even after we pledged to be honest with each other."

She lowered her gaze, unable to look at the disappointment in his eyes. The ticking of the clock grew louder. Eventually, he broke the silence.

"Were you never going to tell me about the brat?"

She drew in a sharp breath.

"Deny it if you dare."

Meggie shook her head. "I cannot."

"That bastard Hanson was the man who ruined my sister. You gave birth to his child!"

She shrank back under the force of his anger,

and he raked his hand through his hair—hair she knew to be soft and silken, hair she loved the feel of under her fingers.

"I knew you were keeping a secret from me, Margaret," he said.

"You did?"

"Aye, but, fool that I am, I'd assumed you were with child. *My* child that is, not another's."

Her heart shuddered. "Dexter, surely you're not accusing me of…"

She was interrupted by three sharp knocks on the door.

"For fuck's sake!" he roared. "Am I to be plagued by everyone today?"

The door opened, and Charles's face appeared, pale with fear.

"Mr. Peyton's here to see you, sir," he said.

"Can't you see I'm busy?"

"He insisted." The footman flinched as if expecting a blow. "He said there are several documents requiring your signature, which were due to be issued today."

Dexter swore.

"Bloody Hanson! Not content with ruining my wife, his timewasting threatens to ruin my business."

The footman glanced at Meggie and widened his eyes.

Dexter rose to his feet. "Tell Peyton I'll see him in the parlor," he said. "As for you," he turned to Meggie, "Stay in this room until I return. I'll deal with you later."

He ushered the footman out of the study and slammed the door behind him.

I'll deal with you later…

He'd used those same words the day he had Milly thrashed for swimming in the lake.

Anger replaced fear. How dare he threaten her! Did he think to punish her as he saw fit if she did anything he happened to disapprove of?

Yes, he did. And the law was on his side. He could do whatever he wanted with her. And nobody would stop him.

But, worse than the fear of punishment was the knowledge that she'd lost her husband's trust.

And his love.

She rose from her seat and opened the study door. Charles was nowhere to be seen. Raised voices came from the door across the way. This was her chance. She tiptoed across the hallway, pulled open the main doors, and ran out into the street.

THE SUN HAD disappeared, and Meggie increased the pace to warm her limbs. She should have taken her shawl, but her instincts had told her to leave the house as soon as possible.

After a while, she heard footsteps from behind, and she stepped up the pace. At the end of the street, she turned and headed toward Hyde Park. The footsteps drew closer, and a ripple of fear threaded through her.

Someone was in pursuit.

She turned into a side street and broke into a run, then slammed into a wall of muscle.

Two hands grasped her arms, and she wrinkled her nose at the stench of cologne.

"Steady on, lover! Your eagerness is showing," a familiar voice said.

She looked up into George Hanson's eyes. With a cry, she struggled to break free.

"Kicked you out already, Megs?"

"Leave me alone!" she cried.

"Oh, Megs," he said. "I thought we'd renewed our friendship."

"You were never my friend," she said. "But you've made one fatal mistake."

"Which is?"

"You've killed the goose, George," she snarled. "I don't care who else you tell, for you've told the one person who matters to me. And my husband won't care enough to buy your silence."

He tightened his grip, and she winced.

"Unhand me," she said. "Now."

"You heard the lady," a new voice said.

George's eyes widened, a hint of fear in their expression.

Meggie turned to face the newcomer.

Tall, with thick black hair, he wore a dark cloak capable of melting into the shadows. A mask concealed the upper half of his face.

His shadow, cast by the moonlight, stretched across the pavement. "Unhand her," he said, "or you'll suffer the consequences of assaulting a lady."

"Lady!" George scoffed, "she's nothing but a…ow!" He reeled back as the newcomer slammed his fist into his face.

"Leave," he said. "Now. If I see you in London again, I'll shoot you."

"You wouldn't dare," George said. "I'd have you arrested."

"A difficult accomplishment from beyond the grave, but you're welcome to try."

George's eyes widened, and, like all bullies, he quaked in the presence of a stronger opponent. He turned and fled.

"Major Hart, what are you doing here?" Meggie asked.

"I could ask you the same thing," Devon Hart replied. "Why are you on the streets at this hour, and why are you buying that man's silence?"

She hesitated. His eyes showed compassion, and she believed a loyal heart beat in his chest. But blood ties ran deep. Loyalty to his brother would triumph over any compassion for her.

She shook her head. "I can't tell you that," she said. "I must go."

"Has my brother already driven you away?"

She wiped away the tear which had splashed, unchecked, on her cheek, and a warm hand clasped hers.

"Forgive me, sister, I can see you're distressed," he said. "You're not obliged to tell me anything. Shall I take you home? Dex will be worried."

"I can't go back."

He sighed. "What's my brother done now?"

"He's done nothing," she said, her voice cracking. "It was me."

"A sweet creature like yourself can't have done anything my brother would disapprove of," he said. Why don't I take you home and knock some reason into his addled brain?"

"I deceived him," she said. "I lied to him, and he'll never forgive me."

He glanced along the street, but George was long gone.

"I take it the rather handsome man you were grappling with has something to do with it. Have you been unfaithful to Dex?"

"No!" she cried. "I'd never…" She broke off and shook her head. "It happened before I married your brother."

"And you kept it a secret?" He let out a curse. "Dex bloody *hates* secrets."

"N-no, he knows I wasn't..."

"He knows you weren't a maiden?" His expression softened. "He would have realized as soon as..." he hesitated, "...unless you and Dex never..." He shook his head. "I always thought he was a master at bedsport."

Her cheeks heated with embarrassment. "He found out the day we married."

"That was months ago!" he cried. "Bloody hell, I knew Dex bore a grudge, but he seemed happy with you when I last saw him."

"He was," she said, "until today—when he discovered I had George's child and concealed it from him."

She looked away, unable to bear his disappointment. Strong arms pulled her into an embrace.

"Oh, Margaret!" he cried. "You ran away rather than face him?"

"You don't understand!" she cried. "The last time I saw him that angry, he had a young girl thrashed! He told me he wanted nothing from me but honesty—and I deceived him. But I had no choice. He's said several times that no man should be expected to forgive such a woman who'd borne another man's bastard. I had to keep it from him."

Devon cursed. "Secrets have a way of coming out," he said. "You should have told him. Yes, he would have been angry, for he has a vile temper when he doesn't get his way, but he would have valued your honesty."

"You didn't see him," she said. "I thought he was going to beat me."

"My brother may be many things, Margaret, but he'd never take his hand to you. Why don't I take you home and speak to him? He won't touch you with me there."

"And when you're gone?" She shook her head. "I can't go back."

"Then come home with me," he said. "There's plenty of room at my lodgings. At least you'll be safe."

"I wouldn't want to cause trouble between you," she said. "He might look for me there."

"You can't wander the streets."

"I can return home to Blackwood Heath."

"You'll not find a coach at this hour."

"Perhaps Mrs. Pelham would take me in until tomorrow." She nodded to herself. "Yes, Anne will understand. She's my friend, and her first husband was unkind to her. She told me how he struck her when she spilled his brandy."

"Has Dexter been unkind to you?"

No. He hadn't. Gruff and brooding, perhaps, but not unkind. Every action he took had been for her benefit. He wasn't a man of pretty speeches and overt gallantry—but that didn't mean he loved her any less.

Had loved her.

Devon let out a sigh. "Against my better judgment, I'll take you to your friend, if only to ensure your safety. But my brother will find you eventually. When he sets his mind on something, he won't stop until he gets it."

"Promise me you won't tell him where I am," she said.

"You have my word," he said. "And we Harts always keep our promises."

His words pricked at her conscience and, as if he read her mind, he squeezed her hand. "He'll come round. I'm sure of it. Give him a chance."

Why did he sound as if he were trying to convince himself rather than her?

"MARGARET! MY DEAR, whatever's the matter?"

Anne Pelham ushered Meggie inside the townhouse. "Tippett, go to the kitchen and ask Mrs. Johns for some hot cocoa. Right away!"

The footman, who'd been staring at Meggie's disheveled form, bowed and disappeared.

Anne led Meggie upstairs and into a small parlor. An embroidery frame and half-empty glass of milk sat on the table beside the fireplace, and a small dog snored in the basket on the floor.

"Oh, Anne, forgive me!" Meggie cried. "I've disturbed your evening."

"It doesn't mean I find the disturbance un-welcome," Anne said. "Though I confess, I'm surprised at seeing you again so soon after we parted company earlier today."

Mr. Pelham appeared in the doorway. "I thought I heard voices," he said. He looked at Meggie, and his eyes widened. "Is everything all right?"

Meggie jumped to her feet. "I-I'm sorry," she stammered. "I should go."

"You'll do nothing of the sort," Anne said. "Harold, leave us."

"But…"

"Shoo!" she cried, waving her hands at him.

He rolled his eyes, then disappeared. Anne smiled indulgently. "He may be the master of the house, but, unlike most husbands, he has the good sense to know when he's not wanted."

Meggie bit her lip, and tears stung her eyes.

"Meggie!" Anne cried, taking her hands. "Whatever's the matter? You were so happy earlier today."

Her face paled. "Has something happened to Mr. Hart?"

"N-no, Dexter's well."

"Does he know you're here?"

"No!"

Anne's eyes widened.

"Forgive me," Meggie said. "I-I'd rather he didn't know."

"Whatever for? Has he done something?"

"It's what I did," Meggie said. "He's so angry. He…" Meggie caught her breath, and Anne drew her into her arms. "Don't say any more," she whispered. "There's plenty of time to talk once you've had your cocoa."

Her friend's gentle kindness was more than Meggie could bear. Anne stroked her hair, uttering soothing words as tears stung Meggie's eyes.

After the footman arrived with the cocoa, Anne drew up a chair, settled Meggie into it, and placed a shawl round her shoulders. Then she settled into her chair and resumed her embroidery. The sound of the needle pushing in and out of the frame, together with the gentle crackling of the fire, soothed Meggie's distress, together with the sweet aroma of the cocoa.

Meggie lifted the cup to her lips. Steam swirled above the sweet, brown liquid, and she detected a whiff of brandy. She took a sip, then relaxed back, cradling the cup in her hands.

Footsteps approached, and Anne rushed to the door. Meggie closed her eyes, taking in the crackle of the fire as she heard whispers.

"Harold! What did I tell you?"

"Is Mrs. Hart all right?"

The voices lowered to a murmur of whispers, then Meggie heard the door close, and a rush of silk as Anne resumed her seat.

"It seems Harold needs another lesson in knowing when his presence is not required," she said.

Meggie sat up. "What did he want?"

"That doesn't matter," Anne said. "He's promised to leave us in peace for the rest of the evening." She looked up from her embroidery and focused her gaze on Meggie.

"You can speak freely here," she said. She resumed her attention on her needle.

"Or not," she continued, "as you prefer. But I'll say that any reasonable man would understand that an innocent woman can be blamed for events that are out of her control."

"And you think my husband a reasonable man?" Meggie asked.

"My dear," Anne said. "Men—your husband in particular—have no conception of how they appear to others when they're angry. But your husband is a man of honor. He may not be the most personable man of my acquaintance, but he's a rational creature, driven by reason, not emotion."

"What of his feud with my father?" Meggie asked. "That was driven by vengeance, not reason."

"You think your husband wishes to seek vengeance on you?" Anne asked. "Did you set out to hurt him?"

"No."

"Do you harbor hatred for him?"

Meggie shook her head. "I love him."

"Then tell him," Anne said. "He has no reason to doubt your honesty."

Meggie looked away.

"The best thing you can do is talk to him," Anne continued. "You'll have to do the talking. He's a man of action, not words. But there's nothing you can have done that he won't forgive."

"I-I can't," Meggie said. "Not now."

"You needn't worry about your husband tonight," Anne said, "but you cannot avoid him forever."

Chapter Thirty-Three

WHERE THE BLOODY hell was she?

There was no sign of Meggie in the study. Doubtless, she'd seen fit to hide in her chamber.

The first rush of fury had been tempered by the terrified look on his wife's face. In truth, his anger was directed at that bastard Hanson. How could one man have caused such ruination? His beloved sister, and his equally beloved wife, had been duped into falling in love with that scoundrel.

With Daisy, Hanson had wanted to get his hands on Dexter's fortune. Most likely, with Meggie, Hanson had been after Alderley's.

As for the child…

It took two to make a child. Why, then, should his wife feel the need to conceal it from him? She must have known he'd understand.

Or would she?

He thought back to the day he'd explained Daisy's history. His relief that she'd not fallen pregnant had stemmed from his hatred of Hanson, not out of any disgust at what Daisy had done. Yet, his harsh words to Daisy had driven her away.

And now he'd done the same to Meggie.

"Charles!" he roared. "Mrs. Draper!"

Hurried footsteps approached as the footman and housekeeper arrived.

"Have you seen your mistress?"

"Is she not in the study, where you ordered her to remain?" the footman asked.

Mrs. Draper gave him a sharp nudge.

"Begging your pardon, sir," Charles said, lowering his gaze.

Christ—were the staff afraid of him also?"

"She must be in her chamber," Dexter said. "Mrs. Draper, will you fetch her for me?

"Very good, sir."

"And tell her there's no cause for concern."

The housekeeper exchanged a glance with the footman before bobbing a curtsey and disappearing upstairs.

Five minutes later, she'd not returned.

"Go after her, Charles," Dexter said, crossly.

The footman disappeared after the housekeeper.

When they returned, Meggie was not with them.

"Is my wife indisposed?" Deter asked. "Or, perhaps…" he swallowed his pride, "…she doesn't wish to see me?"

"She's not there."

"Where the devil is she?"

"She's not in the house, sir."

"Don't be ridiculous!"

"He speaks the truth," Mrs. Draper said. "We've searched everywhere." She glanced at the door. "She must have gone out."

"Why the devil would she do that?"

The servants exchanged glances.

His wife—his little Meggie—had run off into the night.

A small ball of fur appeared at the top of the stairs.

"Titan!" Mrs. Draper said. "Where's your mistress?"

The dog trotted down the stairs, then stopped at Dexter's feet and looked up with wide brown eyes.

"Where is she, Titan?" he asked.

The animal whined. Dexter stooped to pick him up, and the animal's lip curled in a snarl.

"Come here, boy." Dexter held out his hand. With a sharp bark, the dog gave him a nip.

"Ouch!" Dexter recoiled. He looked down to see two puncture wounds on his hand. A droplet of blood swelled on his finger.

"Shit!" he cursed. "Godforsaken animal!"

The footman picked up the little dog and cradled him defensively as if expecting Dexter to thrash the creature.

"Dear God, Charles!" he cried. "Stay where you are. What sort of man do you think I am?"

He grimaced. Bloody hell, that bite stung!

"Titan meant no harm, Mr. Hart, sir," the footman said. "All animals bite when frightened."

Or they flee.

What had Devon said?

You've driven all of us away. Don't make the same mistake with your wife.

Dexter had made that mistake. Rather than endure the wrath of a judgmental, bad-tempered husband, she'd chosen the dark of the night and the streets of London.

"Charles," he said. "Fetch my coat."

WHERE WOULD HE even begin to look for her? She liked exploring Hyde Park—she'd often spoken of taking her dog there. But would she go alone?

Halfway down the street, a familiar figure loomed out of the darkness. Clad in a black cloak and living in the shadows, his brother looked every bit the mythical beast.

"Devon!" he cried. "Have you seen my wife?"

"Why on earth would I have seen her?"

Devon's voice held more than the usual note of challenge.

"Do you know where she is?"

"What makes you think that?" Devon sneered. "Perhaps she's come to realize what sort of man you are."

"And what sort of man am I?"

"Bad-tempered, uncongenial, and with an unhealthy obsession with decorum to the detriment of kindness or compassion."

"Bloody hell, Devon, you *do* know where she is!" Dexter fisted his hands. "Tell me what you've done."

"*I've* done nothing."

"Don't play games with me!" Dexter cried. "Where is she?"

His voice caught in his throat, and the challenge in his brother's eyes died. Devon had always been the physically stronger of the two brothers. But his scarred, gruff exterior hid a gentle soul.

Perhaps Devon should have married Meggie instead. With his kind heart, he'd never have broken hers. But Devon pined for another—a woman he could never have.

"Go home, Dex," he said. "Your wife is safe."

"Is she at your lodgings?"

"She refused my offer of sanctuary," Devon said. He let out a mirthless laugh. "She thought you'd seek retribution if you knew I'd helped her. She knows you well."

Dexter itched to wipe the sneer off his brother's face.

"Where is she!" he roared.

"Losing your temper won't win her back," Devon said. "Leave her be until you've calmed down unless you want to lose her."

"I must speak with her," Dexter said. "She's my wife."

"Think of her needs, not yours," Devon placed a hand on Dexter's shoulder and squeezed it.

"Trust me, brother," he said. "Go home."

Devon turned his back and loped off down the road, as silent as a phantom. In a matter of moments, he'd disappeared into the shadows.

Dexter thrust his hands into his pockets. It was bloody freezing. He turned round and made his way back to the house.

"I say, Hart!" a familiar voice cried.

Was the whole world abroad tonight?

Harold Pelham was running toward him. "There you are!" he cried. "I've just been to see you."

"About what?"

"Your wife." He clutched onto Dexter's shoulder and bent over, gasping for air. "I'm going to be in so much trouble."

"Dear God!" Dexter cried. "Is she hurt?"

"N-no..." Pelham drew in a deep breath. "I've not run that fast in years..."

"Pelham, are you all right?"

"Not all of us have your physique," Pelham said. "I ran all the way here. Your housekeeper thought I was going to expire on your floor."

"What the devil's going on?" Dexter asked.

"Your wife's safe."

Thank the Lord!

"Why do you look so distressed?" Dexter asked.

Pelham grimaced. "Because I'm going to get my ballocks chewed off for this. Anne swore me to secrecy."

"Over what?"

"Your wife's with us," he said. "I pray Anne will forgive me, but you have a right to know."

"Then I must go to her."

A hand clasped his arm.

"Don't go in like a charging bull, Hart, or I'll regret telling you."

"Then why *did* you tell me?" Dexter sneered. "To keep your banker sweet?"

"You can be an utter arse sometimes, Hart," Pelham said. "I'm telling you because you're my friend."

"Has she told you what happened?"

"She was very distressed when I saw her, but

my Anne will coax the truth out of her with kindness. You should try it."

Dexter's cheeks warmed with the notion of the gentle Mrs. Pelham knowing his business.

"Have you done something to be ashamed of?" Pelham asked.

When Dexter didn't respond, his friend patted him on the shoulder.

"I'd advise you to take the gentle approach," he said. "It's better to use a sweet bait to snare the woman you love."

"Love?"

Pelham laughed. "You may lack self-awareness, but the rest of us can see that which you're blind to."

"You returned to London a changed man," he said. "The only difference was that you had that sweet woman by your side. For the first time, I saw you look upon another human being with tenderness. If that's not evidence enough, then the fear in your eyes tonight, followed by the relief when you realized she was safe, would convince even the most hardened cynic of how deeply you love your wife."

"Then what do you suggest?" Dexter asked.

"Come back with me now and talk to her," Pelham said. "You'll be doing me a favor, for I'll need someone to share the brunt of Anne's anger."

"Your wife can curse me all she likes," Dexter

said, "as long as she releases my wife back into my care."

"I wish you luck, my friend," Pelham said. "I wish us *both* luck."

Chapter Thirty-Four

"ANOTHER COCOA, MEGGIE, dear?"

Meggie shook her head and stroked the pug on her lap.

"Lady Guinevere has taken a liking to you," Anne said. "Titan looks a lot like her," she continued, setting her embroidery aside. "He has a patch of white fur under his chin, just there…"

She leaned over to tickle the pug's chin.

"Who's mama's good girl, then?" The dog gave a little yap, and Anne laughed. "All right, you can have a treat, for you've taken good care of my friend tonight." She glanced at the clock over the fireplace. "It's getting late."

"Would you rather I left?" Meggie asked. "I have no wish to impose or cause trouble between you and Mr. Pelham."

"Harold does what I tell him," Anne said.

"But I think it's time to retire." She took Meggie's hand. "Things will look better in the morning."

The door opened, and Harold Pelham appeared.

Anne rose to her feet. "Is all well, my love?" she asked. "You look out of sorts."

That he did, hair disheveled, face flushed, his expression could almost be described as guilty.

A shadow moved behind him, and Anne recoiled.

"Harold! What have you done?"

The shadow moved forward, morphing into the shape of a man.

Dexter…

Meggie let out a cry and shot to her feet. Lady Guinevere jumped to the floor with a bark of protest.

As he advanced on her, his body seemed to fill the room. Meggie backed toward the wall, reaching behind her. Her fingers curled round a candlestick, and she picked it up, drawing comfort from its solidity.

He glanced at the candlestick, and his jaw bulged as if he ground his teeth, then his dark gaze focused, unblinking on her.

"Harold!" Anne cried. "What on earth possessed you to betray me?"

"Forgive me, Anne," Mr. Pelham replied, "but whatever's happened between Hart and his wife, we've no right to interfere."

"I promised my friend!" Anne cried. "She trusted me. She values truth and honesty, and you've let her down."

Meggie looked away, no longer able to meet her husband's gaze.

"What about *my* friend?" Mr. Pelham asked. "I did what I thought was best, and I'd do it again."

"Please," Meggie pleaded. "Don't fight on my account."

"Come with me, Anne," Mr. Pelham said. "Let Hart deal with it."

"Harold, I…"

"Mrs. Hart will be quite safe. Isn't that right, my friend?"

Dexter nodded, his gaze fixed on Meggie.

Anne addressed Meggie's husband. "Lay a finger on her, and you'll answer to me," she said. "I care nothing for what the law says."

"Understood," Dexter said, his voice a low growl.

He waited until they were alone, then he gestured to a chair.

"Will you sit?"

Meggie made no move.

"If you believe you're in danger in my presence, Margaret, then sitting or standing, it makes no difference."

"I'm glad you've clarified that," she said, finding her courage. She tightened her grip on the candlestick and sat.

"May I sit, also?"

"Do you need my permission?"

"Yes," he said. "I do."

She nodded, and he sat. He said nothing, but her cheeks warmed under his scrutiny.

At length, he spoke. "Will you tell me your history?"

"Dexter, I-I'm sorry," she said.

He raised his hand. "No, Meggie," he said. "I asked for your history, not an apology. Will you tell me the truth?"

She lowered her gaze to the candlestick and ran her fingertips along the cold, smooth metal, tracing the pattern etched into the brass.

"About the child," he prompted.

The long-buried memory resurfaced—pain she'd spent eight years trying to bury in the darkest corners of her mind.

"Meggie?"

She gripped the candlestick, taking comfort from its solidity.

"I grew up on the Alderley estate," she said, "with the gamekeeper, Mr. Arnold, and his wife. I always wondered why the man from the big house visited me, though he never seemed to like me. But I always had to put on my best dress when he came."

"Did you know he was your father?" Dexter asked.

"Not at first," she said. "I dreaded his visits. One day I ran away before he visited, but Mr. Arnold found me and gave me a thrashing."

She shifted in her seat. Dexter maintained his gaze on her, and she looked away, unable to look into his clear blue eyes.

"When the weather was bad, he came in the carriage and brought a footman with him. Compared to the old man who hated me, Georgie made me laugh. He slipped me a note one visit, then we started meeting in secret." She blinked back tears. "He was the first person to show me kindness, to treat me like I was *someone*—not an inconvenience to be hidden away. I fell in love with him, and I believed he loved me."

She wiped her eyes with the back of her hand. "I thought he wanted to marry me, but after I..." she hesitated, "...after I gave myself to him, he never visited me again."

"Did he not accompany Alderley?"

"No," she said. "I looked forward to every visit, praying Georgie would come. But he didn't. Then..." she swallowed and closed her eyes, "...when I began to feel sick, I realized I was pregnant. I went to the big house to find Georgie."

"And did you?"

"Yes," she whispered. "He said the child could be anybody's, and he threw me out. Then, the next day, he came."

"George?"

"No, my father." She cringed at the memory. "I thought he was going to kill me! Georgie had gone to see him, asking for money."

"And—the child?" Dexter asked.

She closed her eyes, searching for the memory, but the years had eroded the image of her child's sweet face from her mind.

"I called him Billy," she said. "I held him in my arms the day he was born, and for a brief moment, nothing else in the world mattered. There was only him. And me."

"Where is he?"

Meggie lifted her head and met her husband's gaze. "He died," she said, "so you needn't be concerned about my bastard child disgracing your good name. He can't shame you from beyond the grave, can he?"

He shook his head. "Meggie, I'd never say such a thing."

"Wouldn't you?"

This time it was he who lowered his gaze.

"Alderley came and took my baby," she said. "He said I was a whore, unfit to look after the child, and if I defied him, he'd send me to an asylum."

She bit her lip, taking comfort from the physical pain. "I never saw my Billy again," she said. "Shortly after Alderley took him, he sent me to

Blackwood Heath. A month after I arrived, he came to tell me Billy had died of the ague. I asked him if I could visit his grave, but he refused. My son had been placed in a pauper's grave. He said it was the best place for a shameful secret."

Dexter cursed. He rose to his feet, and his powerful frame towered over her.

"How old were you when it happened, Meggie?"

"I was fifteen."

"Dear God!"

"I thought I loved Georgie," she said. "I would never have…given myself to him if I hadn't. I-I should have told you the day of our wedding, but neither of us wanted this marriage, and you were already so angry! Then, when you said about Daisy, about how no reasonable man would accept a woman who'd had another man's child…"

She shook her head. "My child died," she said. "What good would come of telling you about him? You just would have been one more person who wished he'd never been born."

His hand clasped hers, and he caressed her skin with his thumb.

"Do *you* wish he'd never been born, Meggie?"

"No!" she cried. "I wish he'd lived."

"Oh, Meggie," he said, "I wish you'd trusted me enough to tell me."

"Why would I?" she asked. "You were so

angry."

"Not at you, my love. I'm angry at that bastard Hanson and myself. I haven't done enough to win your trust. But, if you permit me now, I'll take the first step."

He lowered himself onto one knee.

"Will you come home, Meggie?"

"I-I don't know."

"Meggie, you did nothing wrong. You were a child who was taken advantage of. As for your concealing the truth from me—*I* am to blame for that. But come home with me now, and I'll do everything I can to atone—to prove how much I love you."

He glanced at the brass implement in her hand.

"You can hit me with that if it makes you feel better."

She lifted the candlestick and inspected it. He straightened and opened his arms in invitation.

"Go on," he said. "It's the least I deserve."

"You'd let me *hit* you?"

"You may do anything you wish if it makes you happy."

She struggled to stifle a smile, and his eyes lit up. "Ah!" he cried. "The idea appeals. And, as you can see, Mrs. Pelham's carpet is a lovely red color, so you can beat me to a pulp with that glimstick without upsetting the décor."

She loosened her grip on the candlestick,

which fell to the floor, and he covered her hand, intertwining his fingers with hers.

"I've always looked down on those who are afraid," he said, "for I believed that to show fear is a weakness. But, tonight, when I thought I'd lost you…" He shook his head. "I'd never imagined what it would be like to be so afraid that you cannot breathe, that your body feels like a thousand daggers are piercing it. And the shame that I was the reason for your flight."

He closed his eyes, and his body shuddered as he drew breath. When he opened them again, they glistened with moisture.

"Come home, Meggie," he whispered, "for I cannot live without you."

She curled her fingers round his. "Yes," she said. "I'll come home."

THE NEXT MORNING, Meggie woke, safe and warm in her husband's arms. Last night he'd taken her home in the Pelhams' carriage and carried her upstairs, not stopping until they reached her chamber. He'd slipped in beside her and held her chastely in his arms while she drifted into sleep.

Some of her burdens had lessened—as if having spoken of it, she'd peeled off a layer of pain.

"Good morning, my love." His face swam into view, and he rolled her over and placed a kiss on her lips.

"Did you sleep well?" He smiled. "Judging by the amount of Pelham's brandy you consumed, I'm not surprised."

"If I recall, you partook of plenty yourself."

"It was only proper to accept his hospitality after imposing on him," he replied. "Besides, his terrier of a wife needed reassurance that I wasn't going to carry you home over my shoulder and tie you to this bed."

A wicked grin spread across his face. "Of course," he said, "I'm still disposed to consider it if you ask nicely. I can put my neckties to good use."

A pulse of longing throbbed deep in her center, and he gave her a knowing smile.

"We can explore that idea another time," he said. "But for now, I should rise. I can hear James scratching about next door. He'll be wondering what I did with my clothes."

He sat up.

"So that's why I was so warm!" she exclaimed.

Her husband was fully clothed, and so was she.

"You fell asleep in my arms," he said, "and I didn't want to wake you."

"But your clothes, Dexter! They're all creased."

"Yes," he said, rolling his eyes. "James will admonish me for taking such poor care of my jacket. Apparently, creases are the devil of a job to smooth out on this material. Still, it'll keep his mind off other things, such as chasing young Francine about."

"Francine will be kept equally busy," Meggie said. "I have a tear in my dress."

"She'll think I've been ravishing you in the drawing room again."

"Dexter!" She slapped his arm, and he pursed his lips in mock hurt.

He climbed out of bed and crossed the floor to pick up his boots, which he'd kicked off last night. She rolled onto her side and watched. Though he was fully clothed, she knew what every inch of his skin looked like under those tight-fitting breeches.

Facing her, he crouched to pick up his boots, giving her full view of his taut thighs and the bulge in his breeches. He looked up and winked, and she blushed.

"Much as I wish to climb back into that bed," he said, "I'm afraid I must be going."

"Are you going to the bank today?" she asked.

He looked away.

"No," he said. "I have another errand I must

accomplish."

"Will it take long?"

"I don't know," he said. "A few days at most. I can't say any more."

"A few days?"

"I'll be back as soon as I can."

"Dexter…"

He silenced her with his lips, claiming her mouth in a soft kiss. Then he dipped his tongue inside her mouth in a slow, sensual dance. A groan bubbled in her throat, and he deepened the kiss. She buried her hands in his hair, running her fingers through his thick locks while he devoured her until there was no air left in the room— nothing left in the world except him.

He broke the kiss, and she looked up at him. His eyes were closed, a small bead of moisture in the corners. Then he opened them, and she was lost in the sea of blue.

"I wish every goodbye could be like this," he whispered.

"Must it be goodbye?"

"I'll be back before you've begun to miss me."

He rose to his feet, blew her a kiss, then disappeared through the adjoining door, and she heard James's muffled exclamation.

Not long after, she heard Francine's timid little knock on the chamber door, and the maid entered. She took one look at Meggie and uttered an exclamation in a similar tone to her husband's valet, laced with a similar degree of disapproval.

"Madame! Votre vêtements! Qu'avez vous fait?"

She smiled at her maid's scolding and stood meekly while Francine undressed her.

By the time she descended the stairs, dressed in a fresh gown, her hair curled elegantly on her head in Francine's unique style, Dexter had already gone. She passed the mirror in the hallway, barely recognizing the elegant woman in the reflection from the terrified young bride who'd entered the house almost six months before.

But what purpose did it serve—being transformed into a lady, if she did not have her husband by her side?

Where had he gone?

Chapter Thirty-Five

EACH TIME DEXTER saw Alderley Hall, he was reminded of the pain that bastard Alderley had caused his family—the lashes on his back, Lilah's childhood torment, Daisy's ruination.

And his wife's heartbreak.

Meggie deserved to know where her child was buried, so she could say goodbye properly. No parent should have to bury their child—but Dexter's brave little wife had not even been granted that.

And it was time Alderley paid for what he'd done.

Dexter leaned out of the carriage window and hollered at the driver. With the crack of the whip, the carriage increased in pace and rattled along the road to the hall, the place where Dexter hoped he'd find all the answers.

Alderley must have spotted him coming. Before he reached the main doors, they opened, and a heavily-built footman stood in the doorway.

"The master's not at home."

"Did he tell you to say that?" Dexter asked.

The man's eye twitched, and Dexter laughed. "If you're going to serve your master properly, you need to be a damn sight better at lying." He pushed past the footman. "Alderley!" he roared. "Come out, you bloody coward!"

"Sir, I hardly think that's proper," the footman said.

"Do I look like I care for propriety?" Dexter demanded. He gestured to a door. "Is that the morning room? I'll wait in there. If your master prefers to remain *not at home*, I shall return to London straight away and issue proceedings to foreclose on his debts. The next visitors to Alderley Hall will be the bailiffs."

Without waiting for a response, Dexter strode into the morning room. The colors looked faded, the curtains frayed, and a distinct smell of damp lingered in the air. A decanter, almost empty, sat on the bureau at the far end of the room. He lifted it up, pulled out the stopper, and sniffed.

Brandy—a cheap one, at that. He set it down, leaving fingerprints on the glass body. He rubbed them together. A thin layer of dust covered his skin, and he wiped his hands on his jacket.

Was this what his old enemy had been reduced to? A crumbling house and a single, thuggish servant?

He approached a chair beside the empty fireplace, then thought better of it when he spotted a dark stain on the seat.

"What do you want?" a voice asked.

Alderley stood in the doorway. He seemed to have aged since Dexter had last seen him. His jacket hung on his frame, and his skin had a grayish pallor as if the evil from within had finally surfaced to rot his body. He leaned on a cane, claw-like fingers curling round the tip.

"Is that how you address family?" Dexter sneered.

Alderley gestured to the chair. "Won't you sit?"

"I'd rather not," Dexter said. "I'm not here for tea. Or..." he glanced at the decanter, "...whatever you have which attempts to pass for brandy."

"Then, why are you here?"

"I'm here about the child," Dexter said.

Alderley's eyes narrowed. "What child?"

"Your grandson."

"I have no grandson."

Dexter folded his arms. "Must we continue this game?" he asked. "I refer to my wife's child. The one you took from her."

Alderley sighed, then shuffled into the room and sat on the stained chair. Dexter could almost hear his joints creak.

"How should I remember what I did?" Alderley asked. "It was nearly ten years ago."

"So, you *did* take her child away from her."

"I did not…"

"Come, come," Dexter said. "You've as good as confessed. You profess to be a man of honor—why not do the honorable thing and tell me the truth?"

"The truth!" Alderley scoffed. "Why should I give the likes of you such favor?"

Dexter folded his arms. "I shan't leave until I have satisfaction," he said. "If you don't tell me what I want to hear, I shall return tomorrow and the day after—and the day after that, until you do."

"Is everything all right, sir?" The footman appeared in the doorway. Alderley glanced from him to Dexter, then his shoulders slumped, and he sighed.

"Yes, Wilkes," he said. "Now, leave us."

Dexter waited until the footman had closed the door behind him, then he raised his eyebrows and waited.

"I gave the child to the cook," he said. "She had a sister in the next county, who took it off my hands. At considerable expense to myself, I might add, but it paid for her silence. And a waste of money it was, too, for the cook told me the brat died shortly afterward." He wrinkled his nose in disgust. "Bloody bastard cost me a fortune from the day she was born."

Dexter gritted his teeth. Was that all Alderley had seen Meggie as—a financial burden? And her child—a waste of money?

"What did the child die of?" he asked.

"Damned if I know. Does it matter?"

"It matters to his mother."

"That disobedient little slut!" Alderley spat. "After all I did for her, she spread her legs for the first man who came along."

"And you took Meggie's child as punishment for her disobedience?"

"It was my right!" Alderley said. "She was bought and paid for—by me."

"Why did you pay for Meggie's upkeep if you hate her so much?"

"Her slut of a mother threatened to tell my wife if I didn't pay for her upkeep," Alderley said. "Then she ran off with the next man she took a fancy to and left me with the brat. But I'd made a promise, and so I stuck to it. I'm a man of honor, Hart. I keep my word."

"A man of honor!" Dexter scoffed. "You'll use the letter of the law—and a contract—to suit your purposes. You twist promises you make to deceive and betray. There's a difference, Alderley, between sticking to your word and sticking to your principles."

"Spare me the lecture on morals," Alderley said. "You've had your answer. Now go, before I ask Wilkes to throw you out."

Dexter laughed. "I'm no longer the helpless child who you beat, and neither are you the man wielding the whip. You get your thugs to do your dirty work for you."

"And what about you, Hart?" Alderley asked. "How did you make your fortune so quickly? By offering the hand of friendship to desperate men in the form of a loan, then profiteering from their misfortune by seizing their assets when they cannot pay the interest?"

He rose to his feet, leaning on his cane.

"Tell me, Hart, are we so different? Or are we just two sides of the same coin? Like black and white on a chessboard, identical in every respect except for how we're perceived. We both use our pieces to secure an advantage over our opponent. Haven't you used your subordinates like pawns? Didn't you intend to use my daughter Elizabeth to suit your ends by marrying a title? In giving you my bastard instead, I did what any other man would do. If you were in my position, you'd have done the same."

"The difference between us is that I no longer see Meggie as a piece to wield against an enemy," Dexter said. "I had thought she was my queen— the most powerful piece on the board. But she's not. She's the king. The one piece I'd sacrifice everything to protect. The one piece, who, without her, the game is lost."

He moved toward Alderley until they were almost touching, chest-to-chest. "That night at cards," he said, "the night you tricked me. You thought you'd sacrificed a pawn, a worthless piece to gain a strategic advantage over your enemy. But you were wrong, Alderley—so wrong. In giving her to me, you conceded the game."

He looked into the eyes of his old enemy and saw nothing but a pathetic man who would never find peace. The hatred he'd harbored for Alderley for so many years had been extinguished.

Now, all he felt was pity.

He offered his hand. Alderley's eyes widened, then he took it. His skin was paper-thin and translucent, blue veins visible beneath. Brown liver spots adorned the back of his hand, which shook with age.

"Perhaps, now, we understand each other," Dexter said. "We'll never part as friends, but perhaps it's time to draw a line under the past and declare a truce."

Alderley nodded and squeezed his hand.

"I'll see myself out," Dexter said. "Rest assured, I won't visit again. Neither will my wife."

As he approached the main doors, Dexter heard voices coming from across the hallway. A door opened, and two people walked out—Elizabeth and a man he never expected to see at Alderley Hall again.

George bloody Hanson.

Elizabeth gave a small gasp, but Hanson smiled, with the same look of satisfaction on his lips the day Dexter had confronted him about Daisy. Elizabeth patted her hair, but she could not conceal her disheveled state, nor the flush of female satisfaction.

"Dexter!" she cried. "What are you doing?"

"I could ask you the same," Dexter replied. "Hanson—what a coincidence you're here also. I had wondered why Fate kept drawing us together, but..." He glanced at Elizabeth, "I suspect there's a mortal hand on the tiller."

The answer to the riddles was sliding into place.

"Tell me, Hanson, what persuaded you to seduce Meggie?" Dexter asked. "Or, should I ask *who*?"

Elizabeth paled and gave Hanson a sharp frown.

Dexter laughed. "How long have you been her creature, Hanson? Eight years?" He turned to Elizabeth. "Tell me, woman, how long had you known you had a sister? Were you jealous of her? Even though she was tucked away in obscurity whereas you were the pampered lady, wanting for nothing? Did you see her as a rival for your father's attention and set out to destroy her?"

She glanced at Hanson, fear in her eyes.

"Let me guess," Dexter continued, "you persuaded Hanson to seduce her so that Alderley would send her away, is that it?"

"She was a slut—a bastard!" Elizabeth cried, "a disgrace to our name! I couldn't have her tainting our reputation. Papa was a fool, spending time and money, which was mine and my brother's!"

"Your brother left for the army as soon as he was of age," Dexter said. "I doubt he'd care."

"But *I* do!" she cried. "And I'll do anything to get what I want. Just like you."

"I don't set out to destroy lives," Dexter said, "nor cheat my way into getting what I want. Was the ruination of an innocent worth it for a few extra jewels?"

"Of course it was!" she cried. "It's a small price to pay if I get what I want."

Dear God—Daisy!

"And my sister?" Dexter asked. "Was she in your way also?"

Hanson shuffled on his feet, the guilt in the air so thick, Dexter could almost taste it.

"Why the devil would you be jealous of Daisy?" Dexter asked. "What was she to you?"

"She was your sister," Elizabeth said. "You were inseparable. You wouldn't look twice at anyone else with her around, and I wanted you for myself. When you rejected me, I had to do something."

"Rejected you?"

"At the harvest festival," she said. "Don't you remember? I asked you to dance, and you rejected me in favor of your sister."

Dexter shook his head. He'd rejected the advances of countless women almost as soon as he'd left boyhood. Had one long-forgotten rejection given rise to such catastrophic revenge?

"Is it true?" a voice said.

Alderley stood in the hall, accompanied by a woman in a plain gray dress with a white apron and a bunch of keys hanging from her waist.

"Elizabeth?" Alderley shook his head. "Dear God, girl, I gave you everything you wanted, and more! Why the devil would you do such a thing?"

"Because I was always second best," she said, "your second daughter…" She pointed at Dexter, "*his* second choice."

"It's time I left," Dexter said. "Alderley, you have enough trouble on your hands without me adding to them."

"Dexter…" Elizabeth pleaded.

"No," Dexter said. "You've no right to call me by my name, Miss Alderley. I daresay Hanson here will accommodate your wishes. I hear he's willing to do anything for a price. But have a care—your father's funds are unlikely to run to a seventh season."

He turned to Alderley. "I pity you, sir. Your problems are considerably greater than mine. I shall leave you to resolve them."

"Mrs. Gordon," Alderley addressed the woman next to him. "Please see our guest out. He'll not be returning."

"There's no need," Dexter said. He turned his back on them and exited the building. As he stepped onto the drive outside, the gravel crunching under his feet, he breathed in the fresh air as if to dissipate the evil from the atmosphere. Footsteps crunched behind him as the housekeeper followed him to the carriage.

"There's no need to see me off," Dexter said. "I'm going."

"I must speak with you," the housekeeper said. She lowered her voice. "It's about the child."

He raised his eyebrows.

"About wee Billy," she said, "the child the master took."

"How do you know about the child?" Dexter asked.

"From Mrs. Dawkins—the cook," she said. "She passed last winter, God rest her soul, but in her final days, she told me about a child her sister took in and the secret she kept. She felt that sorry for that poor girl, but she was too frightened of the master to tell anyone the truth until she knew she had nothing to lose—not even her life."

"I don't understand, woman," Dexter said.

"What are you saying?"

"I dared not ask who the child was, but I knew it was something to do with the young woman the master brought onto the estate—the woman who married you, sir. I'd seen her with Mr. Arnold years before, then she disappeared. But then, she returned last winter, and I wondered who she was and why the master had hidden her away again. But then, he gave instructions for a party, and I saw her again when she came into the house. That was with you, sir, and I told Betty that I'd seen her before, but Betty said I couldn't have because Mistress Elizabeth had told her that…"

"Have mercy!" Dexter cried. "Spare my ears. Can you not cease your prattle and speak plain English? What do you know of the child?"

"That he's alive."

Chapter Thirty-Six

NO MATTER HOW many times Meggie read the note in her hand, she couldn't will it to say more.

Meggie Dearest,

Forgive me, I must remain absent for a while longer. I shall return as soon as I can.

Trust me,
Dexter

She threw a log on the fire, which flared and crackled. Summer was over. Yesterday, as she'd walked Titan in the park, Meggie had felt the crunch of the first frosts underfoot.

Now, with a mug of coca on the table beside her and the little dog snoring in a basket at her feet, her thoughts turned once more to her husband.

Where was he?

When he'd sent her to the country, she'd relished the solitude and dreaded his arrival. But now, she found herself craving him. His silent, brooding presence gave her reassurance; his strong hands made her feel protected. And at night…

At night, his body gave her pleasure.

She glanced at the wall clock—almost time for supper. The smell of ragout had been permeating throughout the house all day. It seemed odd, eating on her own at a table big enough for twenty, in a room bigger than the house she grew up in, but she maintained the ritual. She was a lady now.

A door opened and shut below. Most likely Charles on an errand for Mrs. Draper. He'd said something about needing more logs for the fire, and the basket in the parlor was almost empty.

She heard three sharp knocks on the door.

"Come in!"

The door swung open. A man filled the doorway. His jacket was rumpled as if he'd been traveling for hours. Hair tousled, brow creased, he looked exhausted. But those intense blue eyes focused on her with their clear gaze.

"Dexter!" She jumped to her feet, almost tripping over Titan's basket.

He held his hand up. Tempered by the expression on his face, she stopped.

"What's the matter?"

He moved toward her and took her face in his hands, then brushed his lips against hers. She tasted salt on his skin and breathed in his aroma—woody spices mingled with the scent of dust from the road.

"I have something for you," he said.

"A gift?"

"If you like." He hesitated. "I trust I've done the right thing."

He held out his hand, and she took it. His fingers curled round hers in a tight, desperate grip, as if seeking reassurance. If she didn't know him better, she'd have thought he looked afraid—like a child, uncertain whether he was about to be punished.

He called out. "You can come in now."

A woman appeared in the doorway. She wore a plain dress of black wool and a simple cap on her head where gray curls peeked out. Beside her, gripping her hand, was a young boy with a head of thick, brown hair. He stared at Meggie out of wide, expressive brown eyes, and Meggie felt a shock of familiarity. In his free hand, he held a small posy of flowers. They looked the worse for wear—withered and drooping as if he'd been clutching them for hours.

The woman dipped into a curtsey.

"Dexter, who are these people?" Meggie

asked.

Dexter nodded to the woman. "Go on."

"My name is Mrs. Goode, ma'am." The woman nudged the child. "Introduce yourself, lad, as I told you."

The child bowed. "Pleased to meet you, ma'am. My name is William Goode."

Dexter drew in a sharp breath.

"Did I do it right, sir?" he asked. "Isn't that my name?"

He looked up at Dexter, fear and awe in his expression. Dexter must look terrifying to a small child with his powerful physique, dark features, and arresting blue eyes. Meggie pulled her hand free of her husband's grasp and beckoned to the child.

"Come here," she said. The boy glanced at the woman, who nodded.

"Go on, lad. You must do as she says now."

Meggie crouched until she was at the child's eye-level and held out her hand.

The boy moved forward and took it.

"How cold you are, sweetheart!" she cried. "How long have you been on the road?"

"We left this morning, missus. Just after sunrise."

"That was hours ago!" Meggie said. "Would you like some hot chocolate? It's perfect for warming you up when you've been outside." She nodded to Titan, who slept in his basket. "I took my dog for a walk today, and it was so cold, I couldn't feel my hands! But after a cup of chocolate, they're as warm as toast, now. What do you think?"

"You've got nice hands," the boy said.

Meggie laughed. "You're a gallant little gentleman!"

The boy held out the posy of flowers. "These are for you."

"Why, thank you," Meggie said, taking them. "They're beautiful. You know how to woo a lady."

She looked up and saw Dexter and the woman—Mrs. Goode—both staring at her. Dexter's eyes shone with pride, but Mrs. Goode's eyes were wet with tears, and she let out a small sob.

Dexter placed his hand on the woman's shoulder. "Mrs. Goode, remember my promise. You'll not be parted from William."

"Dexter, what's going on?" Meggie asked.

Dexter stood behind the boy. "Don't you know, my love?"

The boy craned his neck to look up at Dexter. "Did I do right with the flowers—Papa?"

"He's your son?" Meggie asked.

"No," Dexter said. "He's yours."

"M-mine?"

"Look at him, my love," Dexter said. "Look at his eyes. The shape of his nose. That stubborn little chin."

Recognition slid into place, and her heart leaped with hope, pumping blood through her veins, rushing through her ears. Her chest constricted, and she fought for breath as the world slipped out of focus.

"Meggie."

Her husband's voice drew her back, like a lighthouse in the fog, anchoring her to reality, and she focused on the child—the boy who stared at her with the same eyes she saw in the mirror every day.

"Billy…" she gasped, lifting her hand to her mouth. "*My Billy?*" She shook her head. "No, this can't be real. He said you'd died."

She looked up at her husband. "Is this a trick?" she cried. "Why have you done this!"

Dexter grasped her hands. "It's no trick, Meggie," he said. "I went to Alderley Hall in search of the truth about your son. Alderley had manipulated you all your life to control you. So I wanted to know for sure whether the boy…" he broke off, glancing at the child.

Whether he lived or died.

"My search led me to Mrs. Goode."

A tide of hope swelled inside Meggie, but fear tempered her faith. She didn't know if she could withstand any more heartbreak.

"Your husband speaks the truth, Mrs. Hart," the woman said. "My sister was the cook at Alderley Hall. The master there had Billy sent to me, where I looked after him as if he were my own. Begging your pardon, ma'am, but we told Lord Alderley that he..." she hesitated and glanced at the boy, "We did it to protect the little mite, so he'd be left alone. He's a sweet boy, ma'am, and he'll give you no trouble."

"Y-you looked after him?" Meggie asked.

"I always told him he had a mama who loved him and missed him." She wiped her face, and the back of her hand glistened with tears. "My dearest wish was that you be reunited when it was safe. A child needs his mother."

"And what about you, Mrs. Goode?"

"Aunt Fanny will be staying here, too!" the boy exclaimed. "Papa said she can live with us, isn't that right?"

"Yes, that's right, young man," Dexter said, smiling.

"But, sir," Mrs. Goode said, "I'm not Billy's mother. Your wife..."

"Have I not already explained this, Mrs. Goode?" Dexter asked. "Billy will need a nursemaid, and I can think of no one finer than the woman who cared for him since he was a baby. And besides," he glanced at Meggie, "if my wife and I are blessed again, I can engage you to take care of *all* our children."

"Ahem," Charles appeared at the door. "Will your guests be staying for dinner, sir?"

"They'll be staying forever," Dexter said.

"Would you ask Mrs. Draper to prepare two rooms? And see if the cook can stretch the supper for four."

"Perhaps I should accompany Charles," Mrs. Goode said. "The three of you need to get acquainted."

Meggie clutched the child's hand and pulled him to her.

"Billy…"

"Mama."

It was a single word. One tiny word, yet it conveyed so much—the hopes she'd harbored during her pregnancy, while she'd cried in pain during her confinement, then finally, when she'd lain broken and battered in her little bed when Alderley had cursed her wantonness and told her that her son had died.

Yet here and now, she cradled her child in her arms while he uttered the one word capable of shattering her heart.

Hot tears splashed onto her cheeks, soaking into the boy's shirt as she clung to him and cried—for the years she had lost and for the son who had returned.

"Mama?" Billy, her little Billy, curled his fingers and clung to her dress. "Mama, what's wrong?"

"Nothing," she said, "my darling child, there's nothing wrong.

"Then why do you cry?"

"Because I'm happy, my love," she said. "So very happy."

"Do people cry when they're happy?"

"Sometimes," a deep voice said. Strong, warm arms enveloped Meggie and her child, and she looked into her husband's eyes to see the blue clouded with tears. "Sometimes, even the strongest man will succumb to the overwhelming power of pure happiness, a pleasure so intense that words cannot convey how completely, utterly, deliriously happy he is. Sometimes, young man, only tears will do."

"And will *I* be happy, Papa?"

"Yes," Meggie said. "Yes, you will."

Epilogue

Eight months later...

"MAMA! MAMA!"

Meggie's heart skittered at the voice she'd longed to hear. She set her mending aside and grasped the arms of her chair.

"Oh, no, you don't, Mrs. Hart!"

Mrs. Goode rushed to her side. "Doctor McIver told you to take it easy."

"But Billy's home," Meggie protested, "I've not seen him for two months."

"He can come to you."

The door burst open, and a whirlwind entered.

"Billy!" Meggie cried. The boy rushed forward but halted as a stern voice boomed around the room.

"Not so fast, sir! Your mama's in a delicate condition."

"Delicate!" Meggie huffed, trying to stand. "I'm the size of an elephant. It's a wonder you can bear the sight of me."

"My dear, Meggie," Dexter said with a wicked smile, "you know full well that I relish the sight of you—as I believe I made clear twice last night and once again this morning."

Mrs. Goode burst into a fit of coughing, and Meggie felt her cheeks burning. As her pregnancy advanced, her need for his touch had become a craving, which he was more than happy to satisfy. He glanced toward the chair beside the window where yesterday he'd sat back, his hands interlinked behind his neck while she'd ridden him, bringing them both to pleasure. Had any passer-by looked up, they would have seen her.

She might have believed she was turning into a wanton, but Anne Pelham, now expecting her fourth child, had warned her that pregnancy often increased a woman's appetites. And judging by the size of the smile on Mr. Pelham's face when Meggie took tea with them last week, Anne's fourth pregnancy was no exception.

Billy gave a stiff little bow. "Hello, Mama."

Meggie opened her arms, and the boy rushed toward her, and she held him close, burying her face in his hair.

"I've missed you," she said.

"And I, you, Mama."

"Did you have a good time at Eton?"

"Oh, yes!" Billy cried, "I've made two new friends—we're in Godolphin House together. Papa says they can stay with us at Molineux Manor for some of the long vacation."

"Are you working hard?"

"Papa has already asked me that during the ride home," Billy said. "I'm top of my class in mathematics, and I've joined the chess club."

"Excellent!" Meggie laughed. "Mr. Peyton will be pleased. Perhaps he'll include one of your games in his next chess book."

Billy puffed out his chest with pride. "I lent Augustus a copy of Uncle Oliver's book," he said. "He didn't believe me when I said my mama had written a whole chapter. He thinks girls can't play chess."

Meggie laughed. "Girls can do anything," she said.

"Well, I'm looking forward to renaming my business Hart & Son," Dexter said, patting Billy on the head. "Or perhaps, even Hart & Sons."

"What if I give birth to a girl?" Meggie asked.

"Then I'll change my livery to Hart & Son & Daughter," Dexter said, laughing. "That'll cause a stir at the bank!"

Mrs. Goode rose to her feet. "Come along, young man," she said. "Cook was baking sweet buns for your return. Shall we see if they're ready?"

Billy grasped her hand, and she led him out of

the parlor.

"Our son is prospering," Dexter said. "It's a pity Alderley didn't live to see his grandson thrive."

Meggie nodded. Her half-brother James had returned from the army to claim his title as Viscount Alderley. He had a Herculean task on his hands—managing not only a bankrupt estate but a sister who resided there, a bitter woman haunting its shades.

"Billy doesn't need the Alderleys in his life," Dexter continued. "He has aunts enough."

"That he does!" Meggie laughed. "Delilah wrote to say she's coming to help with the baby after my confinement, and she'll brook no denial."

Dexter rolled his eyes. "That's all I need," he said. "Lilah's a hellion. She'll spend the entire visit ordering me about."

Meggie laughed. Dexter's youngest sister had come to stay over Christmas. Meggie had been apprehensive at meeting Delilah, but she'd immediately put Meggie at ease. Lilah's husband, though a duke, possessed a natural warmth. The huge Scotsman had pulled Meggie into a bear-hug and welcomed her to the family. As for their daughter, Flora, Meggie had fallen in love with the flame-haired toddler on sight.

"I won't hear a word against your siblings," Meggie said, "for I love them all."

Dexter sighed. "As do I," he said. "I would

have them all happy."

"Aren't they?"

"All except Devon."

"Your brother will find happiness," Meggie said. "He just needs to find someone capable of seeing the goodness in his heart."

"You always see the goodness in others," Dexter said. "Not everyone possesses that quality." He sighed. "Sometimes, I regret not having the opportunity to see Alderley again before he died. I wish I'd been able to thank him properly."

"What for?"

"For giving me you," he said. "The greatest treasure in his possession."

He lifted her hand to his lips.

"I might have spent the rest of my life merely *existing*—devoted to increasing my fortune and my social status. But you..." He placed a hand on her belly. "You taught me what it was like to *live*."

He leaned forward and kissed her again, his tongue probing, seeking entrance. Gladly, she opened to receive him. Then he broke the kiss.

"Come, my love," he said. "Supper awaits, after which I hope to enjoy dessert."

He took her hand and led her downstairs, his eyes glittering with mischief in anticipation of the night ahead.

The End

About the Author

Emily Royal grew up in Sussex, England, and has devoured romantic novels for as long as she can remember. A mathematician at heart, Emily has worked in financial services for over twenty years. She indulged in her love of writing after she moved to Scotland, where she lives with her husband, teenage daughters and menagerie of rescue pets including Twinkle, an attention-seeking boa constrictor.

She has a passion for both reading and writing romance with a weakness for Regency rakes, Highland heroes, and Medieval knights. Persuasion is one of her all-time favorite novels which she reads several times each year and she is fortunate enough to live within sight of a Medieval palace.

When not writing, Emily enjoys playing the piano, hiking, and painting landscapes, particularly the Highlands. One of her ambitions is to paint, as well as climb, every mountain in Scotland.